CHARMS AND CHOCOLATE CHIPS

This Large Print Book carries the Seal of Approval of N.A.V.H.

A MAGICAL BAKERY MYSTERY

CHARMS AND
CHOCOLATE CHIPS

BAILEY CATES

KENNEBEC LARGE PRINT
A part of Gale, Cengage Learning

GALE
CENGAGE Learning·

Farmington Hills, Mich • San Francisco • New York • Waterville, Maine
Meriden, Conn • Mason, Ohio • Chicago

GALE
CENGAGE Learning

LIBRARY OF CONGRESS CATALOGING-IN-PUBLICATION DATA

Cates, Bailey.
  Charms and chocolate chips : a magical bakery mystery / by Bailey Cates.
    pages ; cm. — (Kennebec Large Print superior collection)
    ISBN 978-1-4104-7166-6 (softcover) — ISBN 1-4104-7166-7 (softcover)
    1. Witches—Fiction. 2. Magic—Fiction. 3. Bakeries—Fiction. 4. Large type books. I. Title.
  PS3603.A8955C47 2014
  813'.6—dc23
                                                              2014015875

Published in 2014 by arrangement with NAL Signet, a member of Penguin Group (USA) LLC, a Penguin Random House Company.

Printed in the United States of America
  1 2 3 4 5   18 17 16 15 14

ACKNOWLEDGMENTS

I am grateful to work with such a terrific team at Penguin/NAL: Jessica Wade, Jesse Feldman, Dan Walsh, Kayleigh Clark, and everyone else whose skill and hard work brought this book into being. Thanks to Kimberly Lionetti at Bookends Literary Agency for her advice and hard work. Mark Figlozzi and Bob Trott provided feedback, and the Old Town Writers Group kept me sane more than they know. I appreciate all the helpful information from the folks at Olde Savannah Garden & Produce, the Savannah-Chatham Metropolitan Police Department, firefighter Todd Bryan, and the Savannah Chamber of Commerce. Any mistakes are mine. And, as always, thank you to Kevin for . . . everything.

CHAPTER 1

The smell of woodsmoke from a distant hearth teased my nose as I surveyed my predawn preparations with a critical eye. My new outdoor fireplace perched in the middle of a twelve-foot circle of gravel, its copper gleaming in the soft light of the lantern. Dry kindling stacked in a rough pyramid in the metal bowl awaited a match, and six mismatched chairs sat at equidistant points around it. Only yesterday I'd purchased the two worn oak ladder-backs from a thrift store; the other four I'd moved over from the nearby gazebo.

Katie Lightfoot, hostess with the mostess.

Tonight's Imbolc celebration would be the first sabbat I'd ever hosted for the ladies of my spellbook club — aka coven. Falling on February second, smack-dab between the winter solstice and the spring equinox, Imbolc signaled lengthening days and the coming of new life. It was a festival that celebrated feminine energy and honored Brigit, the patron of midwives, poets, and blacksmiths. Even people who'd never heard of Imbolc practiced divination and the cultivation of light, since Groundhog Day and Candlemas fell on the same day.

Over in the gazebo where I cast most of my outdoor spells, I'd collected a cut-glass bowl, four white candles, several packets of seeds, and a bundle of cinnamon sticks that I'd tied together with a bright yellow ribbon. Mimsey Carmichael had promised to supply a white flower from her shop to represent snow. Bianca Devereaux would bring champagne from her wineshop to symbolize winter ice melting into spring. Jaida French had made a special candle doused with clove, rosemary, and ginger essential oils, and Cookie Rios had offered to bring something to reflect the birth of spring. I wanted everything to be perfect — the fire, the bannock cakes and mulled cider, the incantation to greet spring and honor Brigit, and the final fizzy toast.

Not that I really needed to worry. The coven was an easygoing group, especially my aunt Lucy. They'd become my best friends since I'd moved to Savannah the previous April to open a bakery. Nonetheless, I'd been a practicing hedgewitch —

and that with initial reluctance — only since Lucy had informed me of my magical heritage ten months ago. I still had a lot to learn. Lucky for me, the spellbook club had taken me under its collective wing, each member instructing me on her own special interests. My primary affinity was for working with plants and herbs in the garden and kitchen, but I was learning tons about other kinds of magic.

Not all of it good.

It turned out there was a significant amount of sorcery going on in Georgia's First City. In my short residency I'd met a few of the other practitioners and encountered unexpected evil.

And then there was Detective Franklin Taite. The spellbook club had called him a witch-hunter, but really he focused exclusively on tracking black magic. That meant he wasn't really antiwitch — as long as you stuck with the good stuff. Fine by me. I had no interest in the dark side. Yet he had wanted more.

You are a candela, Katie, a lightwitch. You have an obligation to use that gift. A calling.

I took a deep breath and pushed the remembered words away. Detective Taite had transferred to New Orleans, where he was no doubt stalking another "hotbed of evil" as he'd once described Savannah.

Nothing melodramatic about that. And nothing like dumping all that crazy information on me and then up and leaving.

A breeze sighed through the air, and I tucked my floral-print scarf tighter around my neck. Even in Savannah it was chilly, in the low forties at five a.m. in early February. The three-quarter moon had set hours before, and the sun wouldn't brighten the horizon for another two. The air was inky black outside the confined nimbus of lantern light around the backyard fire pit, and the cool but humid air caressed my exposed face and hands.

Always an early riser, even a middle-of-the-night riser, I loved working outside in the dark. Margie Coopersmith, my adorable yet sometimes nosy next-door neighbor, had become used to my nocturnal digging and planting and weeding by the light of a bicycle headlamp, and while it earned me a certain amount of guff, it also allowed me not only to garden but to practice my own brand of magic outdoors with little notice.

I loved, even craved, the depth of silence I found so early in the morning. Now, fragrant steam rising from the coffee mug in my hand, it was like venturing into a space that was somehow outside of time. With none of the bustling daytime sounds of traffic and lawn mowers and road construction, there were only quiet stars piercing the dark veil above.

Then a faraway siren broke the spell. A dog barked, and the sound of running water from the stream in the corner of the yard reached my ears, carrying with it the sweet scent of winter Daphne blooming in the garden.

"What do you think?" I asked Mungo.

My Cairn terrier bounded down the steps of the gazebo, where he'd been watching me, bright-eyed and tail wagging.

Yip!

I scooped him up and nuzzled my cold nose into his wavy black fur. "So you approve?"

My familiar answered by licking my ear. I stifled a giggle. Sudden light bloomed behind yellow curtains in my next-door neighbors' kitchen, and I blew out the lantern. It was early for Margie and the three children to be up, so I assumed her husband, Redding, was getting ready for one of his long-haul trucking trips. I'd have to remember to bring Margie and the little ones some goodies from work.

Speaking of work, if I didn't hurry up, I'd be late. There was always a lot to do in the mornings before the Honeybee Bakery, which I owned with Lucy and her husband, Ben, opened for the day's business. Plus, I had to get done with work on time so I could head over to Georgia Wild, a nonprofit environmental group I'd been volunteering for, and then get home in time for the celebration. A hedgewitch's work was never done.

I carried Mungo to the back door and set him down. Inside my little home — once the carriage house for a larger estate, now long gone — the light from the kitschy fringed floor lamp softly lit the warm, peach-colored walls of the living room. Closing the French doors to the patio, I turned away from the short hallway to my left that led to the bedroom and bathroom, and headed for the kitchen. Mungo's toenails made tiny clicking sounds on the old wood-plank floor as he followed me.

Mungo grinned up at me, then looked pointedly at his dish on the floor.

"Okay, okay." I opened the fridge and grabbed an egg. "I suppose you want bacon, too."

Yip!

Located in downtown Savannah only a few blocks from the riverfront, Honeybee Bakery was nestled between a bookstore and a knitting shop on Broughton Street. The bakery was named after Aunt Lucy's familiar, a regal orange tabby cat. Inside, the high ceilings gave it a sense of space, and the deep amber walls encouraged energy and creativity. We'd painted the vertical expanse behind the counter burnt orange to offset the tall blackboard menu where we listed our offerings according to the seasons, customer feedback, and our own whims. The chrome-and-blue bistro tables were the perfect size for laptops and notebooks with plenty of room for mugs of coffee and a tempting pastry or two from the glass-fronted display case, while the comfy matching chairs invited people to stay for hours. The scent of succulent baked goods infused the air and spilled out to the sidewalk. Light jazz played softly over the sound system.

At the far end of the bakery a poufy sofa and two chairs upholstered in jewel-toned brocade surrounded a sturdy coffee table. We'd always had a huge bookcase overflowing with all manner of eclectic reading materials, but the month before, my uncle Ben had talked my boyfriend, Declan McCarthy, into helping him install permanent shelves. Now the Honeybee had a proper reading area, complete with three walls of floor-to-ceiling bookshelves and a hand-painted tin sign that said LIBRARY hanging from the ceiling.

At a little after two o'clock, I found myself counting slices of lemon-raspberry tea cake with a sinking feeling. They were our current hot sellers, along with the gingerbread — studded with gems of candied ginger and oversized chocolate chips — and maple bacon scones. It had been a rather slow morning, though, even for those items. Truth be told, business seemed a little slow all around these days. Of course, it would be for everyone, I supposed. Midwinter was hardly high tourist season, and tourism was the lifeblood of Savannah. I was happy to see a few regulars still lounging at the tables.

Ben was behind the espresso machine, sorting through the mail. He stood at an angle to the kitchen, and the soft yellow light shining down from the high ceiling glinted off his rimless glasses. Though he was in his sixties, his hair and the tidy beard he'd grown after retiring as Savannah's fire chief were a deep reddish blond with nary a strand of gray. The bell over the door rang as two men in business suits entered, and Ben greeted them with a hearty "Hello!"

I frowned again at the almost full row of lemon cake. The ribbons of sticky raspberry

jam swirled throughout beckoned tempt-
ingly. Still, if it wasn't selling, perhaps it
was time to change it out for the new
sandwich cookies Lucy and I had been developing.

"Hey, Lucy," I said as she passed by with
an armful of dishes from the bussing station. "I've mixed up a few filling ideas.
Come tell me what you think."

"Mmm. I can hardly wait to see what you
came up with," she said with a grin, and
bustled into the kitchen.

Soon we were sampling away. I licked a
smear of icing off the edge of my thumb.
"What do you think?" I asked. "The hint of
maple syrup in the peanut butter filling
would complement the maple in the cookies."

We had the outside of the sandwiches
down pat — soft oatmeal molasses disks
made with maple sugar and spiced with
plenty of cinnamon and cloves and a subtle
dash of nutmeg. The cinnamon would
promote prosperity and increased energy
for our customers, and cloves invited protection and healing. Nutmeg, one of my favorite spices for both sweet and savory cooking
(so good in spinach), added an extra oomph
of magical energy.

Now we had to figure out what sweet

15

goodness to put between them.

"I don't know, Katie." Lucy dipped the edge of a cookie into the chocolate buttercream frosting and took a big bite. After chewing slowly and swallowing, she cocked her head to one side and said, "This is awfully good. I like the hazelnut spread, too. And the orange curd." She waved her hand in the air. "Bah. We have to pick one, and soon. I've probably already gained five pounds taste testing."

"I hardly think so," I said, eyeing her trim figure. Lucy was in her mid-fifties, but she was petite and fit and tended to wear natural fibers and funky batik and tie-dyed prints. The only indications of her age were the crow's-feet at the corners of her eyes and the gray that threaded through her thick blond mop of hair.

"But you bring up a good point," I continued. "Why do we have to pick just one? What do you say we make all four and then see which the customers gravitate toward?"

"Oooh — that's a good idea." Lucy bent forward over the stainless steel counter and dipped another cookie into the hazelnut spread. Seeing my look, she said, "What? I'm just making sure — oh, never mind."

I laughed.

My aunt held up a finger, swallowed

again, and said, "Now, what would be the best magical amendments for each filling?"

It was part honest question and part quiz. As Lucy put it, being hereditary hedge-witches meant we were "pure magic in the kitchen," and while the other spellbook club members taught me other aspects of magic, my aunt was my mentor when it came to kitchen and garden magic. Most of our "special ingredients" were simply herbs and spices, but we gave them a little extra bewitching boost. Lucy was great at recognizing what people needed — a little clarity here, a bit of love there, perhaps some protection from outside influences — and gently pushed them toward the baked goods we created that would help.

"Well, let's see," I said. "Orange already increases both physical and mental energy, and hazelnut is good for . . . creativity?" I looked to Lucy for confirmation. She looked pleased and nodded. I continued. "And of course chocolate is already awesome. But what if we added cayenne pepper for a little kick, both in the flavor department and for inner strength and cheer. It's good protection during flu season, too."

Lucy clasped her hands and beamed at me. "Cayenne pepper — just a hint! That's delightful! I'll get some right now."

Suddenly I realized I hadn't heard the shriek of the espresso machine or customers conversing for quite some time. Craning my head around the big refrigerator, I saw Ben counting our receipts.

He looked up and smiled at me. "Just running the register tape."

I glanced at the big clock on the wall. It was a little after five. The Honeybee was closed.

"Oh, no. Lucy, I'm so sorry. I have to go. In fact I'm already late for my volunteer work at Georgia Wild." I looked helplessly at the mess strewn on the counter. "Could you . . . Do you mind?"

My aunt pressed her lips together.

"I'll come in early, make it up to you. In fact, let me just put the food away, and I'll clean up the rest in the morning." I grabbed a paper bag to load with day-old leftovers to take with me.

She stopped me with a hand on my arm. "Katie, stop it. I don't mind cleaning up. I'm just worried about you."

"Worried about me? Why?"

"You're running yourself ragged," she said. "It's like you've got a second full-time job at Georgia Wild."

My jaw slackened in surprise. "Only evenings — and only for a couple of hours

18

tonight since everyone's coming over for Imbolc. It was Mimsey who introduced me to Wren, after all." Wren Knowles was the devoted biologist who worked full-time for the environmental nonprofit. She was also the granddaughter of the oldest member of the spellbook club, Mimsey Carmichael.

"I doubt she intended for you to volunteer there every spare minute — I bet Declan just loves that — and for what? To front-load karma?"

Shaking my head, I turned toward the office. "I have no idea what you're talking about, Luce. I would think you'd approve of my volunteering to help the environment. We're green witches, for heaven's sake." Lucy's reference to Declan bothered me more than I liked to admit. Just the other night he'd complained that he saw me less now than he did before we were a steady item.

Steady. Did twenty-nine-year-olds even go steady?

Behind me my aunt said, "You know very well what I'm talking about. Volunteering for something you believe in is wonderful, but I'm not sure it's for the right reason. I think you might be doing it out of fear."

"Am not," I muttered from the office doorway. Looking over my shoulder, I saw her watching me with wise eyes.

"Ever hear the story of the man who learned death was coming for him, so he went to another town? And who did he meet there but Death himself. You can't escape destiny, Katie."

"Come on, Mungo," I said, picking him up from the club chair where he held court during the days he accompanied me to the bakery. He nestled into my tote bag, and I grabbed my jacket.

Lucy still stood in the same spot.

"I'll see you at eight thirty, then?" I kept my tone light and breezy as I placed some of the unsold baked goods in the paper bag. Honeybee leftovers were always popular with the Georgia Wild staff. "I think you'll like my take on bannock cakes."

"I'm sure I will." Her tone was mild, but her eyes bored into mine until I managed to tear my gaze away.

At least she'd dropped her lecturing tone. I kissed her on the cheek. "Bring a warm coat. Even with the fire it will be chilly later on. Bye, Ben," I called, and hurried out to where my Volkswagen Beetle snugged up to the curb.

Front-loading karma indeed. As if.

CHAPTER 2

But Lucy's words stayed with me as I drove to Georgia Wild. I had to admit she had come awfully close to the truth. A tiny part of me hoped that if I could do enough good on my own — and volunteering was at least mildly virtuous — then I could sidestep that whole lightwitch thing Franklin Taite had told me about. *Gift,* he'd called it.

I didn't quite see it that way.

In fact, ever since he'd informed me I had a calling to remedy dark magic, I'd kind of freaked out. I'd even considered turning my back on my witchy heritage altogether, much like my mother had. But I couldn't bear the thought of denying who I was or losing my new friends. I'd been an outsider my whole life, and now I finally understood where I belonged.

I was a witch, and I wasn't going to stop practicing just because some balding police detective told me I'd be called upon to fight dark magic. Bah.

"What would he know?" I asked Mungo, who was still in the tote bag and buckled into the passenger seat of the Bug. "I mean, I'd know if I had a *calling,* wouldn't I? That's not the kind of thing that someone else tells you. It's the kind of thing that bubbles up from deep inside."

I glanced down to see my familiar tip his head to the side.

"What? You think I feel bubbles?"

Yip!

"Hush."

Well, maybe I did. A little, tiny kind of bubbling.

Front-loading karma. Doing good deeds I was comfortable with so I wouldn't be called upon to do something I wasn't comfortable with.

A car honked behind me, and I realized I'd slowed to a crawl. I shook my head at myself and accelerated. It had been three months since Detective Taite told me I was a lightwitch. How was that different than a white witch? I certainly abided by the Rule of Three that the rest of the spellbook club believed in, which, simply put, stated that everything we did would come back to us threefold — good spells and bad.

I reached over to smooth the fur between

Mungo's ears, and he nosed my fingers. The gesture was oddly comforting, and I felt my muscles relax. "Okay. You're right. I'm worrying about nothing."

Perhaps I spent more time at Georgia Wild than I really needed to, but I was genuinely concerned about the local endangered species habitat that the recently launched nonprofit worked to save. Autumn Boles, the founder, was passionate about every single one of the projects we were involved with, from the small cave housing gray bats on a single acre of land to the cypress-dominated ponds tucked into a particular inland pine forest that provided the perfect breeding ground for reticulated flatwoods salamanders. Working with private citizens, environmental foundations, and donors, Georgia Wild bought what habitat it could and sought agreement from existing owners to preserve all or part of their land if it was habitat intensive.

I believed in what they were doing, and I loved working with Autumn and Wren — the latter a witch like her grandmother, but one who preferred to work solitary rather than join a coven. They were great about accommodating my schedule so I could still put in the long, necessary hours at the Honeybee, and they loved it when I brought

Mungo into the office.

Yes, life was good — and satisfyingly tame. Declan might not be that happy with my hours, but I was spending my time doing things I felt strongly about. Not that I didn't feel strongly about Declan . . . but that was different.

Headlights flashed on in front of the small house on Abercorn Street that Autumn and Wren had converted into the Georgia Wild office. I turned on my blinker and waited as a boxy Jeep veered into the street and accelerated quickly away. Thanking the parking gods, I happily slipped the Bug into the empty spot. A narrow covered porch wrapped around the front of the building, and through the winter gloaming I could see the tasteful sign centered on the overhang: GEORGIA WILD — SPACE AND A PLACE FOR ALL.

I got out and went around to the other side of the car to retrieve Mungo and the pastries from the Honeybee. The blinds on the office windows were already closed. Warm yellow light glowed behind them, a comfortable beacon in the chilly evening. Autumn was probably working late again. That woman worked even more than I did.

Running lightly up the steps, I reached for the doorknob. Unlatched, the door swung open at my touch. My nostrils flared as the odor of burnt coffee boiled through the opening. It seemed to carry another scent — or another feeling — with it. I could have sworn I smelled . . . *dread.* Mungo tensed beneath my other hand, and a telltale shiver crawled across my shoulders.

Sipping shallow breaths, I stepped into the former living room where I did the majority of my work. The door latch snicked shut behind me as my gaze swept over the worn Berber carpet, the Goodwill furniture, the overlapping maps and charts tacked directly to the wallboard. The place was clean if not tidy, functional if not beautiful. Two desks faced each other, each with a halogen lamp trained on piles of papers and brochures and manila file folders. Nothing unusual there. Both desk chairs were empty, as was the solitary guest chair by the front window. The yellow light that had looked so friendly from outside came from the tall floor lamp in the corner next to it. Plants tumbled healthy leaves over the edges of the indoor window boxes.

I tossed the bag of baked goods onto a desk and hurried to the coffee station on the far side of the room, sparing a glance at the darkened hallway that led to Autumn's private office at the back of the house. The thick, dark sludge at the bottom of the coffeepot confirmed long, unattended hours on the hot warmer. Why hadn't anyone noticed the stink?

"Autumn?" I called. "Wren?"

The mournful sound that erupted from the back of the building brought every follicle on my scalp to attention. Mungo whined from inside the tote still hanging from my shoulder. I patted him on the head almost without thinking as I backed slowly toward the exit.

Yip!

His bark startled me so much I almost dropped the tote. At least my gasp made me realize that I had stopped breathing altogether. I deliberately inhaled, mind racing, intuition breaking down in the face of fear — but of what I didn't know. Maybe the fear *was* my intuition talking.

Bright light dawned at the end of the hallway for a brief moment, then vanished. A crash sounded as something moved toward me from the office. I whirled to the door, fumbling at the handle so I could get the heck out of there.

"Katie!"

I paused, turning back. "Wren?" Mungo's head popped up out of the tote.

She staggered into the main office, one

shoulder bouncing off a wall as if she'd had a few too many daiquiris. A framed topographical map of northern Georgia crashed to the floor, spraying broken glass.

"Good heavens! What's wrong?" I hurried to her side, grabbed her arm, and eased her into one of the desk chairs.

"Autumn," she panted, looking wildly around the room.

I knelt on the floor in front of her, careful of the glass shards. Mungo jumped out of the tote and ran toward the short hallway. From the corner of my eye I saw him skid to a stop at the entrance.

Taking both of Wren's ice-cold hands in mine, I said, "Honey, settle down. You're hyperventilating." I looked around the office as if a paper bag would suddenly appear out of thin air. Then I saw the to-go bag from the Honeybee. Standing, I grabbed it, dumped the spicy sweet contents onto the desk blotter, and shoved it toward Wren. "Here. Bend down, head between your knees, and breathe into this."

She obeyed like a child, closing her eyes. The paper bag inflated and deflated several times. She shuddered. I put my arm around her shoulders. "It's okay."

Shaking her head, she straightened in the chair and let the bag drop into her lap.

Taller than my five-nine, and a year younger, Wren Knowles was gangly and bird-boned, knobby-kneed, and oddly ethereal on her best days. Now she seemed a faded version of herself. Her face was white as alabaster against her tangled black hair and her big blue eyes blinked rapidly at me from behind thick, rectangular-framed glasses.

"Now." I glanced over at my familiar who still peered toward the office. "What happened?"

Her hand fluttered to her mouth as if to keep words inside. Gently, I took it and held it in my own.

"Autumn," she croaked.

I waited, the initial feeling of dread that I'd felt upon entering Georgia Wild intensifying exponentially.

"She's . . . dead." The second word came out as a wail.

I'd known, in a way, since seeing Wren stumble out of the back, but hearing the actual words was different that just having a feeling. With an effort, I swallowed. When I finally found the words, they came out in a whisper. "Are you sure?"

Her head bobbed, and a tear spilled onto her cheek. "Look for yourself."

That, of course, was exactly what I did

not want to do. Still, squaring my shoulders, I set my jaw and turned toward the hallway. Mungo leaned his head back and met my eyes, nervously licking his lips.

I took two confident steps before faltering, then steeled my nerves and continued on. At least Mungo stuck close to my heels. The door to Autumn's office had swung most of the way closed behind Wren, but a wedge of bright white shone around the edges. I pushed it open.

The harsh fluorescence of the overhead fixture glared down on the tableau. The desk had been cleared of everything. Well, almost everything. Autumn lay on top of it on her back. Her arms were folded over her chest as if she were in a coffin. She wore black slacks and a white silk blouse. One loafer dangled off her foot, but the other had fallen to the floor where the usual contents of the desktop were now scattered. I stared at the pink pearl polish on her exposed toenails, mesmerized.

After a long moment I forced my attention back to her body. If Wren looked pale, it was nothing compared to the complete lack of color in Autumn's skin now. It looked even whiter than her blouse. Her unadorned fingers curled beneath the cuffs, the natural nails buffed to a high gleam but

29

not polished. Her peanut-butter-colored hair curled around classic features in a heart-shaped face, but her eyes were closed and her lips were a disturbing blue.

As were the bruises on her neck.

Then I noticed the wrinkled, dark red paper peeking out of her right hand. My breath caught and that telltale shiver ran down my back again as I looked up to see the screen saver on Autumn's computer. It was an iridescent blue dragonfly, buzzing from corner to corner, side to side. A dragonfly: my totem, which Lucy had explained served as a kind of metaphysical tap on the shoulder. *Pay attention.*

Pay attention, indeed.

Swearing under my breath, I forced myself to move closer. To place quivering fingertips on her neck.

To hope against hope.

But Wren was right. There was no pulse. Our friend and colleague Autumn Boles was decidedly dead.

CHAPTER 3

The first time I'd met Detective Franklin Taite, he'd insulted me. The next time, he'd revealed his knowledge of real magic in the world, but he'd also threatened me. The third time? More threats, including one to drag me into the police precinct for questioning. Finally, he'd told me I was a light-witch and had a calling to battle dark magic, and a week later he had up and transferred to New Orleans.

Nice.

Now his former partner, Detective Peter Quinn, stood regarding me in the front office of Georgia Wild. I was pretty sure he didn't miss Taite much. He certainly seemed more comfortable working alone. Searching eyes gazed out beneath his shock of thick gray hair. He wore charcoal-colored slacks and a leather sports coat over a crisp white shirt sans tie. A resigned, almost wry expression infused his patrician features.

"I only touched her neck," I said in response to the last question he'd asked me. "And only one time to make sure she was really, you know . . . dead."

"And nothing else?" Quinn asked. "I mean, by now you know better than to touch anything else, right?" Sarcastic emphasis on the *by now*.

I glared at him. "I really liked Autumn, you know."

He relented, looking down. True, I hadn't lived in Savannah for a whole year yet and this was the fourth suspicious death that I'd been smack-dab in the middle of. But in my defense, the first one had Quinn pointing a finger at Uncle Ben as a murder suspect, and I just couldn't have that. And the second one? It had been just a coincidence that Declan and I had stumbled across that body in Johnson Square.

Right?

"And anyone who watches television knows not to touch anything," I said. "Though my fingerprints — and Wren's — are going to be all over this place."

"This one's closer to home, I guess," Quinn said. "I'm sorry about that, Katie. But darn it, how —" He shook his head. "Never mind. It's not like you get into these situations on purpose." His expression was unreadable as his eyes met mine. "Do you?"

I bristled. "You think I enjoy being around so much death?"

He hesitated, then shook his head and looked away again.

Death? Or murder? The image of the blue marks on the dead woman's neck played for a moment on my mental movie screen.

"Why was she lying on the desk like that?" I blurted.

"It appears she was posed."

"Posed? Who would do something like that?"

"Her killer." Quinn watched me, unblinking.

"Oh . . . but . . ." I swallowed, hard. "So it's definitely murder."

"We need to confirm how she died, of course," he said, but I suspected he was thinking of those marks on her neck, too. "In your opinion, might she have committed suicide?"

"I — I don't think so," I stammered. But even as the words came out of my mouth, I realized just how much I didn't know about Autumn. "I don't know," I amended. "Listen, I'm afraid I really can't tell you anything else. I got here after Wren found her, and then I called you." I glanced pointedly at my watch.

Quinn held my gaze for a few more heartbeats. I could feel him evaluating how to handle me. "You don't know if she had any enemies?"

I shook my head. "Not really. She was recently divorced, but I don't know much about her ex. All she said was that her marriage stagnated and then died. And she has . . . had . . . a boyfriend who came to pick her up here at Georgia Wild a few times. Hunter Normandy." He seemed nice enough, yet I hadn't really taken to him. Though I didn't actually see auras, I often sensed them, though only recently had I realized that not everyone had the same experience. To me, auras were kind of like flavors. Call me weird, but some people were spicy and some were salty and some were sweet or bitter. Hunter, on the other hand, didn't seem to have any flavor at all.

Wait a minute. "Wren?"

She still sat in the desk chair where I'd deposited her earlier, a dazed look on her face. Quinn had asked her a few questions, but she'd answered only in whispered monosyllables. He'd soon given up and begun to quiz me. Now she turned her head and blinked at me slowly.

"Honey, do you know what kind of car Hunter drives?" I wanted to be sure before saying anything.

It took her a moment as her mind engaged. She licked her lips. "It's a Jeep. Square-looking thing."

"Like a Wrangler?"

She nodded.

Detective Quinn watched the brief exchange with interest.

I hesitated, then made a decision. "A vehicle like that was leaving just as I got here. In fact I took its parking space out front."

"Did you see the driver?"

"Not really."

"Male or female?"

"Sorry. I only saw a vague figure."

"Don't suppose you noticed the license plate."

I shook my head. "But the driver did seem to be in a hurry. Still, like I said, I don't *know* that it was Hunter."

"Yes, you've made that clear," Quinn said with a slightly puzzled look.

"I just don't want . . . Well, you remember the witness who said she saw Ben . . ." I trailed off, unwilling to point out that Quinn had almost arrested my uncle based on her word.

His lips thinned. "I understand. Just let me check in with the crime scene techs before you go." Frowning, he strode down the hallway toward the sound of clicking cameras and murmuring voices.

"Wren, honey? Shall I call Mimsey?"

She shook her head. "When we're done here."

Detective Quinn returned with a plastic bag in his hand. He held it out to me. Without thinking, I recoiled. Forcing myself to step forward, I peered down at what was obviously some kind of evidence. After a few seconds I recognized the dark red paper Autumn had been clutching in her hand. That she'd presumably been holding this when she died was bad enough. Worse was the energy it gave off — a sickly sense of decay, a deep-rooted rot. I imagined I could actually smell it over the burnt-coffee stink that still permeated the air.

"Does this mean anything to you?" he asked.

With considerable effort, I leaned close enough to examine the crumpled form. "It looks like origami. A bird, maybe? No, a bat. Even crumpled up like that I'm pretty sure."

My words apparently pierced Wren's fog, because she got up and made her way over to where we stood.

"It *is* a bat," she breathed. "A maroon bat."

Quinn turned the bag in his hand. "Maroon, burgundy, whichever. But it does look like a bat."

Wren reached for the bag. Frowning, Quinn pulled it back so she couldn't grab it. "No," she said. "It's a *maroon* bat. A subspecies of bat that was native to this area. *Lasiuris marrona.* The coloration of the fur is somewhat darker than the red bat's, and there is a distinctive kink to the third metacarpal." As she spoke, her voice became stronger.

"What do you mean 'was native'?" he asked.

"The maroon bat has supposedly been extinct for over a decade." She blinked at him. "Except six months ago a small number were sighted in Fagen Swamp. They were reported to us shortly after I came to work for Georgia Wild. What else could this be?" Wren's teeth clamped onto her lower lip.

"I think Autumn had been trying to prevent the sale of that swamp to developers until we could verify the existence of the bats," I said to Quinn. Most of my work at Georgia Wild was grunt work — keeping the donor database up-to-date, filing, and general administrative tasks. I'd heard mention of the Fagen Swamp project, but not for a while.

"Who would want to develop swampland?" he asked. "Sounds like it would be more trouble than it's worth."

Wren's eyes cleared as she explained that a group of investors intended to completely drain the swamp and rebuild it into a world-class golf course. "Autumn was an environmental lawyer who devoted her life to the preservation of unique habitats in order to save the species of both flora and fauna found within them. That was why she founded Georgia Wild. Since learning of the maroon bat sightings, she'd been in contact with the land purchasers' lawyer."

"Who is?" Quinn's pen scratched in the small notebook he'd pulled from his pocket.

"His name is Logan Seward. He works for the investors and the landowner, so he's hardly a friend to us," she said.

"That sounds like a conflict of interest," Quinn said. "Who's the landowner?"

"A man named Gart Fagen. Hence 'Fagen Swamp.' It's been in his family for generations." She frowned. "And now he's willing to sell it off to some faceless group that plans to raze it completely."

"I remember filing some documents about

Fagen Swamp with the EPA," I said.

Wren nodded. "We've tried to get the Environmental Protection Agency involved for a while. They've shown a mild interest in saving that particular habitat because it's the perfect place for gray bats to thrive. They're endangered, but there's already significant protection in the Savannah Wildlife Refuge. However, the maroon bat is considered *extinct.* If there really are some in that swamp, it might light a fire under the EPA."

Quinn looked down at the crumpled paper encased in plastic. "Interesting."

"There are so many places to save, and we have limited resources. Autumn told me she was getting ready to give up on the project." Wren sounded angry.

His eyes narrowed, and I wondered how that might sound to Quinn. Could Wren, in her fervent desire to keep the swamp habitat whole for maroon bats and, presumably, all the other species that thrived there, possibly be considered a suspect in her friend's murder? Quinn had jumped to conclusions about Uncle Ben after all.

Sure enough, he asked, "Ms. Knowles, when did you arrive here?"

"Right before Katie got here. About quarter after five or so. Does that sound right?"

She looked at me, oblivious to where Quinn was so obviously going with his questions.

"I got here about five twenty." I glanced at my watch. It was only a little after six, though it felt like I'd been at Georgia Wild for hours.

"And where were you two the rest of the day?" Quinn persisted.

"I was at the Honeybee, of course. You can't possibly think —," I began.

She put her hand on top of mine and squeezed, finally understanding. "It's okay. I was at Savannah State University all day after having breakfast with my grandparents at J. Christopher's. First I participated in a panel about habitat restoration ecology and then visited two classes to speak with students. It's easy enough to check. I went straight from there to Georgia Wild, and Katie came in right after I'd found . . . well, you know." Her voice broke, and she covered her face with her hands.

I moved to put an arm around her shoulders. "She doesn't have to talk about any more of this right now, does she?" Grief came off her in waves, and I wanted nothing more than to hug her tightly and tell her it was all going to be okay.

Except, of course, it wasn't.

Quinn slowly shook his head. "I'm sorry,

Ms. Knowles, but I'm afraid we really do need to know everything you can tell us as soon as possible."

She took a deep breath and dropped her hands. "I understand." Patting my shoulder, she said, "I'm okay, Katie. All I was going to say is that Autumn had one last ace up her sleeve regarding Fagen Swamp. She decided to talk to one of the investors in the land deal. She thought perhaps Seward wasn't sharing information about the maroon bats with all the members of the investment group, and while they're scattered all over the country, there's one who lives right here in Savannah."

"I didn't know she was going to do that," I said. "Who is it?"

"The CEO of the Dawes Corporation, Heinrich Dawes."

My arm dropped from her shoulders.

Great.

CHAPTER 4

Detective Quinn directed a skeptical look my way. "You didn't know Dawes was involved with this golf course venture?"

I shook my head. "Had no idea."

Quinn knew I had a history with Heinrich's son, Steve. I sighed. Declan would not be happy if Steve came back into my life right now. My jaw set. I'd made my choice between them, and I could make a choice now. I could walk away from this.

I *would* walk away from this.

Gathering Mungo in my arms, I grabbed my tote. "I'm sorry. I have to go. If I think of anything else, I'll give you a call. Wren, do you need a ride home?"

"I have my car."

"You okay to drive?" I wanted to inquire about her Imbolc plans but not in front of Quinn.

She nodded. "I'm fine."

Of course, she wasn't, not really. Neither

was I. Still, I could function, and talking about the thing she was most passionate about had seemed to right Wren somewhat. "Okay. I'll talk to you soon," I said.

Detective Quinn didn't try to stop me as I turned on my heel and marched outside. He came to stand in the doorway as I unlocked my car and got inside. When I looked back at him, he raised his hand, a rather friendly gesture under the circumstances. He was probably delighted that I was staying out of his way.

Good. I didn't want to get on his bad side.

"Perhaps this has nothing to do with dark magic," I said to Mungo as I steered the Bug away from the curb. Never mind the dragonfly. Never mind the shiver that always told me to be on alert, that something important was going on.

"Isn't death bad enough without magic being involved?"

Mungo sighed.

On the way home I broke my own rule about not talking on my cell phone while driving in order to call Mimsey. Wren's mother lived in northern California, and Mimsey was her closest family in town. I tracked her down in her flower shop, Vase Value.

"Oh, my heavens," Mimsey exclaimed

after I'd given her a brief rundown on what had happened at Georgia Wild. "I'll call her right away. Poor thing, finding her friend who passed on like that." She made a tsking sound, and I imagined her white pageboy swinging as she shook her head. "And how are you?"

"Oh, I'm . . ." How was I really? "Actually I'm kind of numb."

"Of course you are, dear. That's to be expected."

"I suppose we should cancel the Imbolc celebration tonight."

Her response was immediate and emphatic. "Absolutely not, Katie! We need this celebration of the coming of the light, especially given the darkness you've witnessed today. But would you rather we had it at my house?"

I was relieved to hear she thought we should continue. I'd been looking forward to it for days.

"Not at all," I said. "I have everything ready. Just have to cook up the bannock cakes and reheat the mulled cider."

"Excellent," Mimsey said. "Do you mind if I invite Wren when I talk to her?"

"That's a great idea. Do you think she'll come?"

"She usually prefers to celebrate by herself, but after what happened today, she might not want to be alone. We'll see."

We ended the call as I was pulling into the driveway of the carriage house. Headlights rounded the corner as I let Mungo out to run in the yard, and a familiar black pickup pulled to the curb. I got out of the Bug and approached as Declan McCarthy stepped to the sidewalk. Despite the chill air he didn't wear a jacket over his PROUD TO BE A FIRST RESPONDER T-shirt and jeans. Tall and muscular, Deck possessed classic good looks: dark wavy hair cut short to meet fire department regulation, a solid planed face, and bright blue eyes. The man even had a dimple when he smiled, for Pete's sake. Looks like that usually came with an ego to match, but being raised by a strong mother in a houseful of four sisters had apparently humbled him.

It had also made him a pretty good cook. I eyed the Tupperware containers in his hand. "What's that?"

"Chili con carne," he mumbled before he pulled me close and his lips found mine.

"Mmm. Nice," I said a few moments later. "The chili, too."

He turned, sliding his arm around my shoulders. I inhaled his scent of newly mown grass and peppermint as we walked across the yard. Mungo jumped around us, wagging his tail in greeting. Declan was one of his favorite people.

"I made a big batch for the guys and thought you might want some, too. Even made up a batch without any onions for the little guy here." His sorghum-laced voice reflected that he was a born-and-bred Savannahian.

I laughed. "Mungo, you are one lucky puppy to have this guy around." My familiar was such a little oink that he'd eat anything, including onions and chocolate and other things that were bad for dogs. When he did get into such things, they didn't seem to affect him, but better safe than sorry.

"Besides," Declan said, "you're having your party tonight, and knowing you, you'll get everything ready for them and forget to eat any supper."

Your party. He knew all about Lucy and the spellbook club. And me. When I'd finally told him the truth, I'd been relieved at his relatively mild reaction. After all, Bianca's husband had left her when he found out she was Wiccan. But Declan had seemed amused that I'd been so nervous about telling him. As time went on, though, I was coming to realize that he really didn't *get* what magic was all about. I'd tried to explain the idea of manifesting a desired outcome through focused intention, but he continued to think being a witch was more of a hobby like knitting or scrapbooking. Then again, Ben probably didn't get Lucy all the time, either. It didn't matter. He'd once told me he'd love her if she went bald or turned orange, so learning she was a witch wasn't a big deal.

Like Ben, Declan was a genuinely good guy. I always felt relaxed and safe when he was around. He was funny and smart and often gave me a break from cooking at home after baking all day at the Honeybee.

Like now. "Thanks for thinking of me," I said.

He squeezed me. "Silly goose. I can hardly think of anything else. And speaking of thinking, have you thought any more about going to Boston?"

For the past couple of weeks, Declan had been urging me to go to Massachusetts with him so I could meet his family. I unlocked the door and we went inside. "I have, actually —"

My cell phone rang, cutting off my words. *Saved by the bell.*

It was my aunt. "I just got a call from Mimsey, and she told me about Autumn. Oh, my gosh, Katie, are you okay? Why

47

didn't you phone me? Are you sure you don't want to cancel tonight?"

"Lucy," I tried, but she kept talking.

"Or maybe I should come over early to help you."

"Lucy!"

"Yes, honey, I'm sorry. Just tell me what I can do."

"I'm fine, really. I mean, it was awful, but I'm okay. Declan is here right now. On the way to his forty-eight hours at the firehouse." I looked at him for confirmation.

He nodded, curiosity practically oozing from his pores.

"Oh, that's good. Have him stay until I can get there," she said.

"He has to get going. And Lucy, I still have to make up the bannock cakes for tonight." Truthfully, I wanted a little space to process having seen my fourth dead body in less than a year. That had to be some kind of record for a mild-mannered baker, and I needed to figure out how I felt about it.

And what to do about it.

So now I said, "I could use a couple of hours to get myself together."

Lucy was quiet for a moment, and I wondered whether I'd insulted her. But when she spoke, her tone was warm. "Of course. I understand. I'll show up at eight thirty as planned. If you change your mind and want me to come over earlier after all, just give me a jingle."

"Thanks, Luce."

"Say hello to Declan for me, okay?"

"All righty."

But when I hung up, I had to say a lot more than hello. He wanted to know why Lucy had been so worried, and the more I told him, the more his eyes widened. By the time I was done, he had me enveloped in his arms again.

Which, frankly, was an awfully nice place to be.

"Why didn't you call me?" he demanded.

Gently, I pushed away. "Deck, I just got home. I haven't had time to call anyone — except Mimsey from the car to let her know about Wren."

"Well, yeah, I guess," he almost grumbled. He liked to be needed. Suddenly leaning forward, he stared into my eyes. "Are you really okay?"

I nodded and tried a smile.

"You are not! Katie, how did this happen? What the heck is going on?"

Waving my hand, I said, "Bad luck, I guess. Worse luck for Autumn — let's be clear. Now listen — I really am okay. And you have to get going, or you'll be late."

"But, Katie —"

"And I promise not to worry about you every single second while you're on duty, obsessing about whether you'll be called out to a fire or a horrible car wreck or some other tragedy. After all, it's what you do, and I have every confidence in your ability to handle whatever comes up."

He gave me a wry look and put his hand on my shoulder. "Okay, okay. I get it. You're tough. But you need to know you don't have to be. Not all the time." His kiss was light and tender.

Chastened, I said in a small voice, "Thanks."

"Call me if you want. Either way, I'll check in with you later."

I sat at my kitchen table and listened to the rumble of his truck engine fade. Mungo jumped up on my lap. The chili called from the containers on the counter. Holding Mungo, I got up and dished out a bowl, one-handed.

"You want some?"

His *yip* was subdued.

I heated his a little in the microwave and put it on his place mat on the floor, and he tucked in. I heated mine to blazing and took it to my own place mat on the table. It was awesome chili: spicy and exotic, deepened with the flavor of, Declan had once confessed, a splash of Jack Daniel's.

Still, my stomach topsy-turvy from the day's events, I managed only four bites before I had to dump it back into the container.

Scottish bannock cakes were traditional fare for Celtic Imbolc celebrations, and having a chance to make them for the spellbook club had thrilled me. After all, baking was a huge part of my life, and now so was magic. I loved how they often overlapped. The old recipes I'd found were for a kind of unleavened fried or baked patty, almost like a thick, oat-laden pancake. More recent recipes included yeast, which would make for a lighter, fluffier interior. I could easily see how the older version could turn out like hockey pucks, but I really wanted to stay as traditional as possible and avoid using yeast.

So I decided to do one of my favorite things when it came to making a recipe (or a spell, I was learning) my own: I used elements from very different recipes to come up with something totally new. That something, it turned out, was sweet and savory and substantial without resembling a dry, flat rock.

I melted bacon fat to begin. After all, when in doubt, bacon is a good place to start with any recipe. Then I added oatmeal, baking soda, and a little salt. In another bowl I mixed together beaten egg, milk, barely melted butter, and a bit of maple syrup, then added it all to the oatmeal. When it was the consistency I wanted — still sticky, but workable with floured hands — I dumped in white raisins, candied orange peel, and some finely chopped bacon. A bit of chewiness and a bit of crunch.

My breath deepened as I worked, the acts of mixing and tasting and testing calming both body and mind. In the kitchen I understood how flavors interacted and how ingredients reacted with other ingredients, heat, agitation, and time. With Lucy's continued instruction, I also knew how to add a little magical oomph here and there. I felt sure, able to trust my instincts.

However, when it came to fulfilling some kind of magical destiny, I didn't feel sure at all. Which I hated because I'd really come to enjoy the burst of confidence I'd developed since living in Savannah. The horrible way that paper bat had felt had thrown me. Ugh.

Pausing for an elaborate shoulder roll, I

pushed the thought away. Tonight was for me, for my friends, for Brigit and her promise of spring. Hope and forward motion.

Except for Autumn Boles, of course.

After kneading the rough dough together with a bit more oatmeal, I formed it into three rounds and then cut the rounds into quarters — also called farls — as I did when making scones. The triangular shapes went onto a buttered cookie sheet to bake up crispy on the edges and tender in the middle.

I could hardly wait to hear the spellbook club's verdict.

While they baked, I changed into warm slacks and a thick sweater, tidied the kitchen, and double-checked the preparations I'd made in the dark of morning. Everything looked fine, so when the bannocks were done, I set them out to cool on racks on the counter and shoved aside the pile of seed catalogs on my tiny kitchen table so I could open my laptop.

Mungo whined softly in the back of his throat. Without taking my eyes off the screen, I scooped him up and deposited him on my lap where he promptly lay down so I could type.

Quickly, I searched the online archive of

the *Savannah Morning News* for any mention of the swampland deal or the promise of a new golf course being built on the outskirts of the city. I knew from past experience that the paper was often the first place to get basic information, but I typed my search request with trepidation.

Heinrich Dawes described himself as a venture capitalist, and I'd heard Steve was trying his hand at the family business since reconciling with his father and joining his druidic "social club." However, Steve was also a former crime reporter turned columnist for the *News.* Most of his columns focused on Savannah business, and I didn't remember seeing any about the land deal. Still, I couldn't be sure.

The enmity between Steve and Declan was almost palpable when they were in the same room. Not only had Steve and I once been on the verge of getting seriously involved, but Declan and Steve had their own issues centering around the death of Steve's brother — who had been Declan's best friend.

When the results popped onto the screen, I frowned. There was a brief mention of Fagen Swamp, but it was from five years before in relation to a strange but irrelevant story about an H-bomb landing someplace in the area in the late 1950s. Apparently the investment group had managed to keep the upcoming deal out of the papers. That didn't surprise me since I knew Heinrich Dawes was a man used to secrets and used to getting his way.

Weeks before, when I'd asked Autumn if getting the word out about the maroon bats in Fagen Swamp wouldn't be a good way to garner public support, she'd agreed but said she wanted some definitive proof of the bats' existence first. Otherwise she thought Georgia Wild would look foolish and lose some of its hard-won reputation. I couldn't disagree with her logic.

So I wasn't surprised when nothing surfaced on the Internet about a maroon bat sighting, and the only two references to Georgia Wild were regarding other projects the conservation agency had been involved with. Then, right before I shut down the computer, I saw an article about the increasing development of natural areas in the state.

Gart Fagen was quoted in the piece as saying that the swamp that carried his family's name was a nasty, fetid place that he'd sell in a heartbeat. The article was dated over two years previously and stated that Fagen lived in Sedona, Arizona. If he liked the desert that much, then it was no wonder he had little interest in keeping his inherited marshland. Now it looked like he was about to get his wish.

Snapping the laptop shut, I said to Mungo, "Come on, little guy. We've got enough time for a quick walk around the block."

Yip!

After slipping on my jacket, I jammed a wooly hat over my ears and opened the front door. Mungo bounded out to the postage-stamp lawn, the whole back half of his body wagging as I caught up. The night air had crisped, and I sucked in a deep, apprecia-tive breath as we set off.

Since the houses on my side of the street backed up to an open space, we set off to circle the block across the way. I kept a brisk pace, but Mungo ran circles around me, get-ting twice as much exercise as I did. Good. He could be a bit of a lazybones, lolling around in the Honeybee office while I worked and rarely accompanying me on my runs.

As I walked, I thought about Declan's repeated request that we go to Boston so I could meet his mother and stepfather. I was fine with meeting whatever family he wanted to introduce me to; that wasn't the issue.

But the proposed trip was just one more symptom of Declan pushing me to get serious, and instinctively I resisted. It wasn't that I didn't care deeply about Declan. It was just that it had been only a little over a year since my broken engagement, and I didn't want to jump the gun. Declan was in his early thirties, and I knew he wanted to settle down sooner than later. Still, I wasn't ready to think about marriage again, and I certainly wasn't ready to think about having a family.

Would my children carry the same hereditary affinity for magic that had passed down to me? If I had a child with Declan, would he dilute the gift, or would it matter at all? After all, some said magic passed through the mother's bloodline.

I could imagine what my father, who came from a long line of Shawnee medicine men, would have to say about that.

At least he'd say something. Mama and I had barely managed a few awkward conversations ever since Lucy — her younger sister — had had the temerity to ask me to move to Savannah and open the bakery with her and Ben. Well, that and telling me I was a witch. Mama had worked pretty hard my whole life to keep that information from me, and was none too happy when I'd embraced the Craft so thoroughly.

We'd circled the block, and rounding the final corner revealed Margie Coopersmith hadn't drawn her front curtains against the night yet. I could see straight into her living room. The coffee table had been shoved aside to make space for a blanket fort. Her five-year-old twins, Jonathan and Julia, had on cowboy hats, and Julia ran around brandishing a toy bow and arrow. Margie's golden ponytail swung forward as she plopped Baby Bart onto the sofa. He turned and slid to the floor, hanging on to the cushions as he watched his mother drop down on all fours to give Jonathan a ride. Bart opened his mouth, and I could hear his delighted squeal all the way out on the street.

Laughing, I asked my canine companion, "Can you imagine my mother doing that when I was little?"

His head tipped to one side.

"Sorry. I forgot you haven't met her." Which made me think about meeting Declan's mother again. Would he ever meet my mother? Did I want him to?

The image of Autumn Boles' bloodless face rose in my mind. Did she have family? Parents and siblings who would miss her? And what about Hunter Normandy? What possible cause could her boyfriend have had to kill her? I'd met Hunter only a few times, but he and Autumn seemed to get along quite well, despite the icky feeling he gave me. The hit I got off him was hard to describe, but it was almost impersonal, as if he wasn't the actual source of it. After all, Autumn had been no dummy. She was unlikely to choose — or stick with — a beau who was violent or otherwise unsavory.

Her ex-husband was another possible suspect, of course. The police always seemed to look at significant others and exes first. Autumn's divorce had been final a few months before, and other than infrequent references to incidents from their past, she rarely spoke of him. I didn't even know his name; she'd always referred to him as "the ex," usually accompanied with a slight eye roll.

Then there was that darn bat she'd been holding. Was it actually related to her death, or had she just happened to be holding the origami when she'd been attacked? And what was *wrong* with it, in a metaphysical sense? I'd have to ask Wren if she'd felt it, too.

Sighing, I wished I could talk to my mother about the whole situation. Lucy was great, as were the other ladies in the spellbook club and my dad, but it wasn't the same. What if there really was dark magic involved? I reminded myself that my mother wouldn't have been the right one to talk to about Autumn's murder anyway. Even if she'd been happy that I practiced magic, she'd still be the same overprotective Mama she'd always been.

Back home, I opened the door for Mungo and inhaled the spiced fragrance of the fresh-baked bannock cakes with appreciation.

And then it hit me. I wasn't angry at my mother anymore. Not for keeping the family heritage of hedgewitchery a secret, and not for being such a pain in the patootie ever since I'd found out about it. I was simply tired of dealing with her stubbornness about magic.

And I missed her.

CHAPTER 5

By the time the doorbell rang at eight twenty, the apple cider was hot and infused with cloves, cardamom, clover honey, and a few black peppercorns. Jaida French stood on my porch, armed with a yellow candle, a bottle of wine, and a worried expression. An attorney by trade and tarot expert by training, she had been teaching me how to incorporate cards of the major arcana into my spell work. Tonight she wore designer jeans and a dark red sweater that glowed like fire against her deep mocha skin. She swept into the living room followed by her familiar, a Great Dane named Anubis.

Tail wagging so hard I thought he'd put his back out, Mungo launched himself off the couch. The two dogs touched noses. Mungo was about the size of the Great Dane's head.

"God, Katie. How awful. How utterly, utterly awful." Jaida set the bottle on the coffee table and threw her arms around me. Her soothing voice ran over me like caramel.

I returned her embrace, surprised to feel hot tears stinging my eyelids. "Mimsey called you, too," I mumbled into her comforting shoulder. She smelled like cinnamon.

"Of course. She called all of us." She stepped back and held me at arm's length, looking me up and down. "I'm so sorry about your friend."

I nodded, swallowing the sudden ache in my throat. "Thanks," I finally managed. "Wren was much closer to Autumn than I was, though." I thought of her stunned face as she'd careened out of Autumn's office. "I'm really worried about her. Mimsey said she was going to try to get her to come tonight."

"And Wren said she would." Jaida laid her coat across the back of one of the wingbacks.

I started to close the door, then saw Lucy's 1964 Thunderbird convertible pull into the driveway behind my Volkswagen. The top, of course, was up, but I could see Mimsey in the passenger seat, and the tall figure in the back had to be Wren.

"Grab yourself some cider," I called to Jaida, and went out to the porch just as

Margie opened her front door to take a look. I waved to her. She waved back and went inside. I'd already told her I was having a book club meeting at my house so she wouldn't die from curiosity when the ladies arrived.

The three women got out of the Thunderbird and hurried toward me. Honeybee strolled leisurely behind them, the very picture of orange-striped feline nonchalance. Lucy wore a black cloak that reached nearly to the ground and had tamed her mop of hair into a thick braid that fell over one shoulder.

Mimsey, even shorter than my aunt and considerably rounder, wore a long, poufy down coat in vivid eye-pounding orange. Heckle, her parrot, rode on one shoulder. The septuagenarian was the unspoken leader of the spellbook club, as much as any group as democratic as ours needed a leader. She practiced flower and color magic as well as a bit of divination. Orange was, among other things, the color of movement and life force, apropos for this evening's festivities, and the bow clinging to the side of her smooth white pageboy was the same traffic-cone hue as her coat. As they approached, I saw Mimsey's usual twinkle had been ousted by worry. Lucy watched me

63

with careful eyes as I greeted them, her face relaxing when I smiled at her.

Wren looked a little better, blinking at me from behind her dark-framed glasses. Her sheepskin coat hung loosely on her thin frame, and tight black leggings emphasized her long legs. "Hi, Katie. Thanks for letting me come tonight. I know covens aren't traditionally open to outsiders, especially for Sabbat celebrations."

I took her arm and led the way inside. "Don't be silly. You're not an outsider, Wren. You could be a member of the spellbook club if you wanted."

"I keep telling her," Mimsey said. Heckle squawked his agreement.

"I know, Gran."

"Mimsey, do you think you'll be warm enough in that coat?" I asked. She looked ready for an arctic expedition, and it was still in the low fifties outside.

Heckle, until now the perfect gentleman, suddenly squawked, "Sarcasm! Lowest form of humor!"

"Hush," Mimsey admonished, but at least she was smiling.

Inside, Jaida called from the kitchen, "Who wants cider and who wants wine?"

We all exchanged glances and answered as one: "Wine!"

As everyone got their drinks, the doorbell rang again. Before I could get there, the door opened and Bianca Devereaux and Cookie Rios entered. The other ladies drifted back out of the kitchen, glasses in hand.

"Hi, guys," I said.

"Hello," Cookie said, the lilt of her Haitian accent evident even in the one word. She took off her long leather coat to reveal a form-fitting dress the same jade as her eyes. These days her long dark hair was high-lighted with subtle blue streaks. She was a few years younger than me, but I felt sure she possessed an old soul.

Tall and elegant, Bianca wore a long black cloak like Lucy's. It was pretty traditional garb for workings, especially outside. As she was more traditional than any of us, Bianca looked the most like what the majority of people thought a traditional witch should look — long black hair, pale skin, penetrat-ing green eyes, and a tendency to wear clothes that swirled and flowed around her. Funny that she was closest to Cookie, the one most likely to break the rules and ignore the Rule of Three.

Though the more I practiced, the more good and bad kept getting mixed up.

Now Bianca shook her head. "Oh, Wren.

I'm so sorry for your loss." She held out a basket that held a hefty bottle of champagne and seven carefully wrapped flutes.

Wren took a deep breath. "Thank you."

As I reached to relieve her of the basket, I saw two bright eyes looking out from inside the collar of Bianca's cloak. A tiny black nose quivered, then disappeared.

"I see you brought a friend," I said.

Her lips curved into a gentle smile. "Puck," she said softly, "come out and meet the spellbook club."

The nose appeared again, then the head, snow-white except for a Zorro mask of black fur around the eyes. In a liquid flash he slithered around Bianca's neck and down her arm to the cloak's pocket where he resumed watching us with those dark, assessing eyes.

Puck was a ferret.

"Oh, he's darling," Lucy exclaimed. "How did he find you?" She asked because of course familiars find their witches, not the other way around. Mungo had shown up at the carriage house the first day I'd arrived there.

"He came into Moon Grapes this afternoon — from where, I have no idea. I was in my office working on the books when my assistant started shrieking like a madwoman. I ran out front and found her standing on a chair. She thought this little guy was a rat." Bianca's smile widened, and she stroked the sleek head. Puck leaned into her hand. "He came right up to me and has been riding on my shoulder or in my pocket ever since. He's still a bit shy, but Colette adores him." Colette was her six-year-old daughter.

"I'm so happy for you," Jaida said.

I leaned down to pocket level. "Welcome, Puck." Straightening, I took the basket from Bianca and gestured toward the kitchen with my chin. "Help yourself to some wine if you'd like."

They liked. When they'd returned, I said, "Now listen, everyone. We're going to celebrate tonight. Right?"

Wren solemnly nodded her agreement as we all exchanged glances.

I grabbed one of my three kitchen chairs to add to the six already set up around the fire. "At least we'll celebrate the best that we can under the circumstances. Now I'm going to go out and get the fire going. Grab your jackets, ladies."

Cookie's eyes met mine, holding my gaze for a long moment before looking away. I realized that she hadn't said a word since her initial greeting. Her face was a careful mask, but I could tell something was bothering her.

"Cookie —," I began.

"Let's get this party started," she said, and led the way outside.

The crackle of the fire warmed my mind as much as the flames warmed the surrounding air. I respected all of the elements, but nothing was as comforting as fire, especially on a cold night after seeing cold death.

Usually I cast in the relative privacy of the gazebo, but tonight we used salt to cast our circle deosil around the fire, beginning and ending in the east and encompassing all the chairs and the small table I'd added at the last minute. The tabletop held a small vase of snowdrops — sometimes called the maids of February and a traditional symbol of Imbolc — which Mimsey had also chosen to represent snow. The bundle of cinnamon sticks tied with a ribbon the color of bright sunshine also rested on the table, along with a felted woolen lamb Cookie had bought from Annette Lander, who owned the knitting store next to the Honeybee, and the cut-glass bowl containing several packets of organic heirloom flower seeds I'd been hoarding for this night. All the items represented the coming of spring and light and the birth of new plants and animals — especially lambs.

On the southern side of the table a mason jar half filled with sand shielded Jaida's yellow candle from the night air. The bottle of champagne Bianca had brought from Moon Grapes was on the western side. She'd gone totally overboard with the Dom Perignon, but I wasn't exactly surprised. Bianca had a talent for making money in the stock market, and tended to spoil us a bit when she could.

Our glasses of wine had been traded for mugs of hot cider, which now balanced on the gravel next to each chair. The bannock cakes filled a tray on the ground in front of the makeshift altar. Puck reappeared and wrapped himself around the side of Bianca's neck. Anubis and Mungo lay between the chairs Jaida and I had chosen, and Heckle perched on the back of Mimsey's chair. He was uncharacteristically quiet after his outburst, concentrating on preening his brightly colored wings. Honeybee stretched out as close as she could get to the fire, almost touching the copper bowl. Purring, she did that squinty thing with her eyes, which made me smile. It was too bad I was so allergic to her.

After the circle was cast, everyone else

took their seats around the fire. Looking around at my friends, I realized yet again how lucky I was to have them.

"Katie," Lucy said, "how would you like to proceed?"

I hesitated, unsure if what I was about to propose was a good idea now. Might as well find out. "I was thinking that I'd like to add a twist to the usual incantation." Reaching into my pocket, I pulled out several sheets of handmade paper and a variety of pens. "I do have something short and sweet to recite, but I'd like to incorporate some burning magic as well. What do you all think about writing down our wishes as spring approaches and releasing them in the fire?"

Mimsey clasped her hands and beamed. "Oh, my stars, Katie. That's a wonderful idea."

Jaida said, "It's certainly in keeping with the spirit of looking forward with anticipation and thankfulness."

The others nodded their agreement. All except Wren.

"Anyone who doesn't want to participate doesn't have to," I said, watching her.

Her eyes met mine, but she didn't say anything.

"Okay, so let's get started," I said, passing around the paper.

There was silence as everyone bent to writing their wishes. In my peripheral vision I saw Wren writing, too. Perhaps this ritual would give her a modicum of peace.

When we were done, everyone rose and moved closer to the fire and to one another. Lucy's gloved hand squeezed my own before dropping away. With a quick glance at Margie's house, I moved to the table. The circle was to protect our working, and I'd added an incantation to create disinterest next door. It seemed to be working.

I cleared my throat. Lucy gave an encouraging nod. I placed the fingertips of one hand on the wooly lamb, plunged my other hand into the bowl of flower-seed packets, and began to recite my short and simple Imbolc incantation.

Hail Brigit, protectress
Of women,
Of children,
Of lambs and babes,
Of seedlings and fledglings,
Of all newborn creatures.

My hand moved to the scented yellow candle and the vase holding the delicate sprigs of snowdrops.

71

With this golden light
We welcome you tonight.
Come February maids
And darkness fades.

I brought my hands out in front of me,
palms up.

Brigit, bless the plants of yesteryear
And carry forward new creation,
Transformation,
Inspiration.
May you heal ill's cost and return joy lost.
Let it be so, in celebration.

"Blessed be," Bianca murmured.

At the last minute I'd added the bit about
healing ills, mostly for Wren. After all, Brigit
was the goddess of healing as well as mid-
wifery, and I figured we could use all the
help we could get. At least no one seemed
to think it was out of place.

I took the paper with my wish on it —
there was only one — and gently placed it
among the glowing red coals. It flamed
bright and quick, releasing a brief puff of
smoke that wended toward the starry heavens. I leaned my head back to watch it go.
One by one the others followed suit.

When we had regained our seats, I passed

around the bannock cakes on napkins decorated with vivid sunflowers.

Bianca took a hesitant bite. Delight replaced her doubt. "Oh! I've had bannock cakes before, and they were simply awful. What's your secret?"

Lucy leaned forward to hear my answer.

"Bacon," I said.

My aunt smiled. Any other night she would have laughed, but nothing was normal tonight.

Cookie snorted and leaned forward, staring into the flames. "I hope you're burning magic works, Katie. Brandon is leaving in a month for a stay in Europe to work on his latest art exhibition, and Xana has decided to close the gallery and go with him as his manager. So I'll be out a boyfriend *and* a job." Her words held an undertone of bitterness.

The rest of us exchanged glances. Cookie was known for holding on to both men and jobs for no longer than four months, and she was already three months into the current cycle. Even if her boyfriend and job with the Xana Do! Gallery weren't going away, she would have been moving on. However, she'd always been the one to move on, and this time the choice hadn't been hers. It sounded to me like Brandon and Xana might be doing more than just touring Europe together in the name of art.

Ouch.

"Oh, well," she said with a shrug. "Something will come along."

Bianca patted her arm. "Does anyone else want to share their wishes?"

"Um," I said.

Jaida cocked her head to one side. "Yes?"

They were all watching me. "I wished for clarity."

Cookie tipped her head to one side. "Clarity?" She took another bite of bannock cake and washed it down with a swallow of spiced cider.

"In what regard?" Bianca sounded puzzled.

"As a candela, a lightwitch," Lucy supplied, with a gentle look. "It must be difficult not knowing exactly what that means."

Wren's voice was raw. "Grandma and Lucy were talking about it on the way over here. I don't really know what a lightwitch is, but it sounds like you're supposed to do something to bring Autumn's killer to justice."

My aunt looked at me apologetically.

"That's what I wish for this spring," Wren went on. "No, *before* this spring. I want justice. And money."

74

I blinked. "Money?"

"Autumn had been funding most of Georgia Wild's day-to-day operating expenses with her own money so the first donations we received could go directly toward saving habitats. I don't have enough to keep it going. Heck, I can't make it without a regular paycheck, small as it is. Autumn willed what she had left to G.W., but that's going to take a while to go through probate, won't it?"

Next to me Jaida inclined her head in reluctant agreement. "How long depends on how complicated it is and whether anyone challenges the will."

"Well, her ex-husband might," Wren said. "In the meantime, Georgia Wild was just getting started, and we were operating on a shoestring. We're waiting on a couple of grants, but the coffers are empty right now. I can get into the nonprofit's bank accounts, but I don't have access to Autumn's. I don't even have the money to pay the rent that was due two days ago."

Bianca looked thoughtful. "Let me do some checking with my bank. I'm sure I can at least cover that for you."

Wren took a deep breath, and when she spoke, her tone had lost its desperate cast. "Thank you. I just need a loan until the grant money comes through."

I was grateful the subject of money had crowded out Wren's insistence that I investigate her friend's murder, but my relief was short-lived. She turned toward me again, and the flames that were reflected in her glasses hid her eyes. I could feel her watching me, though. Willing me.

Bianca popped the champagne cork then, and we toasted Brigit before reversing the circle and watching the fire die down in the copper bowl. As I drained my glass, I wondered whether Dom Perignon was supposed to taste like sawdust.

The party broke up a little after eleven. Though the next day was Sunday, many of us had early mornings — Lucy and I in particular. She had offered to stay the night, concerned about me being alone after the grisly discovery, but I assured her it was unnecessary.

Lucy, Mimsey, and Wren were the last to leave. The Coopersmiths' windows were dark as they got into the Thunderbird, everyone battened down for a good night's sleep before Margie rousted the kids out of bed in the morning to go to church. I was glad to learn Wren was going to stay the night with her grandparents. She slumped wearily into the passenger seat, fastening her seat belt before removing her glasses and rubbing her eyes. She blinked myopically up at where I stood by the passenger window, a tentative smile flitting across her features. It was the first time she'd smiled all night.

I leaned down. "Wren, you know the paper bat Detective Quinn showed us this afternoon?"

"Like I could ever forget it."

One corner of my mouth twisted up. "Right. Anyway, it felt . . . odd to me."

She put her glasses back on and peered at me through the lenses. "Odd how?"

"You didn't get any strange hit off it? Like an aura, but not really an aura? More like a scent or a flavor, but not something you could actually smell or taste?"

She frowned.

"Guess I'm not making any sense, huh?" I said.

"Sorry, Katie. I didn't feel anything but ill looking at that thing." She looked nauseated just remembering. "What do you think it means?"

I squeezed her shoulder. "I wish I knew."

They drove off, Honeybee gazing enigmatically out the window and Mimsey's hand still fluttering good-bye as Lucy turned the corner. I kept thinking of what

Wren had said about the overdue bills at Georgia Wild. It didn't seem fair that she had to worry about that on top of finding her best friend murdered.

Inside, I double-checked that the fire in the backyard was thoroughly out and locked up. My nerves were on high alert, so I brewed a cup of chamomile tea. While the water heated, I picked up the living room, which took about three minutes. There was space for the slope-backed, purple fainting couch, a Civil War–era trunk that served as a coffee table, and two small wingback chairs but not much else. The built-in bookshelves displayed all sorts of knick-knacks and reading material, though most of my spellbooks were up in the loft where I kept my small altar tucked inside a lidded secretary desk.

Hot tea in hand, I shut off the lights and headed into my bedroom. Mungo sprawled on the bed, waiting for me with sleepy eyes. The small lamp on the bedside stand cast a quiet light on the Williamsburg blue walls. Next to it a scented geranium offered a subtle citrus fragrance from its tiny twisted leaves.

Fire or no fire, after spending a couple of hours outside, I was feeling pretty chilled. Rooting through the bottom drawer of one of the armoires that served as my closet space, I pulled out a pair of flannel pajamas. Baby pink with white snowflakes, they weren't exactly what I would have bought for myself, but my mother had always insisted that pink was a good color for me because of my dark red hair. She'd sent the pajamas last Christmas, perhaps forgetting that winters in Fillmore, Ohio, were a bit more severe than those in Georgia. Still, tonight they were just what Brigit ordered, and I donned them with gratitude.

As soon as I had plumped my pillows and climbed under the quilt, my phone rang. Leaning back against the filigreed wrought-iron headboard, I peered at the display. Dear Declan, calling well after Emily Post's recommended cutoff for telephone calls. He knew that I didn't sleep more than a few hours a night, though, and would still be awake.

"Hey, you," I said.

"Back atcha. How're you doing?"

"Okeydoke."

"Katie."

"Seriously, I'm fine. The ladies just left, I'm wearing my flannel pj's, and Mungo is passed out on the bed."

"Flannel pj's, you say. Somehow you make that sound sexy."

79

I laughed. "You are so biased."

"Yep. So, did you hear that Punxsutawney Phil didn't see his shadow today? We're looking at an early spring."

"Just another method of divination on St. Brigit's Day."

"Really?"

"Yep. Imbolc, Groundhog Day, St. Brigit's Day, Candlemas — all pretty much the same thing to different people. So things are slow at the firehouse?"

"So far only a couple of traffic accidents, even though it's Saturday night, and a smoke detector triggered an alarm in a hotel. A false alarm as it turned out. The chili was a big hit earlier, though."

"Here, too." No need to mention that I'd eaten only a couple of bites. My stomach growled at the thought, and Mungo lifted his head to peer at me.

We chatted for a couple more minutes. Then we indulged in a few sweet nothings and said good night.

This time I finished the whole bowl of chili.

CHAPTER 6

A regular routine had developed on Sunday mornings at the bakery. Ben was off, either playing his weekly golf game with a bunch of his cronies or, in bad weather, hanging out with them at the clubhouse. Lucy and I got most of the baking done early so we could cover the register and espresso counter. Croft Barrow generally came in for a double espresso before heading next door to open his bookstore, and Annette Lander from the knitting store on the other side of us popped in a couple of times to indulge in her twice-on-Sunday cookie fix.

"These are on the house," I told Annette as I handed her a selection of all four sandwich cookies Lucy and I had been experimenting with the day before. "All I ask is that you give honest feedback. Especially on the chocolate filling." The addition of cayenne pepper had already convinced me that was our winner.

She grinned. "Can do — and thanks!"

The bell over the door rang as she hurried back to her store with the Honeybee Bakery bag clutched tightly in her hand.

Once a month the spellbook club met to talk spellbooks — yes, we were a real book club, too — after the bakery was closed to the public. But every Sunday morning the ladies of the spellbook club came in to tidy and update the books in the big shelving units in the reading area. Each would bring a few new selections, chosen through spell work or simple intuition to help customers. They'd remove other items they felt had already served their purpose.

So when Jaida and Bianca breezed in around ten a.m. the morning of February third, I waved from the kitchen and called to Lucy for a venti coffee frappe and a large mocha. I loaded up a couple of plates with chocolate chip gingerbread and took them out to the table where the two women had settled. Next to Jaida's elbow, I spotted a how-to guide for upholstering your own furniture and a copy of *Pride and Prejudice.* Bianca had a tote bag of old copies of *Life Magazine,* a copy of *Jitterbug Perfume,* and a coffee-table book showcasing the art of Georgia O'Keeffe.

Did I mention the Honeybee library

housed an eclectic selection?

"Where's Mimsey?" Jaida asked. The older witch usually showed up before the rest.

I shrugged and glanced over at where Lucy was wiping down the front of the glass display case.

She looked up. "Might not come today. Depends on how Wren is doing, I imagine."

"Of course." Bianca nibbled at a bit of chocolate on the corner of her gingerbread. I swore, it took that woman all day to eat a single pastry. I slid onto the chair beside her.

"What about Cookie?" I asked.

Jaida looked up from the business section of the paper. "Job interview." She said it as though I should have known.

"Really? She didn't say anything about it last night."

"She did to us. Said she wanted to have something lined up before the gallery closed," Bianca said. "Perhaps you were inside."

"I guess." But now that I thought about it, Cookie hadn't been hanging out at Honeybee like she used to, and it had been weeks since I'd had any real one-on-one conversation with her. I racked my brain, trying to think if I'd done something to offend her. "What's the job?"

"Data entry at a medical office."

"That doesn't sound like Cookie at all." It wasn't like her to "line things up" ahead of time, either. She always happened into whatever she needed exactly when she needed it.

Jaida nodded. "I know. Wonder what's up with that." She grabbed the main section of the paper and flipped it open. "Hey, did you see this?"

I knew she was referring to the article about Autumn's death on page four. "Yeah," I said. "It mentions Georgia Wild but no details, and they left out my name. Wren's, too, thank goodness."

The sound of the espresso machine flared, and I looked up. A woman dressed in khaki corduroys and a bright green sweater handed a bill to Lucy. Croft had finished his double espresso and left, so besides us, she was the only one in the bakery.

"I hope business picks up soon," I said in a low voice as the woman took her small drip coffee and left. When the bell over the door tinkled again, I looked up hopefully.

Steve Dawes sauntered into the Honeybee as if it were the most natural thing in the world. Which, of course, it was. After all, we were a bakery and open to the public, for heaven's sake. It was just that he hadn't been in since Declan and I started dating. In fact, I'd seen Steve only a couple of times since I'd broken the news to him in November, and then only in passing.

He waved to us as he walked to the display case, and Bianca began to raise her arm in automatic greeting before she glanced at me and suddenly clasped her hands on the table in front of her. Jaida's eyes cut my way, then returned to Steve. He turned to look at me with a grin that revealed blazing white teeth and emphasized the wicked curve of his lips. He had dark brown eyes and a sharp nose, and wore a half-zipped microfleece, deliciously tight jeans, and brown hiking boots. His long blond hair was pulled straight back off his forehead into its customary ponytail. I wondered if he'd replaced the charm in the leather cord that held it. My fingers crept to the wire-thin platinum circle I wore on a chain around my neck. It had been woven into that leather tie until Steve, a druid like his father, insisted that I take it. The only time Declan had asked me about it, I'd told him it was a protection charm — which was true. I simply hadn't mentioned who'd given it to me.

"What looks good today?" Steve asked.

You do. I blinked and looked away. *Declan*

*is so much better for me, though. Really, he
is.*

"Try the gingerbread," Lucy said. "Or we
have maple bacon scones, apple fritters,
mocha shortbread, peach thumbprints,
cherry pinwheels — or if you want something savory, how about a piece of rosemary
shortbread? It's marvelous with chai tea."

"Gingerbread sounds great," he said.

Jaida reached for one of the books on the
table and became instantly engrossed. Lucy
shot a look at me from behind the register.

"Anything to drink?" my aunt asked.

Cappuccino. Dry.

"How about a dry cappuccino," he said.

Lucy spurred the espresso machine into
action.

Steve paid and brought the mug and his
gingerbread over to the table next to where
Jaida, Bianca, and I were sitting. He sat
down in the chair nearest mine.

"Katie."

"Steve."

"I heard about Autumn Boles."

"I'm not surprised," I said. "It's right
there in the paper."

"Are you all right?"

Frowning, I asked, "Did I miss something?
I wasn't mentioned in the *News* article."

"No, but you were involved with Georgia Wild."

I shifted to face him, leaning my forearm on the back of the bistro chair. "And how do you know that?"

"Oh, for heaven's sake, Katie. Of course I keep track of you. Just because you decided you don't want me in your life doesn't mean I stopped caring for you."

"I never said I didn't want you in my life. Only that I didn't think we should be, you know, romantically involved."

Jaida and Bianca gave up any pretense of not listening. Lucy moved closer, industriously polishing the glass of the pastry display that she'd already finished cleaning. Not exactly subtle.

His eyebrow arched. "My mistake. Either way, you do have a tendency to attract trouble. I wanted to make sure you're okay."

"I'm fine." I could hear the strain in my voice, though.

He leaned back and looked at me speculatively. "You found her, didn't you?"

I hesitated a few seconds before shaking my head. "Wren did."

"Wren?" He took a bite of gingerbread. Pleasure flickered across his face as he chewed the tender spicy cake filled with crunchy candied ginger and dark cacao chips.

"Wren Knowles. Mimsey's granddaughter."

He took a slow sip of cappuccino, eyes locked with mine. "There's more. Tell me."

I breathed out a sigh. "I came in immediately afterward. I was the one who called the police."

"Darn it. I knew it."

"What else do you know?" Heck, as long as he was here I might as well ask.

"About what?"

"About the Fagen Swamp deal your father's investing in," I said. "You're working with your father now that you two are so tight, right?"

He glanced at Jaida and shook his head. "God, Katie. You never stop."

"Hey — you came to see me, not the other way around."

He looked around at the other three women who were watching us with unabashed interest. "Well, maybe you need to come to the office if you want to talk about business."

"Do you know Logan Seward?" I asked. "The attorney?"

"He's a colleague." He took a final slug of cappuccino and wiped away the milk-foam mustache with a napkin.

Jaida tipped her head to one side. "Logan Seward? I recently met him. At the courthouse. New to town, isn't he?"

He nodded. "Relatively."

She snorted. "*Relatively* new to Savannah means your parents were born here but your grandparents weren't. You know that."

"Okay." He grinned at her. "Definitely new to town."

"What about Gart Fagen?" I asked Steve.

"Seriously — come by my office. I'll be there most of tomorrow. I'll tell you what I can if you're looking into this. But right now I have to get going."

"I'm not looking into anything," I said. However, I couldn't deny the anger that swept over me at the very thought that someone had killed Autumn — anger oddly mingled with curiosity about the weird, icky energy given off by a silly piece of paper.

"Sure you're not. Whatever. Say hi to Declan for me." He stood.

"There's no call for sarcasm," I said. Steve was more likely to send a burning bag of dog poop to Declan than pass along his greetings.

"No. Really. I don't want to be a sore loser. I get why you made the decision you did. I know it's because I decided to join the society and you don't approve of us."

"It's not —"

He held up his hand. "It's okay. But you're still going to be stuck with me when you need me. I'm not letting you go altogether." He picked up his plate and now-empty cup and moved toward the bussing station.

I followed.

"See you soon, Katie-girl." He bent and kissed my cheek. Stunned, I stood there like an idiot as he walked to the door.

"Don't call me that!" I said as he left.

Books tidied and new additions on the shelves, Jaida and Bianca were getting ready to leave. They'd both slipped on their jackets when Mimsey burst into the Honeybee. Her breath came shallowly, and her bright blue eyes were wide as she looked back over her shoulder.

She wore a bright crimson-and-white-striped tunic over white slacks and pumps even though it was well before Memorial Day. The pearl earrings and necklace reflected the smooth white of her hair. Since she always chose the colors of her ensembles with magic in mind, I had to wonder. Red could be for passion, but the square set of her shoulders despite her obvious agitation made me think she was using it for power and determination. White was the color of pure spirit, purification, divination, and protection. After the last twenty-four hours, we all should have been wearing it.

Lucy and I popped to our feet as the door opened wider and Mimsey gestured at someone on the sidewalk. But it was only Wren following her grandmother.

She looked terrible. Her eyelids were red-rimmed behind the chunky glasses, and her nose was pink and swollen. Worry, or perhaps sleeplessness, had painted dark half-moons under her eyes. She wore the same clothes she'd had on the night before, and today the black leggings made her look thinner than ever. If she'd been numb during the Imbolc celebration, it seemed her friend's death had hit her full force today.

"Oh, honey," Lucy said as Jaida reached out and gave Wren one of her signature comfort hugs.

Mimsey's gaze swept the bakery. "Good, you're not too busy. We have to talk." She settled into a nearby chair, more brusque and businesslike than I'd ever seen her. "You have to find out what happened to Autumn."

"I'm sure the police —," I began.

"Wren, show her."

"Show me what?" I sank back onto my

seat with a sense of resignation. Jaida and Bianca slipped their coats off and settled on either side of me.

"Grandma, she's not going to —"

"Lord love a duck, will you just show her?" Mimsey insisted.

Sighing, Wren reached into her backpack. She fished around a little before pulling something out. She stretched her hand out toward me, then opened it.

I stared down at her palm. Sitting there, pretty as could be, was an origami bat.

Neatly folded from maroon paper.

A shiver clawed its way up my spine.

"Did you make that?" Bianca asked.

Jaida looked mystified. Maroon bats had not been on the conversational menu during our gathering the previous evening.

Wren shook her head.

"Of course not," Mimsey said. "I took her home this morning and discovered that someone had slipped that, that *thing* under the front door of her apartment. She told me it's just like the one Autumn was holding when she found her yesterday."

Beside me, Lucy's quick intake of breath mirrored the alarm that passed between Jaida and Bianca. Mimsey crossed her arms over her ample chest.

I rubbed the back of my neck. "It sure

looks the same to me." At least it didn't have the same weird energy that the first bat had given off, even through Quinn's plastic evidence bag.

Mimsey nodded emphatically. "We came straight over here to tell you. Now you can see why you have to help the police. Wren's life is in danger!"

"Grandma, we don't know that."

Mimsey shushed her.

"I take it you didn't report this . . . gift . . . to the police?" Of course they hadn't, or they wouldn't have the crumpled paper to show me. It would already be in the lab having goddess-knows-what tests done on it.

Mimsey frowned and looked at the floor.

"Mims!" I protested. "I can't investigate a crime *instead* of the police. I can only help them."

She smiled in triumph. Jaida snorted.

Darn it.

"I'm not that worried," Wren said. Of course everything about her belied that statement. Something in my expression must have conveyed my disbelief because she went on. "No, really. At least not about this."

"Perhaps you should be," I said in a quiet voice. "Whoever left this origami model knows where you live, and at the very least

93

it has some connection to Georgia Wild." I felt my shoulders slump. "Probably something to do with Autumn's death, too."

Wren's swallow was audible.

Vindication warred with worry on Mimsey's face.

"What do these things *mean?*" Wren asked in a tight voice. The bat spilled off her palm and landed beside me on the bistro table. Unlike the one Autumn had, it hadn't been crumpled in a fist, and I wasn't looking at it through a thick layer of plastic. If I hadn't known better, I would have thought the detailed folded sculpture rather adorable.

"I don't know." I felt helpless. "Mimsey, did you try to find out anything about it in your shew stone?" She was the only one of us who used a polished sphere of pink quartz crystal — literally a crystal ball — for purposes of divination.

"I haven't been home yet," she said. "But I can try when I get there."

"Katie, the police have declared the G.W. office a crime scene and won't let me back in," Wren said. "I can't work, I can't pay the bills, and now some nutcase is leaving folded bats under my door. I don't know what to do."

Bianca reached into her purse. "Here. At least I can give you the money for the rent."

She extracted a checkbook and began to write. "You said that you're expecting a grant to come through soon?"

"Two," Wren said. "I can pay you back then."

Waving the check in the air, Bianca said, "No, this is a donation. I added in another thousand, but you're going to need more cash soon to keep things going. What about applying for a short-term loan at my bank? I'd be happy to vouch for you."

Wren's eyes welled. "Thank you. I'm willing to try anything. I'll go to the bank tomorrow."

"Sweetheart!" Mimsey was beside herself. "I know you're committed to your work, but will you please focus on the matter at hand? You are in danger!" She turned to me. "And you have to help her. You simply have to, Katie. If you won't do it because you know it's the right thing and because you know you *can,* then do it for me. As a personal favor to me. Will you do that? I'm sure the other members of the spellbook club will help out here at the bakery if you need to leave during the day."

All eyes lasered to me. Lucy's gaze was particularly sympathetic but still unyielding.

"Of course we will," Jaida said. "Cookie, too, I'm sure."

I licked my lips. Mimsey was the senior witch in the spellbook club. If we had been the sort of group to have a high priestess, then she would have been ours. But, more important, she was *Mimsey*.

Stifling a groan, I said, "Okay. I can't make any promises; you know that. But I'll see what I can find out."

She beamed. "Excellent! Now, how shall we start?"

I sighed. Sometimes destiny sucked, but if I was going do this, I would try to do it right.

CHAPTER 7

We needed to know more about the maroon bats and the golf course land deal. My knowledge of both was pretty much limited to what Wren had told Detective Quinn and the unhelpful information I'd gleaned from my Internet search the night before. Unfortunately, Wren could talk about habitat and mating rituals and birth rates and food supplies, but she didn't seem to know any more than I did about Autumn's legal machinations.

Now that I was actually asking these questions, though, I was seized with a kind of anxious urgency. "What about the maroon bats, Wren? You said there was an actual sighting that you and Autumn had been basing all of your work in Fagen Swamp on, right? Was it one of the usual suspects?" Many reports of endangered species came from bird-watching clubs, especially the Savannah Avian Society.

"Not this time," Wren said. "The sighting — actually two of them — came from a man who lives right there in the swamp. His name is Evanston Rickers."

"He lives there? How can you be sure he's not just some kook who wants to keep living in the swamp?"

She looked offended. "I went to see him, and he showed me where he'd seen the bats. He's a zoologist with a focus on herpetology — snakes — and he contacted us out of genuine concern about the bats. He gave me pictures. Unfortunately, they weren't definitive enough. Since then I've gone out several times to follow up."

"But you didn't find anything?" I asked. Pictures could be faked — but what would be the point?

Her reluctance was evident in the shake of her head. "It doesn't mean they aren't there. I've only had a couple of months to try to find them, and while maroon bats don't migrate, they do hibernate in the winter. They're also solitary creatures — not like gray bats that thrive in large colonies. Often you'll only find one, or a mother and her pup. I expected to be able to locate them when it warms up."

I wondered whether she'd added that wish to the ones we'd burnt in the Imbolc fire.

She licked her lips, looked around at everyone, and ducked her head. "Autumn said we couldn't wait until spring, though. She said if we couldn't find something to give to the EPA in the next month or so, she wanted to devote our time to the flatwoods salamander project."

Wren had mentioned that to Detective Quinn. If Georgia Wild was going to give up on the maroon bats — and from the work I'd been doing with them, I'd assumed the project had been a rather minor one to start with — then the sale of the swampland would likely go through. In that case, why kill Autumn over it? Could she have discovered some new information that supported the existence of the bats?

After all, if the murderer hadn't killed Autumn because of the maroon bats, then why had Autumn been clutching the origami version of one with that curious and distasteful signature? And why on earth would someone slip one under Wren's door?

"Okay, here's the deal," I said to the ladies. "We need to tell Detective Quinn about this second origami bat. Maybe the lab can find fingerprints or figure out if the paper is the same as the other bat. I don't know. It really would have been better to have the police come to Wren's apartment when you discovered it."

Mimsey looked chastened.

"Don't worry. He'll be happy to get it now," I said, hurrying to assure her. "Wren, I know you and Autumn were close. Can you tell me a bit more about that boyfriend I may or may not have seen on the street outside Georgia Wild last night?"

Jaida raised an eyebrow. "Oh, really. You didn't mention that."

"I told Detective Quinn," I said. "Wren?"

"Well, his name is Hunter Normandy."

Bianca snorted, though she managed to make it sound delicate and feminine.

"Yeah, yeah. He has a fancy name," I said. So did she, for that matter. "Sounds like a trust-fund baby. Ivy League or something. Though the two times I met him he was dressed in funky vintage stuff — mismatched plaids, Panama hat, stuff like that."

Wren shook her head. "I don't think he comes from money. He's a nice enough guy, though I haven't spent any real time around him. He works at a mortuary."

"Doing what?" For all I knew, he could be their bookkeeper.

"I have no idea."

"What else?" I prompted.

She shrugged. "Autumn didn't talk about him that much. She seemed happy enough, and I know she liked spending time with him. Sometimes she'd compare him to her ex-husband, and Hunter always came out on top."

"Nothing else?" Meaning: *No juicy secrets?* "After all, he was her boyfriend. And you guys spent a lot of time together."

"Autumn didn't talk about her personal life much. I mean, you have a boyfriend and I don't know very much about him, either."

Lucy directed a wry look my way.

"Okay. I get it," I said. "She didn't blather on about herself." Hard to argue with that.

"At Georgia Wild she was all about the business of the nonprofit, and while we were really close at work, we didn't socialize much outside of G.W.," Wren said. "Frankly, we were so busy, we didn't have much time to socialize at all."

"What about her ex?"

Again with the shrug. "The divorce was final about five months ago, but he kept calling. She ended up blocking him from her phone."

My ears perked up at that. Were we dealing with a possible stalker? "Was he threatening? Violent?"

"She didn't say that, only that he wouldn't leave her alone." Wren looked frustrated.

I tried not to sigh. "Okay. So I'll call Peter

Quinn and tell him about the bat and see what's going on. For all we know, they have a suspect in custody."

Hey, a girl could hope, right?

The others looked about as convinced as I felt.

"In the meantime, Jaida and Bianca, would you two mind going with Mimsey and Wren to her apartment? Take juniper berries and basil and sage and anything else that will help with both a personal-protection spell and a home-protection spell."

The four women rose as one. Jaida said, "I'll stop by my house on the way and pick up a fresh Rider-Waite deck. The Hierophant card will add power to a protection spell."

"Well, you're the expert," I said. "Lucy, are you okay taking care of things here? It's slow enough that it shouldn't be a problem."

"Of course," my aunt said. "What are you going to do?"

"Well, first I'll call Quinn. Then it seems I need to go see a man about a golf course."

In the Honeybee office I grabbed my cell phone and sank into the desk chair. Mungo stood up on his hind legs on the floor next to me until I picked him up and put him on my lap. He nudged my free hand with his wet nose until I scratched him behind the ear.

Detective Quinn answered on the first ring, skipping the niceties. "Why am I not surprised to see your name come up on my phone the day after a homicide?"

"So you've determined for sure that Autumn was murdered?"

"Hard to kill yourself by strangulation — at least in a way that would leave actual finger marks on your neck."

I shuddered, remembering, then plowed on. "Finger *marks*. I don't suppose there's any way to get actual fingerprints from skin?"

"It is possible in some cases," he said. "But no such luck in this one. Either the heavy moisturizer the victim used caused the killer's fingers to slip or he wore gloves."

Victim. Ugh. "Do you know the time of death?"

"Late afternoon between . . . Katie, do you have some kind of CSI complex? Or did you always dream of being a police-woman when you were a little girl?"

"What are you talking about? Of course not."

"Then why are you calling and asking me all these questions? Because I have to tell you that kind of behavior would make most investigators very suspicious."

"Good thing you're not most investigators, isn't it? I called because there's some new evidence you should know about. At least I assume it has something to do with the murder." And I'd asked all those other questions because . . . well, because I wanted to know what we were dealing with.

He sighed. "Really."

"Remember that origami bat Autumn was clutching?"

"Yeah . . ."

"Wren found another one slipped under her door when she got home from Mimsey's this morning."

"Hang on. She was at Mimsey Carmichael's?"

"You didn't know? Mimsey is her grandmother. I would have thought you'd have verified Wren's alibi by now."

"Only for the afternoon." His tone was elaborately patient. "Since the medical examiner's office determined that's when Boles was killed."

"Oh. Well, Wren spent the night with her grandparents last night and arrived home this morning to find the folded bat. She brought it to the Honeybee."

Quinn swore under his breath.

"I know, I know," I said. "We put it in a plastic bag, and I can bring it by your office if you want." Police headquarters was only a few blocks away.

"You're at the bakery? I'll come get it," Quinn said. "Is Wren still there? I want to talk to her."

"She was when I came back to the office to call you," I replied, fudging a bit. If I sent him over to Wren's apartment right now, he'd probably stumble into the ladies burning juniper berries and tarot cards and invoking protections.

"Tell her to stay there."

"Okay," I agreed, even though I knew she and the others had probably left already. "So, I take it you don't have a suspect in mind already."

"Katie . . ." Quinn's voice held warning.

"Have you had a chance to talk to Heinrich Dawes yet?"

"He's not at the top of my priority list. Been focusing on finding the boyfriend, Hunter Normandy."

"Makes sense." Even I knew the police usually looked at victims' spouses or love interests in murder cases, and I *had* seen that Wrangler driving away the night before.

Wait a minute. "Finding him? You don't know where he is?"

"Katie. This isn't really your business."

"What if he knows that I saw him? Could I be in danger?"

He hesitated. "I don't think so. But yes, he does seem to have disappeared. Didn't show up for work today, either."

"Really. Do you know what he does at the mortuary?"

Quinn hesitated again, then answered, "He's their primary embalmer."

So much for the bookkeeper idea.

I looked at the clock on the wall, surprised to see it was only a few minutes after eleven. A lot had happened in one hour. "All righty then. I'll let you get back to it. The origami bat will be right here, but we close at one."

"Oh, I'll be there within the hour."

That should give Mimsey et al plenty of time to finish their spell casting by the time Quinn made it to Wren's apartment. Not only had he said he wanted to talk with her, but it was likely that he'd want to take a look at the scene of the crime — if slipping a piece of origami under someone's door could be considered a crime.

I said good-bye and hung up without mentioning that I didn't plan on being at the Honeybee when he arrived. Lucy could hand him a plastic bag of evidence as easily as I could, and I wanted to take Steve up

106

on his offer to help as soon as possible. Next I called Mimsey to let her know Quinn would probably be dropping by Wren's apartment. They were just preparing to set up wards, but she assured me they'd pick up the pace.

CHAPTER 8

With a twinge of guilt that he was still in my contact list, I dialed Steve's cell and waited while it rang.

"Well, well, well. I thought you'd never call."

Didn't anyone just answer *hello* anymore?

"It turns out I really do need to know more about the sale of the swamp," I said. "Are you at home?" Steve had moved into his family's guesthouse, but I'd never been there. I did know the estate had a swimming pool and a tennis court, and I was curious to see the place.

"Actually I'm at the office on this sunny Sunday afternoon."

"At the *News*? Can I drop by?"

"No, at Dawes Corp. Thought I'd take a look and see what I could find out about this golf course thing in case you called after all. Which you just did." I could hear him smiling.

Dawes Corp. Lordy.

"Something happened to change my mind," I said.

There were a few beats of silence before he answered. "That sounds serious."

"It is. Someone threatened Wren."

Mungo nudged my hand again, and I absently scratched the top of his head.

"I'm not far from the Honeybee." He gave me the address on Drayton Street. "Top floor. I'll leave the side door to the street unlocked."

"I'll be there in ten minutes." I hung up.

"He wasn't the least bit surprised that I called," I said to Mungo.

He made a noise in the back of his throat and jumped down to where my tote bag sat open on the floor.

On my way out, I told Lucy where I was going. Her response was a quirked eyebrow that I pointedly ignored.

"Detective Quinn is dropping by in the next hour or so to pick up the bat," I said. "It's in a bag on the shelf under the register. Oh, and tell him I'm sorry Wren and Mimsey left before he could talk to them. My bad. They're expecting him at Wren's apartment, though."

"Got it," she said. "Now scoot."

■ ■ ■ ■

It actually took twelve minutes for Mungo
and me to walk to Steve's office. As he'd
said, it was a sunny Sunday, and the humid
air had warmed to sixty-five degrees. A few
acclimated Southerners hurried by me on
the sidewalk bundled up in sweaters, but I
slipped off my jacket and looped it through
the handles of my tote bag. Leaning against
it, my familiar's head bobbed in time with
my steps.

On the way I thought about bats and
swampland, boyfriends and ex-husbands.
About halfway there, I realized that I was
developing a mental to-do list. I might not
know how to be a lightwitch per se, but in
less than a year I'd developed a knack for
getting information and figuring things out.
Quinn wouldn't be excited about my involvement, but if I stayed out of his way, I
might be able to help in the end. I'd left the
Honeybee feeling strongly protective of
Wren, and now that was joined by the
combination of intense curiosity and a
desire for justice that I'd been so carefully
trying to tamp down ever since I'd gotten
that strange vibe from the first origami bat.

I stopped on the sidewalk in front of the

address Steve had given me. Not surprisingly, subtlety ruled when it came to the Dawes Corporation. Nothing indicated the nondescript brick building held offices at all — no signage, no view into windows revealing office furniture, no parking lot. In front a concrete pathway led from the public sidewalk to three steps and then a large wooden door with a brass knocker. Wrought-iron window boxes on the second and third floors spilled over with bright pansies.

Then a single gargoyle downspout on a corner by the roofline caught my attention. Grotesque but amusing with bulging eyes and bulbous nose, the sculpture had something about it.

It held power. Not the cloying, rotting feel of Autumn's paper bat, but a power I recognized.

Looking down at Mungo, I said, "Feel that?"

Yip!

The Dawes Corporation office would be in that corner of the third floor, and Heinrich Dawes had imbued the sculpted stone with a protection spell — and possibly something else. No surprise there. Heinrich wasn't shy about using his druidic power both personally and in business. I just didn't know to what degree.

I veered off the front path and went around to the narrow walkway that led between the buildings. The side door was indeed open. I entered the dark stairwell, blinking as my eyes adjusted to the dimness. Wending my way up the narrow stairs, I bypassed the first landing and entered a short hallway on the third floor. It ended in an open space thirty-five feet square. Light streamed down from multiple skylights set into the high ceiling, and plush carpet muffled my footsteps. Huge potted ficus trees in each corner reached toward the light above, and more lined the wide stairway, which was visible through a glass wall. Comfortable chairs were interspersed along walls graced with splashy modern art, and an unmanned reception desk sat near the entrance from the front stairs.

Three doors opened off the reception area. The first had a nameplate that unsurprisingly read HEINRICH DAWES. I did a double take when I saw the second name: LOGAN SEWARD.

Colleague indeed.

Steve sat behind an enormous burled-walnut desk in the third office. *His* office, the brass plate told me. I'd thought he was merely dabbling in Daddy's business, and now I reassessed.

"Hello," I said.

He looked up and rose to his feet. "Come in."

I paused in the doorway, then continued in. "Thank you for seeing me on such short notice."

He laughed. "How formal. You're very welcome."

I sat down in the distressed leather guest chair that he waved me toward. There was plenty of room for my tote, too, and for Mungo, whose dark brown eyes were fixed on Steve. He sat back down on the other side of the desk.

Another skylight above offered plenty of daylight to tease out the elaborate grain of the desk, illuminate the dark wood of the bookcases and filing cabinets, and echo off the indigo paint on the beadboard wainscoting that ran around the periphery of the room. A marble sculpture of a bull dominated a corner behind the desk, and a single painting of a stormy country scene hung on the wall to my right. It looked like a Constable — so it probably was — and not a reproduction, either. A kind of fuzzy veil surrounded it, indicating it was heavily warded. I had to give Steve credit for keeping things simple in this plush and ornate space. Despite the palpable presence of wealth, the feng shui felt right.

"I'm intrigued," he said. "This is the third time in a year that something like this has landed in your lap, so to speak. And they do say the third time's a charm."

I grimaced at his pun. "Funny."

"Really, I'd like to help if I can."

That's why you're here. Take him up on it.

Taking a deep breath, I plunged in. "So, what can you tell me about the swampland-slash-golf-course deal?"

He considered me. "Well, you do get to the point."

"Sorry." I leaned forward. "But this isn't exactly a social call. I'd think you'd rather I didn't waste your time."

Amusement flickered across his face. "Tell you what. I'll answer your questions to the extent that I'm able if you'll listen to a proposal I have for you."

Uh-oh. Warning klaxons went off in my mind, but I did my best to ignore them, knowing that if I didn't agree, Steve might usher me out right then and there.

I nodded my agreement.

He smiled. "What do you want to know?"

I sat back and scrambled to gather my thoughts. "What, exactly, is your involvement with the sale of Fagen Swamp?"

"I'm not involved at all. Father is."

"Perhaps I should be talking to him, then."

"Yeah. Good luck with that."

He was right. Heinrich probably wouldn't even take my call. I wondered what Quinn would get out of him, if anything.

"He's a venture capitalist," Steve said. "In this case he's investing capital in the venture of building a golf course — along with a few other people, I might add. Obviously the first step is to purchase the land. After looking at several sites, the investment group decided that the location of Fagen Swamp, which is about halfway to Tybee Island, was close enough to Savannah and the price was right."

"Which has to be completely negated by the fact that it's a *swamp*," I said. "Won't it have to be drained, razed, and then completely rebuilt down to the most basic level?" I struggled to keep the indignity out of my voice.

He gave a kind of facial shrug. "Still at less expense than the other land options."

"And if somehow the land can't be sold?" I asked.

"Bah. That silly bat thing? I don't think they're too worried about that."

Mungo bristled beside me.

"Why not?"

"For one thing, only one person has seen them."

"There are pictures."

He gave me a wry look.

"Okay, what do you know about the landowner, Gart Fagen?" I asked.

"Only what Father mentioned. He's a backwoods kind of guy who inherited the land, but he's not much of a nature nut. Couldn't care less about flying mammals. He's racked up a few gambling debts, not too bad but enough to make him highly motivated to sell. And not that many people want to buy a swatch of soggy swamp."

"Sounds like they're taking advantage of him."

"Hardly. He wants the money, and he's getting it. And the investors are getting a good deal. It's the way business is done, Katie."

"Not so great for the plants and animals that live there, though — whether there are maroon bats or not. You're a druid, Steve. Aren't you supposed to respect and love nature? Isn't the rest of your clan supposed to as well?"

His lips pressed together. "I understand what you're saying, of course. But we are modern druids, and nature takes many forms. They aren't turning the swamp into a concrete parking lot. It will be a beautiful golf course full of natural elements. Not wild, mind you, but it will still be nature."

Whatever you have to tell yourself so you can sleep at night, Steve.

"What else?" he asked.

"Who are the other investors?"

"I can't tell you that."

"But you said —"

"I said I would answer your questions if I could. I only know about Father and Logan."

I pointed to the office next door. "Your lawyerly 'colleague,' huh? So is there some famous golfer behind all this nonsense?"

"Not yet — but there will be."

"Who?"

"From what I know, the investors haven't decided yet. They'll select some up-and-comer who will jump at the chance to design a course and whose name will add cachet to the project."

It sounded like a backward way of going at things. What if they couldn't convince their chosen designer to become involved? Then I remembered how persuasive Heinrich could be — and how he wouldn't be shy about using magic to get what he wanted. It would be interesting to see what the Rule of Three bounced back at him.

"Okay." I stroked Mungo's head and thought about what else Steve might be able to tell me. "Do you know of anyone who would, no, wait . . . anyone who could *possibly* have a reason to want Autumn dead?"

He put his hands behind his head and leaned back in his desk chair. His shirt stretched taut over his chest, and I had a sudden vision of running my hands over his bare torso. Tearing my gaze away, I met his dark knowing eyes. For a split second I wondered if he could read my mind, but I quickly pushed the thought away.

"That's a rather subjective question, Katie. Never mind the fact that I'd never met her." But there was something in his voice.

I suppressed a smile. "No, it's not. You either know of someone who has a possible motive — just possible motive is all I'm asking about — or you don't."

Without taking his eyes from my face, he reached for a pen on the desk in front of him and began tapping it against the blotter.

"You do, don't you?" I urged.

He looked toward the ceiling as if weighing his answer. "Possible motive, I suppose. And I'm only telling you this because . . . well, because you might be able to do

118

something with the information. I'm not sure what, though."

"You are a tease. Plain and simple."

A ghost of a smile touched his lips.

Steve said, "I heard that Skip Thorsen wanted to join the investment group, but he didn't have enough money."

Skip. Did I know that name? "Who is Skip Thorsen, and why would that give him a motive to kill Autumn Boles?"

"He's her ex-husband."

I gaped.

"And he still has a nice big life insurance policy on her."

I tucked that choice bit of information into my mental pocket and plunged on. "What about Logan Seward?"

Steve shrugged.

"You must know something about him."

"Nothing that has any relevance here."

I glared at him.

He ignored me. "So, how are you and your new boyfriend doing?"

I stood and slung the tote onto my shoulder. "Steve, I understand your dislike of Declan. I know what happened when he and Arnie went into that burning building. I'm so sorry for the loss of your brother, but it wasn't Declan's fault. I'm simply not going to sit here and listen to you run down my boyfriend."

He stood, too. "Oh, stop it. How is asking how you two are doing running down your boyfriend?"

"It . . . I could hear it in your tone."

"That's ridiculous."

Was it? Was I manufacturing difficulty where there wasn't any?

He came around the desk until he was standing next to me, his elbow brushing my arm. I tensed but held my ground.

"I said I had a proposal for you," he murmured. "It's nothing terrible, nothing weird. But back at the bakery, you said you didn't want me out of your life. And I most definitely don't want to be out of your life."

"Steve . . ."

"We can't be involved, as you put it, *romantically*. At least not . . . well, I respect your decision, Katie, because I respect you. But we can be friends, can't we?"

I was silent.

His voice was tender. "You chose Declan, not me. I should be the one who is upset, not you. I'm over it. I'd rather have you in my life in whatever way I can than push you away because I'm too pigheaded to understand your problems with my druid clan. Because I do understand."

I felt dizzy, and I knew darn well it wasn't

because Steve was trying any magical tricks. *Cripes.*

"Or would it be too difficult for you to be my friend?" he asked. His breath moved a strand of my hair. "Because you're still attracted to me?"

Mungo growled.

"Don't be ridiculous!" Even I could tell there was a little too much fervor in my response.

He stepped back and held up his palms. "Well, then? Friends?"

I pasted a smile on my face and nodded once. "Sure. Why not?" I turned and walked toward the office doorway.

"See you around, Katie."

"Okeydoke." I kept my tone light. As I walked back down the hallway, I muttered to Mungo, "He's right. There's no reason we can't be friends. He's a good guy."

My familiar made a disgruntled noise in the back of his throat.

"Not a good guy like Declan is a good guy, of course," I assured him.

As we made our way down the last flight of steps, the outside door opened and a man entered the stairwell. In the brief flash of light, I had a good view from above of silvery brown hair surrounding a circular bald spot like a monk's tonsure. Then the door closed, and the man started up in the dim light. The newcomer spotted me and stopped, his hand gripping the railing.

My heart began pounding, and Mungo popped up out of the tote.

"Hello," he said. His dark eyes ran up and down my body.

Yuck.

"Hi." I hurried past him, alert for any sudden moves. There was no magical instinct driving my actions, no intuitive hit; there was only the practical motivation that any woman has when she finds herself in a dark stairwell with a man she doesn't know — especially a man who has the bad manners to so blatantly check her out.

"Hey, can I help you?" he asked as I went by.

"No, thanks." I reached for the door.

He started back down the stairs toward me.

"No, *thanks,*" I repeated, holding out my hand and willing him to keep his distance.

He slowed. Mungo growled low in his throat, a small sound that wouldn't have turned a head on the street, but I felt his enormous will join mine in snarling, feral protection.

The air in the stairwell shifted. The man paled. Stepped back.

I yanked the door open and strode into the welcome daylight. Still, I didn't breathe easy until we were out on the street. In Reynolds Square I sank onto a wooden bench and hugged Mungo to my chest.

"My little wolf. Thank you."

He lapped at my chin with his bright pink tongue.

Yip!

CHAPTER 9

Instead of turning toward the Honeybee, I headed toward the Savannah River. The tantalizing aromas of frying garlic, onion, and roasting pork swirled in the air outside the Olde Pink House as we went by. Mungo's nose twitched, and my stomach grumbled. I ignored it. We crossed Bay and soon wended down to the uneven bricks of River Street. As soon as we were away from traffic, I defied the leash law and put Mungo down. He happily trotted along beside me.

A horn sounded from a boat on the river, low and mournful. The calming water energy washed over me. I paused and lifted my face to the warm sunlight for a few moments, closing my eyes.

"You're it!"

I opened my eyes to see three young girls playing tag. They ran toward the river, squealing, and I couldn't help smiling. As we continued along the wide redbrick walkway, thoughts of Autumn, fate, and magic swirled through my mind.

The only reason I became involved in another homicide investigation was because I volunteered at Georgia Wild. I began volunteering at the nonprofit because Mimsey had introduced me to her granddaughter who just happened to work there. *Just happened to.* I'd liked what Georgia Wild stood for and I'd liked Autumn, but Lucy was right: I'd been trying to orchestrate how I could do something positive and at the same time be in control of my own destiny. In doing so, I'd put myself smack-dab in the middle of a murder case.

Again.

Since Lucy had first told me I was a hereditary hedgewitch — actually since I'd first accepted it, which came a bit later — I'd come to understand that I was a kind of magical catalyst. Sometimes my presence augmented magical workings. Coincidences overlapped, things fell into line, and serendipity was my friend. Also, sometimes things *happened* when I was around. I'd come to accept that, too, though somewhat unwillingly.

Last Halloween, Franklin Taite had told me I was a lightwitch. It was frustrating not knowing what that really meant. I couldn't practice dark magic? Fine by me. But what was it, really?

"Is black magic really black magic if it's for the right cause?" I muttered to Mungo. "After all, hardly anything in this world is really black or white. Most things fall someplace on a continuum of gray. Lucy has often talked about gray magic, and so have the other members of the spellbook club. Is there even such a thing as pure white magic?"

Such a thing as pure white magic?

The amplified words drifted back to me through the early-afternoon air. Stunned, I froze. Mungo sat down, looking up at me. Then I laughed, realizing what had happened.

I hadn't been paying attention as I walked, thinking out loud, and had wandered into the circular patch of pavement in Rousakis Plaza that was known as the echo chamber. One day when I'd picked Bianca up from her wineshop, Moon Grapes, to have lunch, she'd suggested we get something and eat by the water. On the way she'd pointed to a man in plaid Bermuda shorts standing by himself in the middle of the pavement and apparently moving his lips silently. A woman stood nearby, watching him with a smile. Bianca had explained that something about the construction of the area ramped up even the smallest whisper and returned it to the person who had uttered it. However, this was the first time I'd actually experienced it myself.

I laughed again, waiting for the echo, but this time another laugh joined my own. I looked around to see who it was. There wasn't a soul nearby. Puzzled, I looked down at Mungo. His nose quivered as he sniffed the air. He wagged his tail, and a split second later I smelled the sweet scent, too.

Gardenia.

My eyes went wide. "Nonna?" I asked quietly. Now Mungo's tail was wagging so enthusiastically that the whole back half of his body wiggled.

This time, instead of an echo of my own words, I heard the voice of my grandmother — my grandmother who had died when I was nine years old.

Katie . . . magic is always about intention. Make sure your intention is for good, and you don't have to worry.

This was the third time she'd come to me, but only the second time she'd spoken. I was thrilled to hear from her again.

"Oh, Nonna," I whispered. "What if I mess up? No one seems to understand.

What if I need to cast gray or even black magic for some reason, but I can't because I'm a lightwitch who can only cast white magic? What if the good of the many depends on the sacrifice of one? What if my intentions are good, but I still make the wrong choice?"

There are no easy answers. And remember that every group for the good has their warriors — the Jesuits, warrior monks, the yamabushi. You must trust that you have whom you need in your life.

Voices behind me warned of an approaching group of tourists. Quickly, I asked, "Whom do you mean?"

The words returned as a normal echo. My nonna's spirit was gone.

Smiling absently at the family walking by, I picked up Mungo and put him back in the tote bag. Slowly, we returned to the Honeybee. As I walked back to Broughton, I mulled over the brief advice my grandmother had offered. What did she mean that I had to trust that I had whom I needed in my life? Someone I already knew? Someone I would meet? More than one person?

At least I understood what she meant by keeping my intentions toward the good. I tried to do that anyway.

Was it possible I was worrying about nothing? That I was already on the right track?

And what the heck was a yamabushi?

Even with the walk along the riverfront I got back to the bakery before we closed. The door of the Honeybee opened when I was a few steps away. Cookie came out but didn't notice me. She propped it open with the ironwork cat we used as a doorstop and turned to wave to someone inside. The spicy, sweet, and savory scents that were the Honeybee's best advertisement rolled out to entice passersby from the sidewalk. I glanced at my watch. Half an hour until closing. Maybe all those good smells would pull in a few last-minute customers from the Sunday strollers spending some of this beautiful day in Savannah's historic district.

"Hi," I said.

Cookie whirled. "Oh! Katie, you startled me." She wore a black ribbed turtleneck over a black and green plaid skirt. Her long legs were encased in tights, and soft leather boots reached to her knees.

"Sorry. How did the job interview go?"

She shrugged. "Hard to tell."

I laughed. "Usually you can tell right away. In fact, usually you don't actually interview for jobs."

Another shrug. "Things change."

I raised my eyebrows. "Cookie? Is everything okay?"

"Sure," she said, and pushed past me. "See you later." The heels of her boots clicked down the sidewalk with purpose.

Bewildered, I went inside. Lucy stood on a stepstool and wrote on the menu blackboard. Two women sat in the library, chatting over crumb-filled plates, and a man sat at a table in the far corner, pounding on his laptop as if it were trying to escape.

"You're back!" Lucy called when she saw me. She'd donned a hemp apron in a muted orange that matched her blouse.

I smiled and approached. "Good heavens. Everything is positively gleaming."

"It gave me something to do while you were gone. How did things go?" Lucy asked, climbing down.

"It was . . . interesting. Mildly informative."

Lucy looked amused. "And how is Steven?"

"Interesting as well. But not as interesting as Declan."

She raised one eyebrow but didn't comment.

Looking at where she'd been writing on the menu, I saw that she'd lowered the price on the Healthwise Breakfast Muffins we'd recently added to the menu. They were chock-full of carrots, bananas, oats, nuts, honey, and coconut, not to mention a plethora of spices.

She followed my gaze. "I thought if we charged less, more people might try them. Or maybe change the name? They're so delicious, but sometimes people have to be convinced to eat things that are good for them."

"Good idea. Let's see how the price change works, and if you think of a better name, I'm all for it," I said, then nodded toward the kitchen.

She followed me as I put Mungo in the office.

"What the heck is going on with Cookie?" I asked over my shoulder. "She barely spoke to me on her way out. I know she's upset about her love life, but she's been acting kind of weird for a while."

Lucy nodded. "I don't even know that she's that upset about Brandon. You know how well she takes moving on to someone new. Practically insists on it. But she skipped the last spellbook club meeting. I think it's the first one she's missed."

"And didn't she seem kind of prickly at the Imbolc celebration last night?"

She shrugged. "Sometimes Cookie can be

131

a little sensitive."

"Meaning?"

A few moments of hesitation, then my aunt looked me in the eye. "Sometimes she feels like the rest of us judge her. Jaida, mostly, because she thinks Cookie is willing to ignore the Rule of Three, but the rest of us as well. And now you."

"Me? Did I say something that sounded judgmental?"

"Not that I know of. But you're . . . Well, she might feel like a lightwitch would be a little . . . holier than thou."

My lips parted in surprise. "That's ridiculous."

"Of course it is. And perhaps I'm wrong. But I've watched how she looks at you since Samhain."

Oh, for crying in a bucket.

I changed the subject. "Did Quinn come by?"

She looked amused. "He did. Picked up the origami — and a slab of sour cream coffee cake for the road."

"Was he angry that Wren and Mimsey weren't here?"

"More like relieved that he didn't have to field any more questions from you, I think."

I gave her a look.

She grinned. "He said he wanted to check

for fingerprints on Wren's door anyway. Said he was going to pick up a lab tech and head over there."

"Speaking of the Carmichael Clan, have you heard anything from them?"

Lucy nodded. "Mimsey called. Jaida and Bianca helped to set personal wards on Wren. Detective Quinn got there when we were on the phone, and they had just finished setting a protective perimeter around her whole apartment building."

"Wow. Sounds like overkill."

"Can you really overprotect someone?" she asked.

"Yeah. I guess you're right." I touched the metal circle Steve had given me, tucked under my T-shirt on the chain around my neck. Lucy, who had one as well, noticed and smiled.

"I had a brief visit from one of my other guardians," I said. "I stopped by the riverfront on my way back. Nonna came to me in the echo chamber in Rousakis Plaza."

Lucy's eyebrows arched. "Mama?" She knew about my previous encounters with her mother — my grandmother.

"Yep."

"What did she say?" she breathed.

"She told me that as long as I kept my intentions good, I'd be okay. And that I have whom I need in my life."

Lucy's laugh held genuine delight. "Well, I could have told you that. It is so wonderful that you have this connection with her."

I knew my sweet aunt would have loved her mother to visit her from beyond, but it would never even occur to her to be jealous or envious.

"Hellloooo!" A woman's voice, deep and fruity, called back to us from the front of the bakery. In a way, it reminded me of Julia Child.

Craning my head around the refrigerator, I confirmed that it was one of our favorite customers. "Mrs. Standish — how are you?"

Tall and plain-faced, she wore a flowing leopard print tunic over black slacks and a hat adorned with an enormous sunflower on the side that shouldn't have worked with the animal print but oddly did. As I approached, the scent of her expensive perfume reached my nose.

"I'm very well, thank you. I'm having a little get-together this evening and just knew I had to have some goodies from the Honeybee for my guests."

"By all means," Lucy exclaimed, and hurried to grab a bakery box.

"You'll need at least two of those," Mrs. Standish said. "I'd like three of everything

134

you have left in the case. Oh! And throw in two dozen of those delightful cake pops." She pointed to the bite-sized cakes impaled on sticks like frosted lollipops arranged in a large stone jar. "The kiddies will love those."

I grinned. "Good choice."

Mrs. Standish leaned one meaty hand on the counter. "Please tell me you'll be putting your peach pecan mini-pies back on the menu soon."

Lucy and I exchanged glances. "We were planning on offering strawberry rhubarb mini-pies soon."

"I'm sure they'll be delicious. Just remember that peaches and pecans are always in favor around here. I must say, though, I recently heard about your lovely berry shortcakes with the honey whipped cream made up fresh for each order. I simply must stop by and indulge in one soon."

I waved at the bakery boxes Lucy was filling. "You're one of our best customers, Mrs. Standish. Stop in for a shortcake whenever you'd like — on the house."

Her face lit up, belying her murmured protest.

"I insist. We really appreciate your loyalty," I said.

"Well . . . I might be able to make room for one right now. If it's not too much

135

trouble."

I laughed. "We'll have it out in a jiffy."

CHAPTER 10

At one o'clock I turned the sign in the window to CLOSED and was about to lock the door when Uncle Ben came in. I finished with the door and closed the blinds as Lucy greeted him with a warm embrace.

"Stop that," she said with a giggle. "It tickles."

"I thought you liked my beard." A smile crinkled the corners of his eyes behind his rimless glasses. He let her go and asked, "What would a nice witch like you recommend to a customer who wants to improve his golf game?"

"Oh, Ben," she said.

"Specifically putting."

Lucy went behind the display case and snagged a chunk of sour cream coffee cake thick with chopped dates and speckled with poppy seeds. She handed it to him. "Try this."

His eyes widened. "Really?"

"You'll like it, but it's not going to do anything for your putting — though it might relax you. Poppy seeds are sometimes a cure for insomnia. However, if you really were a customer, I'd recommend more time on the practice greens."

Looking rueful, he took the offered plate to a table and sat down. I poured the last cup of coffee out of the drip pot and joined him. It was bitter as sin, but I wasn't about to make a fresh pot right before leaving for the day. Lucy took the empty pot into the kitchen, and I heard the sound of water running.

My uncle spoke around a bite of cake. "Now, tell me about what's going on with that nonprofit you volunteer with. Lucy told me all about how you found that poor woman dead and that Peter Quinn is on the case. Do you know if he's made any progress?"

Uncle Ben had been Savannah's fire chief until his recent retirement inspired him to start the bakery with Lucy and me. He'd known Detective Quinn for years, but I was the one who'd had more contact with the police in the last year. Each time my uncle had been very resistant to my being involved in anything remotely dangerous.

"You sound remarkably calm about the

fact that I stumbled onto another dead body," I said.

He glanced toward the kitchen as the dishwasher started up. "Your aunt can be very persuasive."

I laughed. "I bet." Ben was putty in my gentle aunt's hands. "I did talk to Quinn this morning. It sounds like they're focusing on Autumn's boyfriend and ex-husband. They're probably on the right track, too. I had a little visit with Steve Dawes this morning."

Ben frowned, and I knew he was thinking of Declan.

Lucy hurried over to join us at the table. "You never told me what he said."

"I didn't have a chance to tell you before Mrs. Standish came in. I was hoping Steve would be able to tell me more about the golf-course-development deal, but he wasn't very forthcoming. However, I did learn Autumn's ex-husband has a decent motive for murder."

"Oh, dear," she said. "What's that?"

"Life insurance policy. Money he needed because he wanted to invest in the golf course, too."

"What? Even while Autumn was trying to save the swamp?" Lucy's eyes widened in outrage.

"Well, they were exes," I said. "So it stands to reason they'd have some differing opinions on certain things. Apparently that was one of them."

Ben pushed his empty plate aside. "What's all this about a golf course?"

I outlined the details.

"In Fagen Swamp?" he said. "Well, that is interesting. It would be wonderful to have another world-class golf course in the area —"

I rolled my eyes.

"But that swamp's an odd place," he continued. "Spooky. Though I suppose it wouldn't be once you cut down all the cypress trees and drained away the water. I wonder if they'd relocate the animals?"

"I doubt it," I said. "I take it you've been there?"

"Oh, gosh," he said. "A long time ago, when I was a teenager. Trespassing, of course. Old man Fagen was a tough sort, though. Downright mean. It was a good thing we didn't get caught."

"You don't seem like the kind of guy who would do something like that."

"We all did," he said. "Kind of a rite of passage around here then."

I squinted at him. "Really? I guess boys will be boys. How many times did you trespass for fun?"

He shrugged. "A dozen or so."

"Really?" I asked in surprise.

"It was a . . . compelling place. I don't know how else to put it."

Interesting.

Before we all left, I remembered to load up a bag of Honeybee goodies for my neighbors. At the rate they weren't selling and the rate I was giving them away, we'd be out of business in no time.

On my way home, I stopped by Georgia Wild to see whether the police had released the crime scene yet. On Sunday afternoon, parking was open, and I pulled to the curb only a few spaces away from where I'd parked the night before.

Egad. Hard to believe it had been less than twenty-four hours.

Yellow crime scene tape crisscrossed the door, and I almost pulled back into the street. The blinds were open, though, and I saw someone moving around inside. If it was Detective Quinn, at least I could find out whether they already knew about Autumn's ex, Skip Thorsen.

"I think you should stay in the car," I said to Mungo as I unbuckled his seat belt. "In fact, they probably won't even let me inside."

He climbed out of the tote bag and stood with his paws on the dash of the Bug, watching me as I walked up to the door. When I was closer, I could see that the tape had been removed from the opening. I knocked and called, "Hello?"

A uniformed officer opened the door. He was tall, with closely shorn red hair and a hooked nose. "I'm afraid this business is closed, ma'am."

"Oh, Katie!" Wren appeared behind him. "Please, can't you let her in? This is Katie Lightfoot. She volunteers here and can help me sort through some of these files so we can all leave more quickly."

The promise of saving time seemed to convince him. He stepped back and I walked inside. Wren hugged me, and I could feel how frantic she was.

"Tell me what to do," I said.

"The police think they're done here, but they aren't quite ready to release the crime scene. So they gave me permission to retrieve some files and paperwork so we can at least try to keep working. Officer Feherty here has the unfortunate job of babysitting as I try to organize what to take."

I smiled at Feherty, and he smiled back.

"There are worse duties," he said.

Hanging my jacket on the corner of a desk chair, I looked around. One of the narcissus bulbs Wren had forced in the interior window boxes was finally blooming, the tiny white flower unfurling in sweet scented glory to cover the faint burnt coffee smell that still lingered. The sunlight from outside illuminated the worn carpet and used furniture in a way the soft glow of the floor lamp never could. It also highlighted the sheen of black powder across most of the flat surfaces, both vertical and horizontal: fingerprint dust.

Keeping my hands clasped behind my back, I slowly walked around the perimeter. A few rectangular spots showed where a print had been lifted as evidence. The crime scene techs had even dusted the surfaces of photo printouts that lay scattered on the file cabinet near the printer.

One in particular caught my eye. Even through the dusty sheen I could see it was the satellite photo of Fagen Swamp that Wren had printed off the Internet. I leaned nearer, taking in the features of the place recorded from space. I could see a road winding through an open area before trees hid it. Near the middle of the swamp they thinned again to reveal a bridge that led to a clearing and a small building. It was hard to see more because the powder fractured into an odd starburst pattern that obscured any detail. There were no visible finger-prints, though.

Glancing up, I saw Feherty watching me. Fingerprints or no fingerprints, if I wanted to see more of the swamp, I'd better print out another copy myself.

"It's going to take forever to clean all this up," Wren said.

Returning to where she stood sorting through files, I asked what she wanted me to do.

"The new mailing list Autumn bought to target potential donors is right here. I've already printed the labels. Would you mind addressing the solicitation packets?"

"Sure," I said. "I can do all that at home."

"Thank you, Katie. I know it's grunt work, but it does have to be done. I just want to do whatever I can to keep G.W. go-ing. It's what Autumn would have wanted."

"Of course, sweetie." I gave her a quick hug and started gathering what I'd need: brochures and hard-copy information about Georgia Wild, premetered envelopes, and the sheets of mailing labels Wren had printed out.

"You'll need more brochures. There are

some in . . . in Autumn's office."

We both looked at Officer Feherty. "Can we remove something from in there?" I asked.

"Show me," he said.

I followed him down the hallway. In the open doorway, I paused. The desk where Autumn had been lying was empty, the contents that had been tossed to the floor still heaped in piles around it. Even in the friendly daylight, Autumn's pale face and pretty polished toenails came flooding back. The weird energy I'd felt from the origami bat lingered much like the coffee smell still did out front, but there wasn't any sweet narcissus energy to cover it in here. Suddenly woozy, I grabbed the door frame.

"You okay?" Feherty asked.

I took a shaky breath. "Not really." I pointed to a cabinet by the window. "I think the extra mailers are in there."

He opened the cabinet and found an open box. "These?"

I nodded, and he grabbed the box. Together we returned to where Wren was finishing up with her files. Feherty flipped through the contents of the two boxes we were removing.

"Anything else?" he asked.

"I don't think so." Wren sounded worried.

"At least not for now. When do you think we'll be able to get back in here to work?"

"Should be soon."

"Well, okay. Thanks for, um, supervising," she said.

The policeman looked amused. "Sure. You take care, now."

Their eyes met. Oh, my. There was a very strong attraction between those two.

Interesting.

Back in the car I arranged the boxes in the hatchback and buckled Mungo into the passenger seat. Wren and Officer Feherty were still talking on the front sidewalk.

"Right in the middle of all this darkness, I do believe there might be a romance in the making," I said, buckling my own seat belt.

Yip! Mungo agreed.

CHAPTER 11

Margie was unloading the kids from her Subaru wagon when I pulled into my driveway. As soon as I set my familiar on the ground, he veered toward them. The towheaded twins ran to meet him, Julia squealing with delight. I grinned at Margie and grabbed the bakery bag out of the car.

"Brought you a little something," I said. "Healthwise . . . I mean carrot muffins and apple fritters."

"You are a gem! We've been at the park all afternoon and I'm famished." She hefted Baby Bart onto her hip and walked toward me. "Want to come in for a cup of tea? These hooligans can play with Mungo while we have a catch-up."

I glanced back at the box of mailers from Georgia Wild. They could wait. "Sure. I'd love to."

The inside of the Coopersmiths' house was messy but clean. Navigating around the blanket-and-chair fort still standing in the living room, I followed Margie into her kitchen. She put tea bags into cups, filled them with water, and popped them into the microwave while I rustled up plates.

"These don't have a ton of sugar in them, so they shouldn't make the kids hyper," I said, pointing at the muffins.

"Oh, good." Her apple cheeks were pink from an afternoon in the sun. "God knows they're hyper enough as it is."

Steaming cups in hand, we moved into the living room. Margie cleared a space on the sofa, and we both sat down. Bart used a chair seat to pull himself upright and practiced standing for a while. His blue eyes were riveted on the action inside the blanket fort. Through a gap I saw his siblings building a Lego masterpiece. The bottom of the blanket moved as Mungo's black nose worked under it. He peeked out at me, all adorable and sweet.

Or at least I thought so until I realized he was boring holes in my apple fritter with his eyes.

"You've already had enough," I said. "I happen to know Lucy slipped you three whole slices of bacon at the Honeybee before we left."

A low whine rose in his throat.

I shook my head. "If you keep being such a chowhound, you're going to weigh twenty-five pounds. And I'm not carrying around twenty-five pounds in that darn tote bag."

He sighed and wiggled backward into the fort.

"I swear, sometimes I think that dog actually understands you," Margie said, licking crumbs off her lips.

"Only when he wants to." My tone was wry.

"Ha. I know exactly what you mean."

"The JJs?"

"Redding."

I laughed.

"Oh, heck. I'm probably just as bad. That's what happens when you get married. You settle into each other, I guess. Stop listening to every little thing because so many words have already been said." She took a sip of tea. "You're not at that point with your handsome firefighter, of course. You're still in that goofy stage where you can't tear your eyes off each other. Or your hands, I bet."

I snorted. "Oh, I don't know that we've ever really been that bad. Our relationship is more . . . down-to-earth." I'd been going to say *practical,* but that sounded boring.

Margie frowned. "But you love him, right?"

"Of course." Not that I'd come right out and said it.

"And Valentine's Day is coming up."

Crap. I'd nearly forgotten. Since I didn't watch much television, I didn't get the constant reminders from the jewelry stores that gold and diamonds equaled love. I could only hope that Declan didn't buy into that idea.

"What are you getting your beau?" Margie asked.

"I honestly have no idea. What are you doing for Redding?"

She grinned. "I'm letting him dump the kids at his mother's and take me out to dinner."

I pointed at her. "Good plan."

"Oh, I'll get him some silly card, too. But we don't go in for gifts much anymore. Sheez — keeping up with birthdays and Christmas is enough."

Jonathan came out of the fort and crawled onto her lap. She gave him a chunk of Healthwise muffin and told him to share with his sister. He climbed down and went back into the fort, dutifully minding his mother. Then he gave Mungo a piece before I could say anything.

Mungo swallowed and grinned.

"You've lived here your whole life, right?" I asked Margie.

"Sure have."

"Do you know anything about Fagen Swamp?"

She settled back on the sofa cushion. "Holy crumb! I haven't thought about that place for ages."

"So you know it?"

"More than I should. I went to high school with Gart Fagen. He used to throw some wild-ass parties out there when his daddy wasn't around." Her eyes cut to her children. Bart had crawled into the fort and was systematically throwing the oversized Legos out the door.

"Why, Margie Coopersmith," I said. "Are you telling me you attended 'wild-ass' parties? With drinking and such?"

She gave me a look. "How do you think I met Redding?"

"No kidding?"

"No kidding."

"What was Gart like?"

"Kind of a jerk, actually. But why on earth do you want to know about him? He moved away years ago."

So I told her about volunteering at Georgia Wild, the maroon bats, and all the rest, ending with Autumn's murder.

Margie stared at me. "Killed? That's terrible. Just awful." She shook her head. "And all because of that stupid swamp."

"Well, that might not be the case. Her death might not have anything to do with her work at all." I drained the last of my tea and stood. "But it might. And I have a box of mailers for Georgia Wild to put together, so I'd better get going."

Margie stood, too. "You keep safe, Katie."

"Believe me, I'll do my best."

I heated up the last of Declan's firehouse chili for my supper and fixed Mungo one of his favorite meals: shrimp fried rice with peas, carrots, and lots of soy sauce. Then I hauled in the mailers and spent the next few hours of my evening upstairs in the carriage house loft, slapping labels on Georgia Wild pleas for funding while an old Doris Day film droned in the background to keep me from going crazy from boredom. Even with that distraction, thoughts ping-ponged through my brain. Most of them were about Fagen Swamp. It was past time for me to see the place.

As the movie credits came up I reached for one of the last brochures to stuff into yet another mailing packet. My fingertips brushed against something solid, something definitely not paper. Pulling the brochure box toward me, I peered down and then reached inside. A small box had been nestled beneath the Georgia Wild literature — specifically a dark blue ring box, and darn if it didn't have one of those chain jewelry store names embossed in gold on the top.

The ring inside was prettier than any I'd seen during the frequent advertising that had interrupted *The Pajama Game.* It was heavy and silvery, so my guess was platinum. The central diamond was small, but the metal surrounding it was an elaborately filigreed hexagram. It had an art deco flair to it, with two tiny diamonds on the sides surrounded by tiny platinum hearts.

Mungo jumped onto the settee and sniffed at the ring.

"What do you think?" I asked. "This was in Autumn's office, so I assume it belonged to her. But why stuff it down in the bottom of a box like that?"

He didn't have an answer to that, but I thought of what I'd done when my fiancé had broken off our engagement. The cheap ring had swirled down the toilet quite nicely. It was possible this had been Autumn's wedding ring.

Closing my hand around the ring, I shut my eyes and concentrated. Mungo leaned against my arm, offering to help if he could. The ring felt warm in my hand, but I could have been imagining it. After what seemed like a long time but was probably only a minute or so, I began to feel that the piece of jewelry was quite old — decades at least, perhaps a century.

Opening my eyes, I ruffled the fur around my familiar's neck. "Well, duh. Of course it's old. Just look at it. Good goddess, I suck at divination." With a sigh, I returned the old ring to its newfangled box and put it in the carton with the assembled and addressed mailers. I doubted that it had anything to do with Autumn's murder, but I'd inadvertently removed it from a crime scene and needed to let Detective Quinn know about it. Besides, maybe it was worth some real money that could help out Georgia Wild.

I called Wren, but she didn't know anything about the ring. Then I asked if she'd go with me to Fagen Swamp the next day and introduce me to Evanston Rickers. She reminded me that she planned to go to the bank in the morning. Impatient, I didn't want to wait. Heck, now that I'd made the decision to go, I would have gone out there that night if it had been any kind of real option.

"What's this Rickers guy like?" I asked.

"Kind of odd, but aren't we all?" was Wren's not-very-helpful response. "He's a herpetologist from Oregon. He's doing some kind of ground-truthing study in the swamp."

"Herpetologist as in reptiles?"

"You got it. Snakes specifically in this case."

Snakes. Ugh. "What's 'ground truthing'?"

"Taking an actual count of species — flora or fauna — in any given area as opposed to taking a sampling and using that to extrapolate a figure. Probably more than you need to know."

"Sounds very scientific."

"I told you he was a scientist and not some kind of nut," she said.

As we rang off, I considered my options. Bianca often had free time during the day, so I called her next.

"Sure, I'll go with you, Katie. What time?"

"How about nine tomorrow morning?" That would give me time to get most of the baking done for the day and help Lucy and Ben through the morning rush . . . if there was one.

"Sounds good. I'm meeting Cookie for

155

breakfast at Clary's Cafe. Can she come, too?"

"Why not meet at the Honeybee?" I asked. Was the youngest member of the spellbook club working that hard to avoid me?

Bianca was silent for a few moments, then said, "Okay, confession time. I joined Savannah Singles. You know, that online dating site? I've hardly gone out at all since my divorce, and I'm sick and tired of being alone. Cookie's been helping me weed through the possibilities. I want to be careful who I respond to."

"Good for you," I said. "But I don't know why you kept it a secret from the rest of us. We all want you to be happy."

"It's kind of embarrassing. It turns out there are a lot of weirdos out there, especially when you say right in your profile that you're Wiccan. However, I don't want a repeat of what happened in my marriage, so I'm not removing it."

Bianca's husband had left her in a blazing huff when he found out she was practicing the Craft. Too bad for him.

"So I'd like to wait until I at least have a prospect or two before I tell the others," she said.

"Gotcha. Well, I'm glad you're being careful — and heaven knows Cookie is good at evaluating men."

"She's nixed every single one so far." She sounded discouraged.

"Be patient," I said. "Someone perfect will show up when they're supposed to."

She sighed. "I guess so. See you in the morning."

I hung up and the phone rang in my hand. I checked the caller ID: *Mary Jane Lightfoot.*

I debated briefly, then gave in to the incessant ring. "Hello, Mama."

"I suppose you were out with your little club last night, lighting a candle for Brigit," she said by way of greeting. My mother's words were clipped. Sarcastic.

My heart sank. I shouldn't have answered.

"Actually, everyone came over here," I said with forced cheer. "We celebrated in my backyard. I just got a new freestanding fireplace."

"I bet the neighbors love that."

I'd so enjoyed honoring Brigit with the spellbook club. Now that memory faded with every word my mother said.

So I pushed back. "I made bannock cakes with raisins and orange rind, and Jaida made a candle just for the ritual."

My mother's sigh was loud and long.

157

"And Lucy insisted on champagne, I suppose."

"Well, yeah."

She made a very unladylike snorting sound. "You can thank my mother for that. Lucy got it from her."

I gripped the phone tighter. This was the first time Mama had brought up Nonna Sheffield in reference to magic. "She did?"

"You don't think it's something new, do you? Good heavens, Katie. None of this nonsense you're playing with is original. I don't know why you're so fascinated by it all."

Already stretched thin from fatigue and a couple of really lousy days, my patience snapped. "Are you ever going to forgive me for being your daughter?"

"What?"

"You heard me. I inherited my affinity for magic from you and Daddy, but you seem to blame me. I'm sorry you turned your back on this gift, on the honor of being more tuned in than others to the web of reality, on your own abilities, but I'm not going to do that. It's not nonsense, and I'm *not* playing with it."

She didn't say anything, and I thought I'd stepped over the line. Still, we'd been dancing around this very conversation for months now, and I was too frustrated to stop.

"I love you. I miss having you in my life, but if you can't forgive me for simply being who I am, then I don't know what else we have to say to each other."

I heard her take a shaky breath, and then a little sniffle.

"Mama?"

"It's not you that I can't forgive, Katie." Her voice wavered. "It's me."

I was stunned. "But Mama — why?"

"I knew when I was pregnant with you that you'd inherit what you call a gift. And I should have known it would be even stronger because of your father. We used to practice together, you know, and I was aware of how powerful he was. Is." She cleared her throat and repeated, "I should have known."

"You act like it's a curse."

"Maybe it is. It can certainly be dangerous."

Well, I couldn't argue with that. In my short time practicing, I'd been magically attacked as well as physically attacked. And then there was that whole lightwitch thing, whatever that was about. It probably would not be a good idea to tell Mama about that right now.

"Listen," I went on. "I'm not sorry, and you shouldn't be, either. I guess I can understand how you were worried when I was a child that I might do something irresponsible. So you didn't tell me. But don't you see? I did something anyway, only I didn't know it. I didn't understand what had happened."

"Oh, no, Katie. What did you do?"

"I'm sure there were lots of things, but a big one was when I was in the fourth grade. The kids were teasing me about being an Indian princess."

"Well, you are, in a way."

Yes and no. Daddy was descended from a long line of Shawnee medicine men, and somehow his Indian heritage had come to the attention of my classmates. I remembered that my best friend back then, Monty Nye, had thought it was cool when he found out. He'd probably told the others.

"The teasing started to turn kind of ugly," I continued. "It scared me, and I told them to leave me alone."

"So?"

"I *told* them," I said, infusing the word with my Voice.

"Oh," she breathed. "Oh, no."

"Those kids obeyed, too. None of them were ever my friends after that. They totally ignored me, all the way through high school."

"I had no idea. I'm so sorry."

I shook my head, even though she couldn't see me. "No, no. I'm not asking for you to be sorry. Not now. It's all in the past, and I've forgiven both you and Daddy for not telling me who — or what — I was. But now I know. And now I have other people around me who understand and accept me. I'm not an outsider anymore, Mama. Not here." I closed my eyes. "So could you try to forgive yourself, if that's really the problem between us? Please?"

There was a long moment of silence; then she said, "Yes. I'll try."

"Okay, then."

"Katie?"

"Yeah?"

"I love you, too."

Smiling, I opened my eyes to find Mungo watching me. "Good night," she said. "And Happy Imbolc, honey, even if it is a day late."

Before heading off to bed, I texted Declan since he hadn't called to say good night. When he didn't respond right away, I knew he was probably out on a call. Pushing away the pang of worry that always struck when I

161

realized my firefighter boyfriend could be in a dangerous situation — right *then,* not just in theory, I went into the kitchen and started up the laptop. Searching for *Evanston Rickers* netted me a profile on the University of Oregon Web site. A picture of him standing in the front of a lecture hall showed a man in his late forties to early fifties with dark hair and a short beard. He was a tenured professor of zoology with a special interest in the study of snakes and other reptiles. Currently he was listed as being on sabbatical.

So he was a visitor to Georgia, not a native of the area. That made me think he had less of a vested interest in the swamp than I had come to assume.

While I was at it, I did a search for Logan Seward. He had a Web site of his own. It was simple, lauding his legal credentials and community involvement without being terribly specific about either one. There was no mention of any association with the Dawes Corporation or Heinrich Dawes in particular. His contact information gave a phone number and e-mail address but no physical address.

The studio portrait of him, however, told me enough. He was the man who had been coming up when I was going down the back stairwell to Steve's office.

Curiouser and curiouser.

My phone buzzed then, alerting me to a text. It was from Declan: *Car wreck, everyone okay. Can't call but thinking of you.*

Breathing a sigh of relief, I texted back. *Thinking of you, too. Be safe. See you tomorrow.*

The phone vibrated again as I was drifting off, one hand resting on Mungo's back.

Count on it, darlin'.

CHAPTER 12

Bianca swept into the Honeybee right at nine the next morning, her cashmere skirt coat swirling around tall leather boots. Cookie followed on her heels. She'd replaced her usual form-fitting garb with a bulky sweater worn over skinny jeans. Her blue-streaked hair was piled into a clip at the nape of her neck. Bright-eyed and pink-cheeked, they greeted Lucy and Ben before Bianca called to where I was removing warm shortcakes to a cooling rack. "Are you ready, Katie?"

"Will be in two shakes," I said, untying my green gingham apron and hanging it on the wall with the rest of our collection. Hurrying into the office, I fluffed up my short hair and changed out my neon green sneakers for hiking boots. I'd donned jeans and a long-sleeved T-shirt that morning in anticipation of our swamp visit, and I now grabbed my jacket and bag before joining my friends who were still standing by the front door.

Mungo had acquiesced when I'd asked him to stay home today, settling onto the small settee in front of the television where he was no doubt watching soap operas with the occasional break to nibble on the selection of egg salad, macaroni and cheese, and leftover chili that I'd arranged for his dining pleasure.

God. That dog.

It turned out I could have brought him along. Puck poked his smooth head out of Bianca's coat as soon as we hit the street, black nose twitching at the air.

"Hi, little guy," I said to him, then to Bianca, "Do you know how to get there?"

"Her GPS will," Cookie said.

Of course she'd have GPS in her Jaguar, but I didn't really care for the implied *duh* in Cookie's tone. Bianca looked at her with a puzzled expression as she pushed the keyless entry button on her keychain. Once I'd climbed into the back of the cherry red sports car, though, I couldn't have cared less. Just sitting on that heated leather seat made me feel like royalty.

I settled back and fastened my seat belt as we headed toward Tybee Island on Bay Street. The road changed names twice before becoming the Island Expressway.

"Any luck with the online dating?" I asked.

Bianca sighed. "There was one guy I really liked. Nice-looking, decent job, a couple of years older than me. But Cookie said no."

"You could tell from his profile that he's looking for someone with money. You must be very careful about that, Bianca."

"Any news on your job interview?"

"I'll find out in a couple of days."

"What was it again?"

"Data entry," Cookie said, staring straight ahead.

"Where?"

"Candler Hospital."

"Good benefits, huh?"

"I guess."

The conversation was starting to feel like wading through molasses, so I let it drop. On the other side of Wilmington Island, the pleasant voice giving driving directions from the dashboard instructed Bianca to turn right onto a narrow paved road that curved through grassy marshland. As the road narrowed, the cattails grew taller and more frequent along with swathes of giant cutgrass. The number of trees increased. I recognized black gum and cypress.

"Oh, look!" I pointed to an alligator sunning itself a mere fifty feet from the road. It blinked at me slowly, and its craggy mouth seemed to smile. The thing seemed inordinately large.

"I bet they're all over this place," Cookie said. "I wonder how many animals live here."

That gave me pause. Not only how many different species, which was what Wren was always talking about, but how many actual animals? Actual lives that would likely be lost if the golf course development went through. There I sat, encased in luxury and peering out the window at a big flock of ring-necked ducks on a small pond, geese paddling among them. Red cardinals flashed colorful plumage among the branches, and other waterfowl waded or swam or flew.

Bianca pointed to a foot-long fawn-colored bird with a long curved beak and speckled breast. "That's a brown thrasher."

"Pretty enough," I said.

She caught my eye in the rearview mirror. "It's the state bird of Georgia."

"Oh. My bad. This is a birder's paradise," I said. Then, "Uh-oh."

The NO TRESPASSING sign looked freshly painted.

Bianca drove right by it. "Wren said she'd been out here to talk with this Rickers guy, right? I think we can take our chances."

"Yeah," I said. "From what I saw online, he seems geeky rather than someone who would take after us with a shotgun."

Cookie made a sign in the air.

Bianca's eyes cut sideways, then returned to the ever-narrowing strip ahead.

"What was that?" I asked.

"A little extra protection." Her words were clipped.

"I don't know much about magical gestures yet."

"I didn't recognize that one," Bianca said.

"It's one of my little voodoo things," Cookie said. She didn't quite keep the sarcasm out of her voice.

The pavement ended, and Bianca slowed the Jag to a crawl on the dirt road. We rounded a curve to find a covered wooden bridge. It led to a small island surrounded by a natural moat. A log cabin sat in the middle, smoke curling out of the chimney like something out of *Little House in the Big Woods*. An old Chevy pickup was parked along one side. Planks rattled below as we crossed the bridge and came to a stop in the circular open space in front of it.

The nice GPS lady spoke. "You have reached your destination."

We got out, and the smell of the swamp hit me hard. Cookie wrinkled her nose, and

I realized I might be alone in my appreciation of the strong earthy scent rich with the musk of compost. To a gardener like me, it signaled fecundity, possibility, and the circle of life. Around us birds called and hooted. Everywhere you turned, bald cypress trees reached muscular, prehensile roots down into the water to steady their dark trunks. The arching canopy above, barren of green this time of year but draped heavily with the Spanish moss ubiquitous to the area, shattered the sky into small blue shards that seemed very far away indeed. The humid air thrummed with life energy.

"Do you feel that?" I asked the other two. They nodded.

The door to the cabin opened, and a man stood framed in the doorway. I recognized Evanston Rickers from his online photo.

"Can I help you?" His voice was a deep basso profundo.

Tall and angular, he wore jeans and a plaid flannel shirt, but that was where any resemblance to a lumberjack ended. His solid black wavy hair had grown out and now fell just below his ears. Gray threaded his Van Dyck goatee, and high cheekbones set off dark, almost royal blue eyes. Long fingers gripped the doorjamb.

I stepped forward. "Dr. Rickers?"

"Indeed I am. And who, if I may ask, are you?"

"This is Bianca Devereaux and this is Cookie Rios." I indicated my companions.

"Ladies." He nodded to Cookie and then turned his attention to Bianca. Their eyes met for a long moment, and then his attention flicked down to the ring finger on her left hand. When he looked away, she looked like she'd been hit with a stun gun.

Uh-oh. Perhaps her time spent on Savannah Singles had been a waste, but our trip to the swamp may have already been worth the drive.

Cookie saw it, too, and pressed her lips together as she tipped her head to the right and considered our new acquaintance.

"I'm Katie Lightfoot." I stuck out my hand.

He squinted at me. "And?"

"I believe you know Wren Knowles. We're also associated with the Georgia Wild environmental organization." I left out that my association was entirely unpaid and my companions were involved only because they knew me. "We're following up on the maroon bat sighting here in Fagen Swamp."

"Where's Wren?"

"She's busy with other work," I said, fudging.

One side of his mouth turned up in a half smile. "I thought the bats were a dead issue."

I couldn't quite keep the surprise out of my voice. "Did Wren tell you that?"

"No. The attorney for the investment group that's planning to destroy this place. According to him the deal is going through."

"But you saw the bats," I said.

Rickers crossed the twenty feet of dirt between us. "Oh, yes. Three times I saw them, but I can't prove it."

"Of course you took pictures," Bianca said.

Rickers nodded. "I managed a few. Wren said they weren't good enough. They were either too blurry or looked like red bats. See, besides the deeper coloration, maroon bats have an extra bend in their third metatarsal. What you might think of as their third finger. I wanted to enhance the photos, but she said they could be called fake then."

I spoke. "May I ask how you know so much about maroon bats? I mean, I'd never heard of them, and they've supposedly been extinct for at least ten years."

He smiled. "I'm a zoologist."

"But your specialty is snakes," I said.

His eyes narrowed, though the smile remained. "Indeed. But I'm still quite knowledgeable about other species. I have to be."

"I'm sure that's true," Bianca said. By now she was twisting a lock of her hair like a high school girl. Puck's head popped out of her pocket, but Rickers didn't seem to notice.

His mouth widened in a slow, appreciative smile. "Thank you, Ms. Devereaux."

A splash to my right made me turn just in time to see a long slithery tail slip underwater. Too small for an alligator, and too long.

Speaking of snakes.

I was fine with spiders and salamanders, appreciated frogs and toads, mice, and even rats. But I hated snakes with a thoroughly unreasonable but primal passion, and I was in the middle of a swamp that was probably chock-full of them.

"Cottonmouth," Evanston Rickers said. "Fagen Swamp has a lot of them, as well as brown water snakes, rainbow snakes, mud snakes —"

I raised my palm to him. "And birds." Nice, feathery, pretty birds.

"Of course. That's a white ibis." He gestured toward a white bird on a log two hundred feet away. Its long pink beak curved halfway down its body, and you couldn't tell where the face started — the eyes looked like they were set right into that pink beak. It stood on one leg, the other tucked underneath.

Rickers pointed up. "And there's an osprey nest — plenty of those. Oh, and those are the neighborhood turkey vultures. They usually like more open habitat, but that pair seems content to keep me company on my little island here."

Dark eyes blinked down from two remarkably ugly, featherless red faces.

"Can you show us where you saw the bats?" I asked. What the heck — it couldn't hurt.

He blinked, hesitating, then said, "Don't see why not. Follow me." He took off for the bridge.

I trotted over the wooden planks and caught up with him, the other two behind me. "You rent the cabin?" I asked.

"For now. I'd offer to buy it if I thought it would do any good. But I can't afford to purchase the whole swamp, and that's what needs to happen in order to save it." Passion leaked around every syllable. So despite being an outsider, he obviously felt genuine concern. "This is a unique and precious place," he went on. "Autumn is trying desperately to find a buyer who will keep it in its natural form."

"Another buyer," I said. "Of course. That way Fagen will be rid of land he doesn't want, and the swamp won't turn into a golf course."

I heard whispers behind us and looked back to see Cookie and Bianca with their heads together.

"Ms. Boles is doing a good job, but she has encountered a great deal of resistance from the investors who want to destroy this land," Rickers said. "Still, she's stubborn and smart. I'm glad she's spearheading the conservation effort."

The realization set in slowly: He didn't know Autumn was dead.

"Um, Dr. Rickers? I'm afraid I have some bad news for you."

He slowed, leading us single file down a narrow path through the grasses and cat-tails gone to seed. The trees on either side grew closer and taller. I scanned the ground for anything that looked reptilian.

"What now?" he asked over his shoulder.

I decided it would be best to simply state the truth. "Autumn Boles was killed in the Georgia Wild offices two days ago."

He stopped so suddenly I almost ran into him. Bianca did run into my back before catching herself. Pivoting to face us, Rickers said, "You're kidding me."

The look on my face must have been answer enough.

"Killed how?"

"She was strangled."

A speculative expression settled across his handsome features. "Is that why you're out here? Because you think one of the potential buyers came after her?"

The raw accusation surprised me. Of course, he didn't seem to know Autumn was on the verge of giving up the fight for Fagen Swamp, which would effectively remove any motive from the investment group.

Except — if he didn't know she was turning her attention elsewhere, it was possible that at least some of the investors didn't know, either. Steve hadn't been worried about the existence of maroon bats nixing the real estate deal, probably because his father wasn't worried. However, someone in that group could still have had a motive to remove the founder of Georgia Wild from the equation. After all, there was that mysterious folded bat — times two.

I couldn't tell Rickers about the origami. Detective Quinn would have a fit if I went around broadcasting details of his murder case, and with good cause. Plus, I didn't know this guy from Adam.

I settled on saying, "We're here to find

175

out more about the extinct species of bats."

He let out a long, slow breath and turned his focus to the wooded marsh around us. "So are *you* going to do something about the sale of this land?"

"I don't know," was my honest response. "We will if we can." As unlikely as that seemed.

Cookie crowded up beside me. "Are you worried about having to leave this place if it's sold?"

He shrugged. "I'm going to have to leave anyway, when my sabbatical is up in another six months. This isn't personal."

Perhaps that was why he'd seemed surprised but not terribly upset upon learning Autumn had been murdered.

He turned and continued on. We exchanged glances and followed in silence. A minute later the path opened into a clearing. The cypress trees were taller here, some reaching over a hundred feet over our heads. It seemed excessively warm for February, and I wondered if the swamp created its own microclimate. There was definitely some kind of energy at work here, but I couldn't tell whether it was natural.

"There." Rickers pointed at a dead trunk leaning against two live trees. It was gnarled and pocked from rot and animals looking for food. "Maroon bats aren't cave dwellers like many other species. They roost in dead logs and under the bark of some trees. I saw two tucked into that crevice there. When I came back with my camera, they were gone. I started carrying my camera all the time after that and caught two more — or maybe the same two — jammed under that broken shard." His finger moved higher.

We tilted our heads back, and in an instant I lost interest in the dead tree. Behind the cypress we were looking at another that loomed higher. Much higher.

"That tree has to be at least a hundred and fifty feet tall," I breathed. "And old. It must be terribly old." I lowered my gaze to Evanston Rickers. "How old do they get?"

"I've heard they've found bald cypress as old as twelve hundred years," he said, still studying the white weathered wood of the trunk directly in front of us.

It was more than age and size that drew me around the alleged bat roost toward the cypress. It exuded power. What I had taken for the distilled life-energy signature of thousands of animals was actually coming from that tree. It felt foreign, but at least it wasn't the sticky feel of decay like the origami bat or the dark rusted-metal sensation of true evil I'd witnessed once before.

It wasn't unpleasant at all, in fact. But it was most certainly the strongest *pull* I'd ever experienced.

"Ms. Lightfoot!"

Rickers' voice stopped me.

I whirled around. "I'll just be a sec."

Cookie's eyes were round with alarm. "Come back now, Katie. We need to get going."

Bianca looked between us, puzzled.

"I was just going to warn you that there's a cottonmouth den a few yards in front of you," Rickers said. "I advise that you find another route."

The cypress still called. For a brief moment I actually considered risking the snakes.

I'm thinking of walking through a den of cottonmouths? Oh, dear. Something's oh-so-very not right.

"Katie, come on," Cookie urged. She put some of her Voice into the words.

It ran off me like water off a ring-necked duck, but the fact that she had felt a need to use it was enough to get my attention. With an effort, I retraced my steps and led the way back down the narrow path to the bridge.

What was the deal with that tree? Had Cookie felt it, too? Even as I walked away, it tugged at me with its silent whisper.

The whisper lessened as I crossed back over the bridge and saw that a shiny black Land Rover was now parked next to Bianca's Jaguar.

A Land Rover identical to the one Steve drove.

CHAPTER 13

When we reached the Rover, no one was inside. Rickers turned toward the cabin and saw the door was ajar. He strode toward it, fury written on his face.

I was surprised to see the man I'd seen in the Dawes Corporation stairwell come out of the cabin to meet him. Leaning to the side, I tried to see if Steve was inside as well, but Rickers reached out and slammed the door closed behind Logan Seward.

"How dare you enter my cabin without my permission?" Rickers fumed.

"It's hardly your cabin." The attorney reached down with his handkerchief to brush dust from his expensive-looking shoes. A gray flannel touring cap hid the bald spot I'd seen in the stairwell, and his sports jacket didn't look like it was off the rack. Still, there was something unrefined about him. The accent was southern, but not local. I hadn't lived in the South long enough to be able to identify where he was from. At least he wasn't as creepy in full daylight with other people around.

"I may pay for the ownership month by month, but by God it's mine as long as I do," Rickers said. "Not even Fagen can just barge in there unannounced."

"Well, that's why I'm here, Evanston. To give you this." Seward slapped an envelope into the other man's hand. "Notice to evacuate within sixty days."

Rickers stared down at the envelope and then back up at Seward. The muscles along his neck and jawline worked. "I thought you said I'd be able to finish my work here."

"Things have changed."

Things. Had Autumn's death made such a difference to the land deal?

He gave his shoes one last dusting and moved to the driver's side of his car. Looking me in the eye, he tipped the front of the pretentious-looking touring cap. A narrow ray of sunlight glinted madly off a silvery pinky ring. "Ms. Lightfoot." And to Bianca and Cookie, "Ladies."

I inclined my head. "Mr. Seward?"

His hand froze on the door handle. "Yes?"

"Why are you driving that car?"

The smile almost reached his eyes. "Of course you would recognize it, wouldn't you? It happens that I walked to work today, and when I found I needed to make this" — his eyes darted to Evanston Rickers and back to me — "unexpected journey, I borrowed the Land Rover. Satisfied?"

"Why wouldn't I be?" I asked, resisting the urge to make a tart retort. Something about the guy made me itchy.

"Good day, Ms. Lightfoot."

"Mmm-hmm," was my tepid response.

"How do you know him?" Bianca asked as he drove away. Rickers eyed me with suspicion.

"We haven't formally met. However, he's driving Steve's car."

Steve must have told him who I was. He would have, of course. Because that ring on Logan Seward's pinky finger was very similar to the one I wore around my neck. There was only one source for those rings. I wondered where he'd tattooed the druidic sigil each member of the clan sported.

I glanced at Evanston Rickers. He'd opened the envelope and was reading the contents, his face white.

"We'll be going now," I said to him. "Thanks for your help."

He looked up, eyes blazing. "Georgia Wild needs to stop the rape of this land. No one else will help. *Please.*" Power echoed in the word. Magic? Simple passion? An echo of the power of the tree? His attention returned to the notice to vacate, and the moment passed.

"I'll tell Wren about what just happened," I said. I knew it was lame, but it was all I had to give him.

"You do that," he said.

"What do you think?" Bianca asked. "Smart, active, good-looking. And that deep, sexy voice? Whew!" She was referring to Evanston Rickers, of course, and she wasn't asking me. Her dating adviser was sitting in the backseat while I rode shotgun this time.

Cookie leaned forward and put her hand on the back of my seat. "It would be better if he didn't have to leave in two months."

Bianca laughed. "Oh, but what a fun two months it could be."

I blinked. "Bianca!"

"What? Cookie can play the field. Why can't I? I never said I wanted to get married again. I just want a little company. And some fun. If I knew it would only last a couple of months, I might not even tell him I'm a witch."

"Well, that is simply stupefying. Don't you want a relationship to be honest? If you lie to him, he might lie to you — threefold."

Cookie made a noise in the backseat. "So now omission is a lie? You didn't seem to see it that way when you were flirting with Declan and the poor man had no idea you were spending your time casting spells and juicing up the Honeybee baked goods with magic."

I bit down on a retort and counted to ten. "You're right. I was getting used to the idea of being a witch myself. Until I did, I couldn't talk about it with someone I was just getting to know. And in the end, I did tell him and it turned out fine."

"Ladies, please don't bicker. Maybe you're right, Katie. Maybe I should think more about exactly what I want."

We were all quiet for a few miles. Then I couldn't help saying, "What about that tree?"

"The giant cypress?" Bianca guided the Jag smoothly around a curve in the highway. "You seemed quite drawn to it."

"Really drawn to it," Cookie said from the backseat.

"Didn't you two *feel* it?"

"No," Bianca said at the same time Cookie said, "Yes."

"Well, there was something going on, but I didn't associate it with that tree," Bianca said.

"You were distracted by the man candy," Cookie said.

Bianca rolled her eyes before glancing over at me. "So what's the deal with that tree?"

I looked back at Cookie. "Do you know?"

She shook her head.

"Me, neither. But whatever is going on with it is *strong.*"

"And it hooked you. I saw it," Cookie said. "I think you should stay away from it."

Bianca frowned.

"You're probably right." I imagined I could still feel the pull of the cypress, calling to me across the miles in a wordless whisper.

Steve picked up on the third ring. "Hello, Katie-g— sorry."

Well, at least he was trying. "I have a bone to pick with you, Mr. Dawes."

"Uh-oh. But I'm afraid I'm in the middle of something. Can I call you back?"

"Sure," I grumbled.

"We need a berry shortcake," Ben called from out front where he was ringing up a young couple with a baby at the register.

I hurried to the kitchen to construct the shortcake for Ben's customer. First I split the giant, biscuit-shaped shortcake with the tines of a fork and laid the lower half on a plate. Macerated strawberries, blackberries, blueberries, and stewed and sweetened gooseberries piled on next, followed by a layer of honey-balsamic whipped cream, a few more berries, the top of the shortcake laid across at an angle, another dose of whipped cream, and a sprig of spearmint topping the whole tower of sweet goodness.

"Two forks?" I asked as I set it on the table in front of the couple.

Their eyes widened at the giant treat, just as Mrs. Standish's had, and they nodded. I handed them the forks already in my hand and returned to the kitchen.

Fifteen minutes later Steve still hadn't called me back. I was putting a batch of thumbprint cookies into the oven and was thinking about trying him again, when the devil himself came in the front door. He spoke to Ben and gestured toward where I was wiping my hands on a dish towel.

I heard him say, "Katie wanted to talk to me."

Ben came into the kitchen. "Dawes is out front," he said, his brow knitting. "Said you called him?" He couldn't keep the dis-approval out of his voice. He'd encouraged Declan and me to get together almost from the day we met.

"Tell Steve I'll be out in a minute," I said.

I finished loading up another sheet with cookie dough and let Steve cool his heels a bit while I gathered my thoughts. It wasn't that I was avoiding him, but Ben made me feel self-conscious about seeing him.

That's ridiculous, Katie. You can be friends with anyone you want.

Worrying about it was stressful and unnecessary. I decided right then and there to take back my power; Steve and I could be friends, but I had no interest in being best buddies. As for the tension between Steve and Declan, that was, unfortunately, their problem.

Marching out front, I found Steve in the Honeybee library eating mocha shortbread, drinking his usual cappuccino, and idly flipping through one of the old copies of *Life Magazine* Bianca had brought in. He was casually dressed in a forest green long-sleeved T-shirt and hiking pants.

He put down the magazine as I plopped down on the sofa next to him. Kim Novak was on the cover, a Siamese cat sexily draped around her shoulders. The picture made me think of Bianca and Puck.

"Not sure how, but you manage to pull off that color," he said.

I looked down at my apron. It was electric chartreuse, and I'd chosen it to match the high-tops I'd changed back into when we got back from Fagen Swamp.

Shrugging, I said, "All right — spill. Who the heck is Logan Seward?"

A smile quirked up one side of his mouth. "You do get straight to the point."

"And?"

"What exactly do you mean?"

"You know darn well what I mean. I was there when he told Evanston Rickers he has to leave the swamp in two months. Your lawyerly 'colleague' isn't exactly subtle." I pulled at the silver chain around my neck, drawing out the protective ring Steve had given me months before. "Logan is a member of the Dragoh Society, isn't he?"

Steve inclined his head. "He told me he ran into you this morning."

"He recognized me. You'd already told him who I am."

"After you came to the office yesterday afternoon. He asked me about you after he saw you leaving. Found you quite attractive and wanted to know more about you. So I told him a little, leaving out that you're a witch. He'll probably find out from one of the other druids sometime, though. And I told him you have a boyfriend." The last word sounded a little tight, as if he'd had to

188

squeeze it out. Still, his face remained impassive.

Wait a minute. "Why did he need to know I have a boyfriend?" I wasn't fishing, just clarifying.

"He mentioned something about buying you a drink."

Logan Seward wanted to ask me out? I wrinkled my nose. "He's a little old for me, don't you think?"

Steve raised one shoulder and let it drop. "May-September romances aren't exactly unheard of."

It was true. But with the vibe I got from Seward, there was *no* chance that was going to happen. "Where's he from?"

"Kentucky. Elizabethtown."

I sat back on the sofa as I put it together. "He's the cousin. Nel's cousin who the Dragohs were planning to recruit to flesh out your numbers."

"Did recruit, actually."

"And the Dawes Corporation hired him," I said.

"Sort of. He's not an employee per se, but we do have him on retainer."

"How's that working out?"

Steve hesitated. "It's early days yet."

"Meaning?"

"This real estate transaction is the first

real legal work he's done for us."

"So he's new to Savannah, recruited out of the blue to join an ancient group of druids, and dumped right into the offices of Dawes Corp. At the very least he needs to show that he can cut the mustard to be in your club," I said.

He held his hand and made a waffling gesture. "Sort of. It would be nice to know what we're dealing with."

"How far would he go to prove himself to the other Dragohs?" I wondered out loud.

"Oh, Katie. You can't really think —"

I held my hand up. "I've had exactly two encounters with Mr. Seward, and neither was particularly pleasant. I don't know what to think. Do you happen to know what he was doing Saturday afternoon?"

Steve looked troubled, then shook his head. "No idea."

"He sure didn't waste any time kicking Evanston Rickers out after Autumn was killed."

"The guy who lives in the swamp? Tell me about him." He made a face. "I think he intimidates Logan."

"What kind of a druid is intimidated by a college professor?" I asked.

The bell over the door dinged, and I half stood to see whether Ben and Lucy needed help with the newcomers. Two couples milled in front of the menu board, trying to make up their minds.

I sat back down and continued. "The short story is Evanston Rickers is a zoologist on sabbatical from the University of Oregon to study critters in Fagen Swamp. He spotted a small number of maroon bats. Wren says twice, but he said he saw them three times. Either way, as a zoologist he's qualified to make the identification. He's fervent about saving the swamp habitat — not to mention an extinct animal species."

"Not very happy about being evicted."

I held up my palms. "Who would be? Especially after he'd been told he'd be able to continue his work."

Steve studied me. "What else?"

Of course he could tell there was something else. I debated what to tell him. What the heck — at least there was a chance he would understand.

"There's a tree in the swamp," I began. "A big cypress. *Big.*" I paused. "Powerful."

"Powerful how?"

"I don't really know," I said. "There was this crazy charge to the atmosphere. And it called to me — not in words, but . . . you know?"

His thumb stroked his chin. "Logan never

191

mentioned it."

"Bianca didn't feel the call, either, but her attention was . . . elsewhere. Cookie felt something, but not as strongly as I did. She certainly noticed the effect it had on me."

"Fascinating. Reminds me of when you smelled burning hair and no one else did."

I shuddered, remembering. "Mungo smelled it, though. I wonder if he'd be affected by the tree."

Steve said, "I might have to make a trip out to Fagen Swamp myself."

"You've never even been there?"

He shook his head.

"Steve! At the very least you need to see the place your father's company is trying to destroy."

He pressed his lips together. "You're right."

I looked at my watch. "Cookies are about ready to come out of the oven. Did you come all the way over here just because I called?"

"I wanted to find out about Dr. Rickers, and I knew you'd be curious about Logan. It seemed a good subject to talk about in person."

Taken aback, I said, "That was nice of you."

"I can be, you know. Nice, I mean. And I

thought you might be interested in another nugget of information I learned this morning." He drained the dregs of his cappuccino and stood. "Skip Thorsen — Autumn Boles' ex? He notified Father that he's no longer interested in buying into the golf course."

Frowning, I asked, "Why not, especially if he has the money now?"

"I don't know. Maybe the insurance company won't pay. Or perhaps they won't pay soon enough. He could even have found something else to invest in."

"Huh. Okay, thanks for letting me know."

"I'll let you get back to work," Steve said. I walked with him to the door, dodging the group of tourists as they left. Ben's eyes followed us.

Before Steve left, I asked, "Does Thorsen have a real job?"

"He's a dentist." He raised his hand to Ben in farewell and went out as another customer entered the bakery.

A steady trickle of people came in after that. We worked our way through the sudden flurry. After a good forty minutes, things settled down a bit. Most of the customers had left after making their purchases, presumably returning to their desks for a few more hours of work. The sofas in the library were full of chatting clientele, however, and a few bistro tables were still full, too.

I began restocking the display case. We'd had a run on the lemon-raspberry tea cake, which pleased me. Out of the four sandwich cookies, the peanut butter and chocolate fillings seemed to be winning out over the others. Maybe we'd end up sticking with two varieties in the end.

Ben sidled over as I worked. "Declan came in with some of the crew while you were gone. He was disappointed that you weren't here."

"Darn it. I'll give him a call in a little bit."

"Surprised, too."

"Bianca, Cookie, and I went out to see Fagen Swamp this morning. Didn't Lucy tell you?"

"Of course. But you didn't tell Declan."

My brow wrinkled. "No, I didn't. And I doubt that he tells me everything that he does. Unlike you and Lucy, we aren't married." Even if we were, I couldn't imagine having to report in on every activity, nor would I expect him to.

Ben continued, unfazed. "Steve Dawes sure seems determined to stay in your life." Disapproval laced his tone.

I shrugged. "I guess so."

He pushed his glasses up on his nose. "He's not good for you."

Bending to place the last slice of tea cake in the back of the row, I weighed how to respond. My uncle had mentored Declan in the fire department for years and viewed him as almost an adopted son.

Standing upright, I turned to him. "Steve is trying to help me find out more about Fagen Swamp and the golf course deal his father is involved in. That's all." At least I thought that was all. "Declan *is* good for me. That's what's important."

Relief settled across Ben's features as the bell over the door signaled another customer. I smiled at him, glancing over to where Lucy had been tidying the espresso prep area.

She wasn't paying a whit of attention to our conversation, though. Transfixed, she stared wide-eyed toward the door.

I whirled to see what had snagged her attention, and I caught my breath, stunned. Standing just inside the Honeybee, the newcomer took in the room, soaking in every detail. She wore a tweed suit and pointy-toed beige pumps that matched her handbag. Freckles scattered across her ski-jump nose, and her hair was the same red-blond it had always been, though now it came out of a bottle. Her lower lip was firmly clenched between her teeth.

"Mary Jane!" Ben said, walking toward her with both hands extended in welcome. "You've finally come for a visit."

CHAPTER 14

Lucy came out of her trance and rushed toward her sister. They embraced for a long moment right in the middle of the bakery. Customers watched for a few seconds but soon lost interest. This was obviously a family thing.

When Lucy turned away, I saw her eyes were wet. I approached my mother more slowly but hugged her just as hard.

"What are you doing here?" I asked. "We only spoke last night, and you never mentioned coming to Savannah."

Mama smiled ruefully. "It was a bit of a surprise to me, too."

"I don't understand."

"Let's just say I was instructed to get my tail down here. So I did."

Lucy and I exchanged glances. "Instructed?" she asked.

Mama pressed her lips together. "By Mother."

My fingers flew to my throat. "Nonna?"

Ben frowned in confusion. Mama raised her eyebrows and gave me a knowing look. Suddenly aware of all the people in the bakery, I took her arm and said in a low voice, "Let's go back where we can talk."

Lucy was right behind us, leaving Ben to fend for himself. His baffled gaze followed us through the kitchen and into the Honeybee office. Closing the door behind us, Lucy moved to perch on the edge of Mungo's club chair and gestured at the swivel desk chair. Imagining how my mother would react to having a dog in the bakery, I was glad he'd stayed home.

She sat down, smoothing her skirt over her knees and crossing her ankles. "You might have mentioned your nonna's visits."

I gaped at her. "Are you kidding me? You wouldn't talk about the simplest of spells, about *anything* having to do with magic for the last year. How could I tell you about Nonna . . . ? Hey, wait a minute. How did you find out?" I looked at Lucy. "Did you tell her?"

She shook her head and looked at the floor. "Mary Jane might not have spoken to you about anything magical, but she didn't speak to me at all."

My mother reddened. "I'm sorry about

that, Luce."

Lucy was quiet. She'd been deeply hurt and angered by her sister's actions. Mama had cut Lucy off a long time ago when she'd turned her back on the Craft in an attempt to keep me safe.

"Did Nonna tell you?" I asked.

She shook her head. "When Mother came — while I was in the bathtub, of all places, she didn't bother with news updates. You light a few candles, have a glass of wine, listen to a little Rachmaninoff, and the next thing you know your dead mother is filling the room with her flowery perfume and telling you to stop acting like an ass."

"She didn't say that," I scoffed.

"Oh, I just bet she did," Lucy said with an amused expression. "She was never one to pull punches."

Mama nodded. "Told me to stop acting like an ass and to start being a good mother again. Let me tell you, there is nothing like a voice from the past to goose you into doing what's right."

"But we had already begun to make up," I said.

Lucy looked surprised.

"Last night on the phone," I explained.

"Apparently that wasn't good enough. 'Get down there and see what Katie is up

199

to. Embrace it. She needs her mother.' When I told Skylar, I'm afraid he spilled the beans about her visits to you in the past. How she —" She swallowed. "How she saved your life. So you see why I had to come."

"Well, whatever the reason, I'm glad you're here." It wasn't exactly a lie. I *did* want to see my mother, but it wasn't the best timing. We had a lot to work through, a lot to heal. Between the search for Autumn's murderer, trying to keep Georgia Wild afloat, and my usual duties at the Honeybee, I didn't know how I would find the time to spend with my mother.

"How long are you going to be here?" I asked.

"Indefinitely."

Oh. My. "I see." I pasted a bright smile on my face.

"It's all right if I stay with you, isn't it?"

The smile froze on my face as I struggled to find the right words.

Lucy saved me. "Oh, you don't want to do that, Mary Jane. Katie's carriage house is adorable, just perfect for one person, but she doesn't really have the room for a houseguest. Come stay with Ben and me. Our guest room is all ready, and you can have your own bath."

It was the private bath that changed Mama's mind. I sent a grateful look to Lucy, who acknowledged it with a twitch of her lips. Now, there was someone who knew how to be truly good.

"Are you sure Ben won't mind?" my mother asked.

"Of course he won't."

The funny thing was, Lucy was right. Ben loved having houseguests, and he was curious as all get out about my mother. His natural gregariousness would go a long way toward smoothing the rocky patch between the two sisters.

"Let's go ask him," I said. The tight quarters were making me claustrophobic.

When we trooped back out to the front of the bakery, Ben was busy but handling everything all right. Since he was steaming milk, I stepped to the counter to take the order of the next waiting customer.

"Don't you have any *fun* drinks?" asked the scowling woman. Deep frown lines testified to her ongoing bad attitude, and her hands were jammed into the pockets of her stretched-out cardigan.

"We pretty much stick to the regular stuff," I said with cheer. "Since the Honeybee is a bakery more than a coffee shop, we focus more on fun pastries, cookies, cakes, and the like."

"Well, maybe you should up your game, missy." She stomped away.

I certainly wasn't sorry that she was taking her grumpy energy out of the Honeybee.

"Why, that was so *rude*," Mama said from where she stood beside me.

Lucy joined us. "What do you think the best thing would have been for her?"

Guilt stabbed me. I should have thought about how to make her feel better, not been glad when she left. Looking down at the counter, I mumbled, "It's hard to know since I don't know why she's in such a foul mood. Maybe a little bergamot for general peacefulness? Plenty of that in a cup of Earl Grey tea. And olives for stress." For some reason I'd added kalamata olives to a few of the sourdough loaves I'd baked that morning.

Lucy patted me on the arm. "Don't worry. She'll be back."

"How do you know?" I asked.

"Because she could have gone to a coffee shop in the first place, but she came here because something inside told her we could help her."

"But I didn't." I sighed.

"Like I said, you'll get another chance."

My mother had been listening to our

exchange. "So that's what the Honeybee is all about? Using your" — she glanced around — "talents to help your customers?"

"For heaven's sake, Mary Jane!" Lucy's voice rose. "What did you think?"

Customers turned their heads toward us. "Lucy," I said.

She went on in a lower tone. "Katie, of course, has other powers, and she's a consummate pastry chef. But of course we employ hedgewitchery here in the bakery."

My mother's forehead wrinkled, and an ominous look entered her eye. "What do you mean Katie has other powers?"

Lucy put her hands on her hips and leaned forward. "Your daughter is a catalyst and a lightwitch," she whispered. "And so far that has manifested in her being a tool of justice."

I snorted. *Tool of justice.* Sheesh.

Jerking her head back, Mama stared in outrage at her sister first, then at me. "Meaning?"

I shrugged, but Lucy plunged on. "She brings killers to justice. It's happened twice so far, and now she's going for a hat trick."

"Oh, come on, Lucy," I said. "Don't you think that's a bit dramatic?"

"A hat . . . You mean . . . *Katie,*" Mama hissed. "Is that why Mother had to save your life?"

Holding up my hand, I said, "Remember what Nonna told you. 'Embrace it.' "

Mary Jane Lightfoot's jaw clenched and her nostrils flared, but I had to give her credit when she said, "I'll do my best. Now, are you going to show me around the bakery or not?"

As predicted, Ben loved the idea of my mother staying in his and Lucy's townhouse for as long as she saw fit. After I showed her around the kitchen and the reading area, Mama started in on the questions about how we applied herbal craft to our recipes. Finally I had to quietly point out that our customers didn't know that the rosemary Parmesan scones would promote fidelity — or any of the other intended effects of our baked goods.

"It's not that we're trying to fool them," I said. "But some people don't know that they need help — or believe in our particular methods. We're only trying to help."

Mama settled onto one of the bistro chairs in the corner with one of Bianca's copies of *Life Magazine* while I mixed the sourdough to slow rise until the next morning and prepped as much as I could for the next day's baking. As long as she was occupied, I went into the office and called Declan.

He answered on the first ring.

"I heard you came by," I said. "I'm sorry I missed you."

"Me, too, darlin'. It's hard to go cold turkey from you for a full forty-eight."

"You do say the sweetest things. But you make me sound like a bad habit."

"Oh, no. A very good habit." His deep voice dropped even lower. "At least I get to see you tonight."

"Um, I think that can still happen," I said. "But I have some news that might, er, interfere."

There was silence on the other end of the line.

"Less than an hour ago my mother showed up here at the Honeybee, completely unannounced."

"Oh! Katie, that's great. Isn't it? I mean, I'll get to meet your mom before you meet mine."

"That's true. But Deck, don't be surprised if . . . Well, let's just hope things work out between us."

"I want that very much," he said fervently. "As long as it's the right thing for you."

Now, *that* was just one of the reasons why Declan was so good for me.

■ ■ ■ ■

"This is amazing," my proper mother said around a bite of rosemary shortbread after I'd rejoined her. "You are so talented. I mean, I've always known that, but I — I'm really proud of you."

I tried to hide my surprise.

"Now, tell me about this killer Lucy implied that you're trying to find."

We were in the lull that generally hit between lunchtime and the late-afternoon rush for caffeine and sugar. So, haltingly at first and later with my words tumbling all over one another, I told her about Georgia Wild, about Wren and finding Autumn and the maroon bats and Fagen Swamp. When I finished, she was quiet for a long time. I began to regret sharing so much.

"You say your environmental group needs money? How much?"

Ah. She had decided to focus on something nice and safe.

"I don't know. Bianca is loaning Wren enough to cover the rent for the month, and she applied for a loan this morning. Apparently there is some grant money that will come through eventually, but not right away."

"Have a bake sale."

"What?"

"You should have a big bake sale — a huge bake sale — to benefit Georgia Wild. It will make them some money, and it will be a great promotion for you. I know you're busy, so I'll be happy to organize it."

"You know," I said, thinking through her suggestion. "That might help. You are a wonder, Mama."

She ducked her head but looked pleased.

"Lucy," I called, "come hear Mama's idea."

About two o'clock Wren and Mimsey came in. They seemed joined at the hip these days, but I could see why. Mimsey was crazy worried about her granddaughter, and Wren had been through enough trauma that she wanted her grandmother around.

I knew what that was like.

Mimsey took to my mother immediately, despite knowing about her tortured relationships with magic, with Lucy, and with me. I filled them in on the visit Bianca, Cookie, and I had made to Fagen Swamp, and Wren shared her experience with the loan officer at Bianca's bank.

"I know he'll do his best, especially since Bianca vouched for me, but I got the feeling from some of his questions that there might be some doubt about whether a nonprofit can pay back a loan."

"What about the grant money?"

"I have to take him more paperwork tomorrow to prove that it's coming. That might do the trick."

"In the meantime, my mother came up with an idea. Tell them," I said.

Ben came over to listen while Mama told everyone what she had in mind. "I know it would have to be soon — say, three days — and that will be tricky," she said. "Still, that should be enough time to put up posters and let organizations here in town know. I'll contact the paper, and Ben said he'd contact the members of the Downtown Business Association, who would then pass it on. If we could send out to your local mailing list right away, they might receive the notice in time." She looked at the ceiling, and I could practically see the smoke coming out of her ears. My mother had a passion for fundraising that had gone to waste in the small town of Fillmore, Ohio.

Wren bounced in her seat. "Katie, did you address those mailers last night?"

"They're in my car, ready to go."

"You know what we could do? Make up stickers announcing the bake sale and slap them on the mailers. If we hurry, we could still make today's mail."

I glanced at my mother. "That will commit us, though. And I really don't have the time to do much more than extra baking. Do you really want to spearhead this?"

She nodded vigorously. "I'd really like to help."

"I'll contact our printer to make the stickers," Ben said. "We've done a lot of work with them, and I'm sure they'll be able to turn something like that around today."

"Perfect," Mama said. "Where are the mailers?"

"In my car," I said.

Wren stood. "Let's go get them."

I hurried into the office to get my keys and the jewelry box with the filigree ring that I'd stuffed into my bag, then out to the sidewalk where Wren waited.

"I'm parked across the street, but hang on a sec. I wanted to show you that ring I told you about on the phone last night." I extracted the diamond ring from its case and held it out to her. It glinted in the sunlight. "Do you know if this belonged to Autumn?"

She squinted at it through her glasses before slowly shaking her head. "I've never seen it."

"Hmm." I returned it to the box and stuffed it in my pocket.

Traffic was light, and nary a tour bus guide could be heard. That was unusual, to say the least. We crossed, and I unlocked the car.

Loaded with a box apiece, we started back across Broughton.

"I guess I'd better give it to Detective Quinn since it came from a crime scene," I said. "It looks to be worth some real money, too. Maybe it's included in Autumn's will?"

Tires squealed on the pavement, and I whirled to see a late-model SUV careening around the far corner.

"Where's the fire?" I muttered as we paused to let it go by. Without warning, it veered into the oncoming lane and headed straight for us.

"Katie!" Wren screamed.

Dropping the box I was holding, I turned and pushed her as hard as I could. At the same time I *pushed* against the metal monster bearing down on us. Wren fell between the Bug and the car parked in front of it, crying out as she hit the curb. I twisted my torso up onto the hood of my car, arms and legs pinwheeling as I rolled over to the sidewalk on the other side. I thumped to the ground, landing on my hip and arm.

The pain registered someplace in the back of my mind, but I was too focused on staying alive to pay much attention.

A hideous crunching sound ripped the air, and Wren screamed again. The engine gunned loudly. Metal screeched on metal, groaning as it folded and crumpled. The Bug hid most of the SUV from my view, but I could see a heavy black tire far too close to my head and a flash of the white roof above as it backed away. Another tooth-numbing screech rent the air; then rubber squealed on the pavement. The roar of the engine receded as the vehicle accelerated away.

After a small eternity, I gathered my wits and pushed myself to my knees, absently grateful that for once I wasn't wearing a skirt.

"Wren!" I was yelling even though she was only a few feet away. "You okay?"

"I think so." Her voice shook.

Standing on wobbly legs, I took two steps to find she had crawled onto the sidewalk. She looked blearily up at me. It took a few seconds before I realized her glasses had been knocked off. Retrieving them from the sidewalk, I held them out to her. "At least they're not broken."

She didn't reach for them. "No, but I'm

pretty sure my arm is."

"*Wren!* Ohmygodhoneyareyouokay?" Anguish rolling off her, Mimsey was upon us, followed immediately by Lucy, Ben, Annette from the knitting shop, Croft from the bookshop, about fourteen total strangers . . . and my mother.

Who stood blinking at me as though she didn't know me at all.

CHAPTER 15

"I'm okay, Grandma, I'm okay." Wren tried to stand but yelped when her wrist accidently touched the fender of my car.

Ben pushed through the primarily female crowd and carefully helped her to her feet.

"I called 911," Croft announced.

"Thanks." The response was automatic. Everything was automatic. I felt like a robot.

"What happened?" Ben demanded.

"A car, some kind of SUV, came around the corner and . . . I'm not sure what happened after that," I said. "For no reason, it came right for us."

"Did anyone else see anything?" he asked, looking around at the crowd. I heard him as if from a great distance, and then someone said from very far away, "The sunlight flashed off the window, so I couldn't see inside." Other voices gabbled agreement.

Sirens approached, and I realized I was now sitting on the curb without knowing how I got there. My mother was dabbing at a cut on my arm with a damp towel. She was talking, but I couldn't wrap my mind around what the words meant. She looked up and seemed to be talking to someone else. Strong arms lifted me, and I looked up into a pair of loving blue eyes.

"Deck," I said, "put me down. I'm okay."

"The hell you are." His arms tightened protectively around me.

I wanted to close my eyes and let him take care of me. Sleep. Not deal with anything. *No. I can't do that. Get it together.*

The world came back to me in an audible rush. Colors were brighter, individual beads of humidity collided against my skin, and the afternoon sunlight swirled through the air. I could smell diesel and spice and Declan's shampoo, hear his heart beating like a sledgehammer and his breath that sounded like a tsunami as he carried me into the Honeybee and over to the reading area. It was as if everything had somehow become more *real.* With eerily calm fascination, I took it all in, even as my senses began to fade back to normal. The whole experience lasted only ten seconds or so, but I knew the memory would remain with me for the rest of my life.

"Honest, I'm fine," I managed to say.

Something in my voice must have been different, because after one gauging look into my eyes, Declan tentatively set me on my feet, his hands on my elbows as I eased onto the sofa.

"Wow. That was weird," I said.

"It's called shock."

"Maybe." But it had been more than that. I looked around. Mama had followed us in but was hanging back. I waved her over. "You two have met, then?"

Declan looked at her, and something passed between them. Suddenly they were both grinning.

"You do know how to make introductions exciting," he teased.

I noticed he was still in uniform. "You're here professionally?" I asked.

"We were doing building inspections nearby. Got here in two minutes. But I'd hardly call any response to your almost getting run down in the street professional. You scared the bejesus out of me."

"Me, too," Mama added.

"How's Wren?"

"She's on her way to the emergency room. Ben and Lucy are still talking to the police outside. I'll be right back."

I started shaking all over.

"Adrenaline rush," Declan said in a soothing voice. I wondered how often he had to use it in his line of work. "Give it a few minutes and you'll feel better."

My mother returned with a glass of water clenched in both hands. The liquid trembled, and I saw how upset she was. "It's okay, Mama. I feel" — *amaaazing* — "fine now."

Her eyes never left my face as she put the glass down on the coffee table and sat next to me.

"McCarthy?" called a voice. "You available?"

Declan looked at me, and I nodded. "Go ahead. Do your job. I'll be okay."

After giving me a quick squeeze, he went back outside. For the first time in almost a year I was alone with my mother.

"What did you do out there?" she whispered. Her eyes shone an iridescent green to my heightened senses. "That truck was coming straight for you."

"The driver must have swerved." I wondered if I looked as flushed as I felt. With each heartbeat, I felt the ebb and flow of blood in every vein and artery.

"They didn't swerve." Mama crossed her arms over her chest.

I giggled. I didn't mean to, but it escaped before I knew it was there. Clamping my hand over my mouth, I struggled to maintain a sense of decorum. It wasn't hysteria — it was just that I felt so strangely *good* after I . . .

"I pushed it away," I said.

She blinked, but then she said in a new voice, "I've never seen anything like it." Resignation and perhaps a little wonder were mixed in the words.

"Did anyone else notice?" I asked in alarm.

"Lucy might have — she was looking out the window, too. But your light would have obscured it from most people." She bit her lower lip. "I must say, you were rather subtle despite the urgency of the situation."

Now I was staring at her. My mother had gone from trembling to practical in less than a minute. Grabbing the glass, I sucked down half the water.

"My *light*?" I asked after swallowing.

"That blinding flash." Her eyes narrowed. "You didn't know?"

I shook my head, remembering someone outside saying that the reflection of light off the window made it hard for them to see.

Lucy came in from the street, followed by Ben and Detective Quinn. Ben pointed toward the library. Quinn saw me, nodded, and came over.

I stood, still feeling light-headed. "Detective Peter Quinn, this is my mother, Mary Jane Lightfoot."

He took her hand. "Delighted to make your acquaintance."

"Thank you." She blushed in the face of his full-wattage Southern charm.

"I'm afraid I need to speak with Katie alone, Ms. Lightfoot."

"Mary Jane," she insisted to my surprise. She rose. "I'll be in the kitchen when you're done, Katie."

Quinn settled into a chair and assessed me. "You don't look the worse for wear. Do you want to go to the hospital, get checked out?"

"Nope. I'm okay. I mean, I'm shaken up of course. Someone tried to —" I stopped and felt my eyes go wide. "Quinn, someone tried to kill me!" I hadn't thought the actual words yet, and now the knowledge hit me like a cartoon anvil.

"Maybe," Quinn said. "Are you sure it wasn't an accident?"

I tried to keep my mind on the question and not leap to conclusions. "The driver would have to have been drunk or stoned or . . . I guess it's possible. I sure like the idea better than the notion of someone targeting me."

"If it was deliberate — and that's still the more likely scenario in my opinion — the intended victim was probably Wren Knowles."

"Because she received the origami bat," I breathed. "Of course. Did you find out anything else about it?"

He shook his head. "Same as the one Autumn Boles was holding when she died. It was made from paper found in craft shops and artist supply stores all over the area. I'm told it was mostly sold with a selection of other colors and sizes."

But Wren's hadn't felt icky like Autumn's. Could the first one have given off that aura of decay because of the violence of her death?

Death. Decay. *Embalming.*

"Did you track down Hunter Normandy?" I asked.

He pressed his lips together. "You sure have a lot of questions."

"Like it or not — and I suspect the answer is 'not' — I'm smack-dab in the middle of this mess. Of course I have questions."

He gave me a long look, then finally nodded once. "I guess I can see your point."

Declan came in and beelined over. "Hey, Peter," he said to Quinn. "Listen, hon, I've got to get going. But I'll come over tonight as soon as my shift is over, okay?"

The feel of his hand on my shoulder felt grounding, and I ached for more. "Can hardly wait," I said.

He leaned down and gave me a quick buss, glanced at Quinn, and then returned for a proper kiss. Ruffling my hair, he murmured, "I'm so glad you're okay."

Quinn watched him go. "Does he know you're still seeing Dawes?"

I stood. "I am not 'seeing' Steve. We're simply friends."

He rose, too. "Especially now that he can give you the lowdown on the golf course deal."

I looked away.

"Aha! I knew it. Well, his father was remarkably unhelpful on that count. Anything you might want to share with me?"

I opened my mouth, then closed it. "All of a sudden you don't seem to mind me asking questions."

One side of his mouth turned up. "I'll take information anywhere I can get it when I'm investigating a murder."

Good. "He didn't tell me very much. However, he did mention Autumn's ex-husband. You've talked with him, of course."

"Yesterday."

"Did you know he had a life insurance

policy on her?"

"As it happens, I did." Quinn sounded impatient.

"Did you also know he wanted to buy into the deal at Fagen Swamp with Heinrich and the rest but didn't have enough money?"

A low whistle at that. "Interesting."

"Except he's withdrawn his bid to be part of the investment team. I don't know why."

"Hmm. Anything else?"

"Logan Seward gave the man who rents the cabin in Fagen Swamp sixty days to leave. It sounds like the sale of the land is going through unless we can find definitive proof the maroon bats really exist."

Quinn patted me on the shoulder. "Good to know. You keep this up and I'm going to have to see about getting you on the payroll."

I rolled my eyes. "Ha-ha. And does Logan Seward have an alibi for Saturday afternoon?"

"Not a very good one. Said he was in a bar watching the play-off game. Some other patrons remember seeing him, but no one can say exactly when he was there. Eyes on the game and all, plus it sounds like he kept to himself."

"Hmm. Oh! Wait a second. I just remembered that I have to give you something that

I found yesterday."

Curiosity marked his expression as I retrieved the jeweler's box.

I reached into my pocket and held the box out to him. "It's a ring I found in one of the cartons that Officer Feherty let me take out of Georgia Wild yesterday. I'm sorry, but I'm afraid I touched both the box and the ring."

Quinn opened the lid and took out the ring. I guessed I shouldn't have worried about handling it.

"Feherty missed it?" he asked.

"Yeah, but it was buried in the bottom of a full box of brochures. Plus, the CSI techs had already gone over the place. Don't be hard on him."

"I'll try not to be too much of an ogre about it." He replaced the circle of filigreed platinum in the jeweler's box, put it in his pocket, and stood. "You be careful, all right?"

"Count on it," I said.

The gawker knot from out on the street had moved into the Honeybee. Twenty or so people milled around, asking questions and sharing their thoughts.

"Why was there an ambulance? Was someone hurt?" This came from a concerned-looking gentleman wearing a felt fedora.

"Really? A hit-and-run?" A thrill ran through the teen boy's voice.

"Did anyone get the license plate number?" asked Croft Barrow, and I mentally cheered his practical approach.

"Only the last two digits. I told the police everything I saw. But it happened so *fast,*" said a ponytailed woman.

"Did you see how fast that SUV was going? And how it totally crushed that car?" said a matronly sort to her friend.

My heart sank. Was she talking about the Bug? I'd been in such a daze when Declan picked me up that I hadn't even noticed. I made my way through the crowd to the window, only to find that a police van blocked my view.

Steve Dawes walked by on the sidewalk outside, carrying one of the boxes of mailers that Wren and I had dropped. Annette Lander followed with the other one. Steve opened the door for her, and they came into the Honeybee.

"These were scattered all over, but we got most of them," Annette said, setting her box down on a table. Steve put his on the chair next to it.

"Thank you," Ben said, hurrying to take them into the office.

Annette turned toward me and put her hands on her hips. "What the heck happened out there? I'm in my shop ringing up a skein of organic cotton for a customer and suddenly, *crash*!"

I winced. " 'Crash' pretty much sums it up."

"Well, at least you didn't get hurt." She looked worriedly at the door. "I'm sorry, but I really ought to run. I left the shop open."

"Go," I said. "And thanks again for your help."

"You bet." She lifted her hand and hurried out.

"And thank you, too," I said to Steve, who still stood by the boxes of mailers.

"Sure." His eyes examined mine, then moved on to the rest of me. "You're all right?"

"I'll have some bruises, but I'll be okay. How did you know what happened?"

"A little bird told me," he said.

"Steve —"

"Gotta go." And with a quick squeeze of my shoulder, he left.

I turned to see Ben coming toward me. My uncle took my elbow and steered me into the kitchen. Mama had stepped in and was quickly loading plates and cups into the big dishwasher. "We can handle the bakery for the rest of the day," Ben insisted in a low voice. "This rush won't last long, once they get their fill of muffins and gossip, and Lucy called Cookie. She doesn't have to work at the gallery until this evening, and she's coming to help out."

"But she doesn't have to," I protested.

He wasn't listening. "Will you please go and take a nap? You're suffering from shock, and you don't even realize it."

"Oh, I am not," I said.

"You're pale as can be, darlin'. I've never seen you so white."

He had to be making that up. Maybe the sun did scatter a few freckles like Mama's across my nose, but I'd inherited more of Daddy's Shawnee complexion than her light Irish skin.

"Besides, I can't sleep during the day," I argued. "I barely sleep at night. And I don't even know if my car is drivable after that jerk ran into it."

"I took a good look at it," he said, looking over to where Lucy was frantically trying to keep up with the influx of the curious. "The Beetle has a pretty good scratch on it and a dent in the fender, but it's fine otherwise. The Toyota that was in front of it, though? Pretty much a total loss."

"Oh, no. Do we know who owns it?"

"Looks like a rental."

For some reason that made me feel better.

"Mary Jane, maybe you could drive Katie home? Lucy and I can come pick you up after we close the Honeybee at five."

My mother stepped in and said quietly, "Of course. I'd love to see your house, sweetie."

"There you go," Ben said. "Go spend some time with your mom. Show her the carriage house and all that you've done with the yard." He hurried over to the register to help my aunt.

I sighed and looked at Mama. "I guess you're stuck with me."

She smiled a worried smile. "Ben is right. We'll go to your house, have a nice cup of tea and a chat."

"Hang on," I said. "I'll be right back."

She turned back to the dishwasher, and I went into the office. I retrieved my tote bag and then quickly turned on the computer screen. One quick online search later and I was ready to go. Together we wended our way through the customers crowding the Honeybee. No one seemed to be in much of a hurry, and Ben and Lucy had everything under control. They both waved as we left but didn't break away from what they

226

were doing.

Out on the sidewalk, Mama held out her hand. Reluctantly I gave her my keys. Carefully looking both ways, we crossed the street. A uniformed woman with a camera was snapping picture after picture.

She lowered the camera when we approached. "You the owner of the Volkswagen?" she asked.

I nodded.

"Just finished up with it. All yours."

"Thank you."

I stood on the sidewalk, surveying the damage, hands on my hips. What I saw shook me. It could have been worse — really, it could have. In fact, it probably should have been worse, given the velocity with which the big white SUV had been coming at us.

Ben was right: The damage to my car was minimal. But the red Corolla in front of it was another story. The driver's side door had been pushed halfway into the seating compartment. The front quarter panel was crumpled and bowed, the bent metal jammed right up against the tire. The hood was open, and a faint hissing sound emanated from the radiator.

Push or no push, if Wren and I hadn't gotten out of the way, we'd be dead.

227

My mother was watching me. "You saved your friend's life, you know. Shoving her out of the way. And . . . well, you know." She got in and pulled the door closed. I went around to the other side, fuming at the SUV driver.

It seemed more useful to be angry than afraid.

"Mama?" I said. "What do you think about making a little side trip before we go home? Frankly, I'm way too jazzed up for a cup of tea and a sit-down just yet."

She turned the key, and the engine coughed, then roared to life. The radio blared classic Southern rock, and I reached over to turn it off. "What did you have in mind?" she asked.

"I want to stop by the dentist's office and make an appointment."

The look she gave me was skeptical at best. "Why not simply call?"

"It would be better to go in person."

"Katie. Even I know better than that. What are you up to?"

Unsure of how she'd react if I told her, I nonetheless opted for honesty. "The dentist I want to go see is named Skip Thorsen. He's Autumn Boles' ex-husband."

"Autumn is the woman who was killed?"

Good heavens. My mother had just ar-

228

rived in town and had already witnessed either a freak accident or someone trying to kill her daughter. Add to that she found same daughter involved in a murder investigation, however peripherally.

"Right," I said. "You really are taking all this rather well."

"I'm not, really. But I'm doing my best to fake it."

I laughed, and she smiled in return. I had to give her a lot of credit for trying so hard.

"So I want to go by his office and see if I can get a hit off him."

"A hit."

"You know. A feeling."

"You can do that?"

I shrugged. "Sometimes. It's not consistent or . . . clear most of the time." I thought of Hunter Normandy and how he'd felt so flavorless to me. Now I had to wonder if that had to do with his job as an embalmer. I could understand why he might wall his psyche away, whether consciously or unconsciously, from the work of preparing the dead for the next step on their spiritual journey. However honorable it might be, sometimes it had to be hard. Nonetheless, I couldn't be sure that was why he seemed like such a blank to me. And what about the way the two different origami bats had felt? I had no idea what to do with that.

"It would also be good to know whether or not Skip Thorsen was in his office all day," I said. "Or if he left for a while this afternoon. Like an hour or so ago. And I wouldn't mind knowing what he drives."

She stared at me. "You mean like a white SUV?"

Slowly, I nodded.

Mama put the car into gear. "Where's his office?"

I pulled out the printout I'd made before we left the bakery and began reading off directions.

CHAPTER 16

My mother was quiet as she drove my Volkswagen, merely nodding her understanding
of the directions to Skip Thorsen's dental
office. Downshifting, she turned left on
Whitaker Street and headed out of the
historic district toward Midtown. My guess
was that she was still upset about witness-
ing my instinctive move to protect Wren and
myself with magic. Or maybe it was witness-
ing her daughter's actual power after trying
to deny it my whole life.

I debated what to say, finally settling on,
"When was the last time you practiced?"

She didn't answer at first, and I wondered
whether she regretted her impulsive trip to
Savannah even if it was at Nonna's urging.

Nonna. I wondered why she hadn't shown
up to warn me like she had when I'd been
in danger before.

"The last time I cast, it was a garden spell
to heal blossom end rot on some tomatoes

your father planted," my mother finally said. "Our next-door neighbor, Mr. Osborn, saw me, and even though what I did was subtle — spraying a healing tea of bay and lavender and burying moss agates near the base of the plants — a few nights later he caught your grandmother performing a fertility spell."

"Lucy told me that story," I said.

"Did she tell you our mother was naked as a jaybird?"

"She was . . . *what?*"

My mother grinned. "Oh, yes. Your nonna practiced old school."

I giggled for the second time that day. "Old Mr. Osborn must have been downright scandalized."

The smile dropped from her face. "All of Fillmore was scandalized. Small town like that, news travels fast. There was a meeting at the city hall, and they even talked about arresting your grandmother for public indecency. But it was the incantation that really set things off. She was ostracized, ridiculed, and you can bet everyone looked at us sideways as well."

"I had no idea," I said quietly. "It must have been awful."

"It was a conservative little town," she said, turning right at a stop sign when I pointed. "Still is. Your dad and I talked about moving, starting fresh, but it was my home and I didn't really want to. Mother completely refused to be bullied out of town, and I couldn't leave her there alone. Your dad said to ride it out, that people would forget. I don't know if they ever did. Your nonna was considered a crazy old witch until the day she died a few years later, but people seemed okay with Skylar and me." She looked over at me, then back at the road. "And you. I wasn't going to risk that. I thought we did the right thing, not telling you about your abilities."

"That's it," I said. "On the right."

She pulled to the curb a half block past the address I pointed out and shut off the engine. Turning to face me, she said, "I don't know that it was right, especially given the degree of ability you possess. If I was wrong, I'm sorry. I never, ever wanted to hurt you or cause you unhappiness. I was just doing the best I could."

My throat worked, so tight I couldn't speak. I didn't know what to say anyway. "Oh, Mama," I finally managed.

She blinked away tears and reached over to give me an awkward hug. Clearing her throat, she said, "Enough drama. Let's go see a dentist."

Dr. Thorsen's practice was in a building that also housed a real estate agent, a CPA, an orthopedist, and a dermatologist. A sterile hallway led to a closed door with a melamine placard on it. I pushed the handle down and went in, Mama on my heels.

The waiting room held six chairs upholstered in tough, dark-colored fabric, two small tables displaying neat stacks of magazines, and a large marine tank full of brightly colored fish. Recessed lighting shone down from above, a cool light that didn't make up for the lack of windows. In one corner a pile of plush pillows was surrounded by toys ranging from building blocks to a cast metal fire engine to handheld electronic games. A reception counter ran along one wall. Behind it, shelves of charts and files stood at attention, and a closed door no doubt led into the inner sanctum of reclining chairs, drills, spit sinks, and all the rest.

The waiting room was completely empty, as was reception, but I could hear the sound of quick keyboard strokes from around the corner.

I rang the bell on the desk. Moments later a petite woman leaned around the partition. Her blue-black hair was gathered into a bun high on her head, and she peered at me over a pair of zebra-striped reading glasses. "May I help you?"

"I'd like to make an appointment with Dr. Thorsen," I said.

"I'm sorry. He's not seeing any patients for a few —"

"The doctor isn't taking any new patients," interrupted another woman as she joined her. The newcomer was older, with a mannish chin and an assured demeanor. Her name tag said CHARLY.

"So he's not in?"

"Not today," Charly said. The bespectacled receptionist faded back, and I heard the typing begin again.

"That's too bad." I took a leap. "How is Skip doing?"

Her expression softened. "You're a friend?"

For some reason I didn't want to lie, which was funny because I was usually pretty good at it when I needed to be. So I simply smiled and said, "I'll track him down." That wasn't a lie, either, not if I could help it.

"All right," she said.

"Thanks anyway," I said, and then to Mama, "Let's go."

We had turned to leave when Charly said, "If you're really his friend, maybe you can help. He's not doing well at all since her death."

"Poor Autumn," my mother said.

I kept the surprise off my face, but it wasn't easy.

Charly grimaced. "Tragic, wasn't it? Skip has cancelled all his appointments for the next few days." She hesitated, then plunged on. "He appears hell-bent on spending all his time at the Old Familiar."

"Oh, no," I said.

"Thanks for letting us know," Mama said.

Outside, she asked, "Is the Old Familiar what I think it is?"

I nodded confirmation. "It's a bar."

"Uh-oh."

We began walking. I looked up and down the street but didn't see anything like the vehicle that had nearly killed Wren and me. It had to have been pretty smashed up, too, and whoever had been behind the wheel was unlikely to just leave it in his usual parking spot.

"The driver of the SUV could have been drinking," I said. "Might explain a lot, actually. I mean, it was very sudden, but I didn't feel any blatant malevolence from the inside of the vehicle. On the other hand, I could

236

have missed it. There was a lot going on at once."

"Blatant malevolence," she repeated.

"I wonder if he's at the Old Familiar now — and if so, whether he was there earlier this afternoon."

We'd reached the Bug, and Mama unlocked it. Fingers on the door handle, she said, "Well, I for one could use a drink."

I blinked. "Well, okay then."

The Old Familiar was a takeoff on an English pub except for the menu, which was distinctly Southern. Along with your ale, stout, or porter, you could snack on boiled peanuts or chow down on a full Low Country boil complete with spicy shrimp, corn on the cob, sausages, and red potatoes. As we approached, the smell of garlic, onions, vinegar, and beer seeped out around the door.

We stood just inside, blinking against the sudden dimness after the bright sunshine. The space was small, with only enough room for thirty or so people if some were willing to stand. Six dark wooden booths lined the wall to the left, and a heavy mahogany bar curved along the wall opposite, studded with tall stools and complete with a brass railing to rest your feet on. A mirror behind glass shelves reflected glittering bottles of liquor and their colorful contents. Rockabilly played over the sound system.

On a Monday afternoon there were few customers and one bartender to tend to them. A couple sat in the booth farthest from the entrance, jammed together on one hard bench and completely immersed in each other. A large man with a magnificent head of blond hair sat slumped at one end of the bar with a pint of something dark in front of him. He didn't look around, either, but if anyone in the place was Dr. Skip Thorsen, it was him.

I wiggled onto the bar stool one seat away, and Mama sat on the other side of me. Her tweed suit was out of place in the joint, but at least she didn't look like a tourist. The big guy's gaze wandered over to my bright green high-tops and stayed there, his eyes bleary and red-rimmed.

Yeah. This was the guy.

The bartender, short and caramel-skinned, came toward us, swishing a towel over the counter more from habit than a need to clean up. "Getchoo?"

"I beg your pardon," my mother said.

"What. Can. I. Get. You?" he repeated.

"There's no need to be sarcastic. I'll have

a glass of your house Cabernet Sauvignon, please." Proper, cosmopolitan Mary Jane Lightfoot. Never mind that she had been born and bred in a town of fewer than six hundred people.

"I'll have a Guinness," I said. On top of the adrenaline that had recently whipped through my vitals, I hadn't eaten any lunch. Something substantial was in order. "And some buttermilk hush puppies and fried green tomatoes if the kitchen's open."

"Sure," he said, writing down the order and taking it through a door to the back.

I heard a pan clang from the other side of the wall. The bartender returned and poured our drinks. My mother's nose wrinkled after her first sip of wine, but she didn't say anything. We made small talk about the bakery and her plans for the bake sale until our food came, then dug in.

The fried green tomatoes crunched when I bit through the crispy coating, their sour flavor combining perfectly with the sweet cornmeal and garlic aioli dip. Suddenly I wasn't just hungry; I was ravenous. I plowed through my portion and started in on the hush puppies — tangy with buttermilk and rich with onion and whole kernels of corn, crisp on the outside and fluffy tender inside.

Mama nibbled on one of each but urged

the rest on me.

I took her up on the offer, eating until only crumbs remained and two inches of Guinness were left in my glass. If I'd felt okay before, I felt pretty darn good now. The guy two seats down watched my snarf fest with mild interest.

"Say, aren't you Skip Thorsen?" I asked pretty much out of the blue.

The big blond guy's head snapped up. "What's it to you?"

I widened my eyes. "Nothing. Gosh. Sorry."

He took a sip from the pint glass. At least he wasn't pounding it back. "No. I'm sorry. You're a patient? I'm sorry I don't remember you."

Shaking my head, I said, "Not at all. I work at Georgia Wild, with Autumn."

His eyes filled. "Autumn's dead," he said. Grief flowed off the poor man, so raw that it was hard to be in the same room with him. But I'd asked for this, and I'd see it through. I felt rather than heard Mama slip off the stool next to me.

"I know. I'm so sorry. You must have loved her very much."

He barked a humorless laugh. "Oh, I did. Still do, for that matter. Doesn't matter whether she divorced me or is gone, I still feel the same." It was obvious he'd been drinking, but he wasn't sloppy, only very open to conversation. There would be no need to use my Voice.

Not that I would have anyway, of course.

I felt bad taking advantage of the situation. On the other hand, love was a powerful emotion, and complicated. It wouldn't have been the first time someone had been killed because they rejected someone who loved them.

"I heard about your divorce," I said.

"Her idea, not mine. Kept trying to get back together, but she wasn't having any of it." He wove a little on the stool, then took another pull at his beer.

"The situation at Fagen Swamp must have been a sticking point between you."

He looked confused. "What the blazes is Fagen Swamp?"

"It's the land Heinrich Dawes and his group of investors are buying to turn into a golf course."

The confusion stayed right where it was. "What does that have to do with Autumn?"

Now I was puzzled. "She — through Georgia Wild — was trying to save that land. It's habitat to a huge number of species of animals and plants." No need to go into the whole maroon bat thing.

241

His face cleared. "I didn't know she had any interest in that land at all. I hadn't talked to her for months. She blocked my calls." The tears welled again, but he blinked them away. "God. I wanted to invest in that stupid project. I wonder if she knew."

"I don't think she did," I said truthfully.

"So you're part of the investment group?"

"Nuh-uh. I didn't have the money. Though now I do — or will." He rubbed both hands over his face, the very picture of defeat and sadness. "But I'm not going to spend that money."

"What do you mean?"

"I don't want it. When the check comes, I'm giving it all away." He slumped down, elbows on the bar, and stared at the bottles on the shelves. "Giving it all away."

Mama slid back onto her stool. "Something is buzzing in your bag."

"Oh! My phone. Excuse me," I said.

Skip waved his hand absently in the air.

It was Margie. What the heck?

"Hi there," I said into the phone.

My next-door neighbor spoke so fast her words tumbled over one another, making it hard to understand her. "Oh, thank goodness you answered. I've tried everything I can think of, but I don't have a key to your house and you lock everything down so

242

tightly I couldn't figure out a way to get in."

My heart beat faster. "Slow down, slow down. Now what happened?"

"I don't know what's wrong!" Margie almost wailed. "He just keeps howling."

Fear stabbed through me. "Mungo?"

"Yes! It's been over an hour, and he won't hush. I'm sure something's wrong, but I can't see him through the window. He sounds like he's right by the door."

Slapping a bill on the bar, I said, "Thanks for calling. I'm on my way."

CHAPTER 17

Mama didn't argue when I asked for my keys, and in minutes we were buzzing toward the carriage house. Seat belt clenched in one hand and the other gripping the inside of the door, she stammered out, "I t-talked to the bartender when you were speaking with the dentist."

"Will you relax? I'm not even going over the limit." I eyeballed the speedometer. "At least not much."

She ignored me. "He said Dr. Thorsen had been in the Old Familiar since ten o'clock."

I slowed for a turn. "Ten in the morning? Oh, dear. That's not good at all. That poor man is utterly devastated by Autumn's murder."

"Tragic," she said, loosening her death grip on the oh-my-God handle an iota.

"I'd like to help him," I said. "Maybe you could show me a healing spell?"

"We'll see," she answered as I pulled into my driveway.

Margie came running out of the house, Baby Bart bouncing on her hip. She'd been watching for my car, of course. I boiled out of the driver's seat. Sure enough, a mournful canine cry pierced the air.

"Mungo!" I called, and ran for the door. He fell silent as soon as he heard my voice.

"I can't imagine what's wrong with the little guy," Margie panted as she climbed the porch step. My mother came up right behind her, concern furrowing her brow. I slid the key into the lock and pushed the door open.

Mungo ran out and, dancing on his hind legs, planted his front paws firmly on my knee. Earnest brown eyes bored into mine. I picked him up and ran my hands over him. "Does something hurt?" I asked.

He frantically sniffed my face and neck, huffing into my ear as he surveyed me for damage. My familiar was as worried about me as I was about him. Maybe more.

I looked at Mama. One side of her mouth turned up. "So this is the famous Mungo."

Squeezing him tighter, I said, "More like infamous. Thank you so much for calling, Margie. For trying to get to him. I don't know what happened, but he seems fine

245

now." His pink tongue darted out and lapped at my chin.

"Maybe something sad happened on one of those soaps he likes to watch," Margie joked.

The baleful look he directed her way was completely lost on her.

"Margie Coopersmith, this is my mother, Mary Jane Lightfoot."

Margie held out her hand. "Well, I'll be darned. So nice to meet you! Katie didn't mention that you were planning a visit."

My mother smiled and shook her hand. "Nice to meet you, too. It was a . . . spontaneous decision to come see my daughter."

"Make sure she shows you all around Savannah. We're pretty proud of the place." She was already moving back toward her house. "I have to run. Better see what the JJs have managed to get into the two minutes I was gone."

We waved good-bye, and still clutching my dog as if he were going to disappear into thin air, I went inside. When I looked back, Mama was bent over by the rosemary star topiary by the front steps. She saw me waiting and straightened to join me without commenting. Lucy had planted it the day I'd moved south for protection, good luck, and assurance I would always remain in power in my own home — all this before I'd ever even heard the term hedgewitch.

I snuggled my nose into my familiar's neck. "I'm so sorry. Of course you knew something was wrong. It was an SUV . . . Oh, never mind, my little wolf. Just know I'm fine, just fine."

My mother laughed. "You were always particular to dogs."

"Were Sookie and Barnaby your familiars?" I asked. They were the Labrador retrievers we'd had when I was a child.

"Not mine. I've never had a familiar." My mother sounded sad, and I wondered if Cookie minded being the only one of the spellbook club without a familiar now that Bianca had Puck. "Sookie was your father's, though. And Barnaby — well, I always suspected he was yours."

"Really?" I liked the idea. Mungo apparently did not — his nostrils flared. "Barnaby has been gone for over a decade," I said. "There's no reason to be jealous." I glanced down and saw the frantic scratch marks on the bottom of the wood door. Poor little guy. I turned him around to face my mother. "Listen, I have someone I want you to meet."

Mama leaned forward and took his furry

face in her hands. "It's very nice to finally make your acquaintance. I'm Katie's mom."

His nose quivered, and then his mouth opened in a big doggy grin.

Yip!

"You little flirt." I set him down on the wooden floorboards.

Mama put her hands on her hips and surveyed the small space. Her eyes traveled over the sparse furnishings.

"You really did start over here, didn't you?"

I'd sold or given away pretty much everything I owned before I left Akron to start the Honeybee with Lucy and Ben. The only things I'd brought with me had been clothes, a few books, and my favorite cookware.

"I did," I said. "Though Lucy and Ben surprised me with the bed." I led her into the bedroom where the scrolled ironwork headboard of their gift was silhouetted against the Williamsburg blue wall.

"It's all lovely," she said. Back in the living room, her gaze rose to the loft above, stopping on the secretary desk. The front lid was closed as usual, since I opened it only when I wanted access to the contents. "I remember that piece — and what Lucy used it for." Her eyes flicked to me. "Your altar?"

"Yes."

A ghost of a smile crossed her face.

It didn't take long to point out the bathroom and kitchen. Then I led her through the French doors to the small covered patio. She paused, but I took her hand and pulled her out to the backyard, past the new fire pit to the curving gardens I'd designed with love and created with sweat. Mungo ran ahead of us, turning to wait by the blooming Daphne bush. Its sweet scent filled the air.

"In the summer this area is planted with vegetables, with a few herbs thrown in. Right now only hardy greens, alliums, and brassicas are doing well in the cold." I pointed to the cold frame. "I'll be putting starts in there soon, though. And over here is the real herb garden — medicinal plants as well as culinary."

"And magical," she said.

"And magical," I agreed.

"You have natural water on your property?" She pointed to the stream that ran for a few feet across the back corner of the vegetable garden.

"How lucky is that? I never knew how handy it would be for casting."

She pressed her lips together, saw me watching, and forced a smile. Turning, she began walking toward the gazebo. "This looks new."

"I had it built. The carpenter wanted to paint it, but I wanted to be able to see and touch — and smell — the bare cedar."

Stepping up to the interior, she ran a finger over the smooth wood of the broom handle leaning against the wall. Then she looked down and raised her eyebrows. I'd painted a purple star in the center of the floor. It was about ten inches in diameter and outlined in white — not an obvious pentagram, but useful nonetheless.

"This is your sacred circle," she said as Mungo ran inside and lay down smack-dab in the middle of the star.

"My favorite place to cast, outside with the elements but not, you know, *in* them. And no one notices me in here." At least so far. "Though I haven't been dancing around out here naked, either. I think that might garner some attention, circle or no circle."

"Hmm. Witches have largely given that up since the advent of wooly sweaters. Still, on a hot summer's night . . ."

I felt myself beginning to blush and turned away. Mungo bounded out of the gazebo and rolled in the grass. I laughed. "Silly bear."

Suddenly he stood to attention, looked at the house, and streaked across to the French doors.

Yip Yip Yip Yip Yip!

What on earth? Alarmed, I ran across the yard and opened the door. He dashed inside, heading straight for the door.

"Is someone here?" I went to the shutter on the window and opened it all the way. There was no one on the front porch, no car at the curb. "What is the matter with you?"

"Katie," my mother said in a strangled voice.

I whirled to see her pointing to the floor in front of the door. "What . . . ?" And then I saw the paper.

The dark red paper folded into a bat.

While Mama and I had been in the backyard, someone had walked right up to my house and slipped it under my door. So much for that rosemary topiary.

I yanked the door open and ran out to the front yard, looking wildly around as if I'd missed someone standing there when I looked out the window. Out on the public sidewalk, I checked left and right, but there was no traffic, and I didn't see any vehicles that seemed unfamiliar. Mungo ran out into the street, and I called him back.

The hinges next door creaked as Margie came out to her porch, Bart clinging to her leg. The JJs ran down the front steps and out to the mailbox. Reaching above their heads, they managed to open the front. Hopping up and down, they tried to reach the mail inside, but the carrier must have shoved it to the back. My mother, who had followed me as far as the driveway, hurried over to help them before I had the chance.

Waving, Margie called, "Thanks!"

Striding past my mother and up the Coopersmiths' front path, I grabbed the railing and stood on the lowest step. Mungo stopped by my heel and sat down.

My neighbor looked surprised. "You're white as a sheet, darlin'."

"Did you see anyone come to my door?"

She craned her neck around to look at the front of the carriage house. "No."

"Anyone on the street in the last ten minutes?"

"Sorry, I wasn't looking."

The one time Margie wasn't keeping tabs on everyone. What good was a nosy neighbor if you couldn't count on her to be nosy?

Bless her heart.

I swore to myself at the same time I pasted

a smile on my face. "Just wondering. I thought I heard a knock at the door when we were in the backyard."

Relief erased the worry from her forehead. "Whew! I thought something must be awful wrong." She eyed Mungo. "You ever find out what the deal was with this one?"

"I think he just didn't want to be left alone today."

She rolled her eyes and smiled. "Oh, brother. You're a spoiled one, aren't you?"

Yip!

"He is," I agreed, itching to get back and take another look at the bat. "Sorry he made such a ruckus."

Margie waved away my apology.

Mama came up then, Jonathan skipping on one side and Julia on the other, their sticky hands firmly enveloped in hers. Jonathan broke loose and ran to give his mother the mail.

She flipped through it one-handed. "As usual — bills and bull." She grinned at my mother. "Thanks for rescuing them. They do love to bring it to me."

My mother smiled. "Those two are delightful. Just delightful." She leaned over and ruffled their blond hair. "Wish I could tuck you in my pocket and take you home."

I watched with a combination of fascination and surprise.

Standing upright, she said, "Come on, Katie. Let's go have that tea before Lucy and Ben get here."

"Uh. Okay. Bye, Margie."

"See you," she said, and went back inside.

"Seeee yoooouuu," the JJs called in unison as we walked away.

Stepping carefully around the origami bat, I closed the door and grabbed my cell phone out of my tote bag. Mungo advanced on the piece of paper lying there so innocently. I mean, it was a piece of *paper*. But one sniff and he went bananas, barking and growling.

"Shhh." I knelt beside him. "You're not going to scare the thing." But I was curious about what had set him off. Holding my hand above the bat, I waited for the feeling of sweet rot that Autumn's bat had emanated.

There was nothing.

"Do you smell something on it?"

Yip!

Quinn's phone rang three times, then went to voice mail. I left him a message about the unpleasant calling card I'd just received and went into the kitchen to find the kettle heating on the stove and my mother surveying the contents of my herb

254

cupboard. She selected three jars and set them on the counter: chamomile for calm, basil for courage and protection, and lemon verbena for even more protection.

My mother might not practice formally anymore, but she was most definitely a hedgewitch at heart. The thought made my own heart warm. So did the fact that she was trying to protect me. I'd learned by now, however, that sometimes the standard magical protections didn't always work when up against dark magic. When up against evil.

While the tea brewed, I locked the back door and checked all the windows. Maybe the SUV had been aiming for Wren rather than me as Quinn had suggested, but now someone had threatened me, too.

Or was it a threat? What did those stupid bats mean?

"I wish Detective Quinn would call back," I said, returning to the kitchen. "I hate leaving that thing on the floor, but I don't want to touch it."

"He will." Mama poured our tea and carried it to the kitchen table. I put some peanut-butter swirl brownies on a plate, and we sat down. I was still hungry.

"How serious are you and Declan?" she asked, peering at me through the steam rising from her cup.

I shrugged. "Serious enough. Definitely exclusive. He's trying to get me to go to Boston to meet his mother and sisters." Part of me was thrilled that she was asking, and without the curled lip she had always used to ask about my former fiancé, Andrew. Another part of me remembered that curled lip and knew it could return.

"Does he know?" she asked.

"That I'm a witch? I didn't tell him at first, but he's known Lucy and Ben for a long time." And his best friend, Steve's brother, had been a druid. "So he wasn't exactly surprised when I sprang the news."

"And he's obviously okay with it."

"Yeah. I don't think he really, you know, gets it, but that's okay. I mean, how could he, not being of a magical persuasion himself?"

"You're right, of course," she said. "Look at Ben and Lucy. He just lets her be who she is. That's a lot."

I hadn't really thought about it in those terms, but the thought made me happy.

"But it doesn't sound like you two are serious enough that I can start thinking about grandchildren," she said. "At least not yet."

Stunned, I took another sip of tea, gathering my thoughts. "I noticed that you were pretty taken by those twins next door."

She sighed, dreamy-eyed as a girl thinking about her prom date. Good heavens.

"So that has me wondering — if you like kids so much, why don't I have any brothers or sisters? Or is it just grandkids that you want because you can send them home to their parents?"

"Oh, no. I love children. But as soon as it became so evident that you had . . . abilities, your father and I came to believe that the double whammy of hereditary hedge-witchery combined with a shamanic bloodline probably shouldn't be repeated."

I honestly didn't know whether to be insulted or not, so I took another sip of tea and shelved her answer for later consideration. Luckily, my phone rang before I had to come up with a way to change the subject.

It was Quinn. "What's this about another one of those blasted bats?" he demanded.

"Someone slipped it under my door, just like they did with Wren."

"When did this happen?"

I looked at my watch. "About an hour ago."

"You were home?" He sounded incredulous. "That's ballsy. Sorry. I mean bold."

"My mother and I were in the backyard. Mungo heard something and alerted us, but by the time we got to the door, no one was there."

"What did you do with it?"

"Nothing. I left it right where we found it. Mungo might have nudged it with his nose — he definitely smelled something on it — but otherwise it's still what I guess you would call 'in situ.' "

"Don't touch it. I'll be right over."

CHAPTER 18

Detective Quinn arrived with a crime scene tech, asked his questions, took a bunch of pictures, and bagged the origami evidence. As he was finishing up, Lucy and Ben drove up in the Thunderbird. They got out, opened the back door, and pulled out to-go containers that smelled amazing even across the yard. Moments later Declan arrived clad in his dark uniform slacks and a light blue T-shirt with the Savannah firefighter logo on it.

"I'm sorry, Katie," Quinn was saying as everyone trooped over to where we stood on the lawn. "There's not a lot I can do. I'll make sure patrol drives by more often, same as for Wren."

My mother pulled Lucy and Ben aside, and I watched as my aunt's eyes grew wide and a thunderous expression descended on my uncle's face. No doubt Mama was telling them why Detective Quinn was making a house call.

"Thanks." I wasn't surprised. It wasn't like I expected the police to post a guard on my house because of a piece of paper.

Declan closed the door of his truck with a *thunk* and crossed the yard to the driveway. He walked around the Bug, shaking his head as he examined the damage with a troubled expression. Then he strode over to where we stood. "Detective Quinn? Did you find the driver of the SUV?"

Quinn wagged his head no. "We're working on it. One witness got the last two digits of the license plate, and we have reports of the vehicle being either a Porsche Cayenne or one of the BMW X series."

"Then why . . . ?"

"He's here because someone slipped an origami bat under my door."

Quinn held up the evidence bag he'd tucked the folded paper into.

Declan frowned, and it occurred to me that he didn't know anything about the bats. Since he'd been working the last forty-eight hours, our conversations had been relatively short and sweet.

Now I said, "Autumn had one of those in her hand when she died. Then someone left one for Wren — and after the hit-and-run this afternoon, we're pretty sure it's a threat.

Right?" I asked Quinn.

"Better to be safe than sorry," the detective said.

Mama drew in a sharp breath, and her fingers crept to her mouth as if she were trying to keep her thoughts to herself. Apparently she hadn't taken the bat seriously before.

My boyfriend put his arm around my shoulders and drew me close. "Don't worry, Ms. Lightfoot," he said. "I'll run off any evildoers." He tried a smile but didn't quite pull it off. His word choice bothered me. Evildoers, indeed. I glanced over to see my mother and aunt weren't smiling, though both looked relieved that I'd have a guard.

"All night?" my mother demanded.

Declan looked uncomfortable. Quinn looked amused.

"All night," I confirmed. I was a grown woman and I could have overnight guests if I wanted. So there.

Still, it was a good thing Mama was staying with Lucy and Ben. The day had been eventful, and by necessity we'd fast-tracked getting to know each other again — better than before, actually — but I still didn't think I was ready to have her hang out at the carriage house with Declan and me all night.

"When will we be able to get into the Georgia Wild offices to work?" I asked Quinn. "We might need to replace some of the donation requests that were ruined after that crazy driver made us drop them."

"We released the scene a little while ago," he said. "You can go back anytime you want."

Declan sighed.

"Have you heard how Wren is?" I asked my aunt.

Lucy grimaced. "She's pretty banged up — she hit her head, and her arm is broken in two places. Mimsey took her home from the hospital — Mimsey's home, of course — about an hour ago and is watching her like a mama bird."

"More like a grandmamma bird. I'm glad Wren wasn't hurt any worse and that she has Mimsey to look after her. She's in the safest place she can be."

I invited Detective Quinn to stay for supper, but he said he had to get going. He drove off, and the rest of us dished out the upscale comfort food Lucy and Ben had brought from Zunzi's: simple hummus with pita bread, lasagna, meat loaf, and their Indian curry stew along with a big romaine salad. We loaded our plates in the kitchen buffet style and went into the living room to

262

find places to settle in and eat.

Sitting cross-legged on the floor, I took a big bite of curry and rice and nearly moaned, it was so good. Silence fell over us all as we dug into the savory repast. Mungo lapped at the dab of hummus I'd put on a plate next to his lasagna.

Ben updated us on the bake sale for Georgia Wild. While Mama and I had been gallivanting around dentist offices and bars that afternoon, he'd had stickers made that announced the fund-raiser, picked them up, and then convinced some of the customers still hanging out at the Honeybee to help put them on the mailers that Steve and Annette had rescued from the street.

"I made it to the post office just before it closed. And as long as the print shop was making stickers, I asked the guy I work with over there to do a quick and dirty design for a flyer, which he did and then copied off a couple hundred of them for me."

Mama looked pleased. "That's wonderful, Ben. I was afraid we'd have to scrap the idea altogether after the . . . events this afternoon." Her eyes cut to me.

Ben grinned. "As mellow as we Southerners sound, we're really pretty good at getting things done down here, you know. I gave out a bunch of the flyers for customers to hand out to their friends, and Croft and Annette both posted them in their stores. I'll e-mail the DBA members tonight and get the ball rolling there."

"I'll help tomorrow," Mama said to him; then to me, "I'm going to fill in for you at the Honeybee tomorrow. That way you can sleep late."

I finished chewing a bite of lettuce and swallowed. "I never sleep late. You know that."

"After your day, I think you'll sleep better than you think tonight. Either way, take it easy tomorrow. Heal up a little."

"That's a good idea, Mary Jane. We're happy to have you," Ben said.

Lucy smiled fondly at her sister. After all the hurt between them, it was an encouraging sign.

Declan looked alarmed. "Heal? Is there something I don't know?"

I shook my head. "Just bruises, Deck. No big deal. But Mama? Are you sure you want to start your vacation by getting up at five in the morning and going to work?"

She snorted. "First off, it's a visit, not a vacation, and it started by learning you're involved in a murder and then watching you almost get run down in the street. Believe me, hitting the kitchen early in the morning will be a welcome change."

I grimaced. "Yeah. Okay, I'll take you up on it." Not because I felt a need to rest and recuperate, but because there was a kind of bond that forms when you cook with someone, a bond that could serve to help mend my mother's relationship with her sister.

Lucy insisted that I keep the leftovers — not that there were many — and she and Ben went out to the Thunderbird. While we were on the sidewalk that wound from the house to the street, my mother put both hands on my shoulders and held me at arm's length, searching my eyes as if trying to read my mind.

"I'm sorry for the last year. I'm glad your grandmother —" She glanced over my shoulder to where Declan waited in the doorway. "I'm glad I decided to come."

"I am, too," I said quietly. "Daddy tried to explain why you kept your secrets, why you were so upset about my embracing the Craft, but I didn't really understand until this afternoon."

"You forgive me?"

"There's nothing to forgive."

We embraced, a nice long mother-daughter hug, and when I backed away, I saw tears in her eyes. I felt them in my own, too.

"Take care of her," she called to Declan.

"I will," was the deep-voiced response.

"See you tomorrow," I said.

She got in the backseat, and Ben drove off. I looked down at Mungo, who was leaning against my ankle. "So that's my mother. What do you think?"

Yip!

Declan helped me put the food away and do the dishes. There wasn't room for a dishwasher in my modest kitchen, so we stood side by side at the sink, washing and drying. I bumped his hip with mine. *Ow.* He leaned over and kissed me on the cheek. Mungo perched on a kitchen chair, watching us.

The very picture of domesticity. It was nice.

"You don't seem very worried about this bat thing," Declan said. "Should you be? Should I be more worried for you?"

"Honestly? I don't know. I mean, I don't have anything to do with the bats or the real estate purchase personally, but who knows how someone demented enough to kill Autumn might connect me with either or both. It could be enough that I volunteer at Georgia Wild. Or maybe the maroon bats are really red herrings."

Mungo groaned.

"Sorry," I said. "I talked to Autumn's ex, Skip, this afternoon."

"This afternoon? *After* the hit-and-run?" He sounded downright scandalized.

"I needed to unwind a little. Besides, Mama was with me."

That seemed to slightly mollify him, but he still didn't look very happy.

"Anyway, I don't think he had anything to do with Autumn's murder. He was awfully broken up — he's been missing work, drinking all the time. It's bad. I'd like to help him." Mama had neatly sidestepped the idea of helping me with a healing spell. Perhaps tomorrow I'd approach her again — or Lucy and the spellbook club. Perhaps my mother wasn't quite ready to cast again.

Perhaps she never would be. The thought made me sad. At least we'd had an honest conversation about why she had kept my witchy heritage a secret.

Honest conversation.

"Deck, I think there's something you should know."

He dried his hands on a dish towel and draped it over the edge of the old-fashioned enameled cast-iron sink. "Sounds ominous. Maybe we should go into the living room."

After we'd arranged ourselves — him

leaning against the high corner of the fainting couch at an angle and me leaning my
back against his chest while classic rock
played low on the stereo, I told him I'd gone
to see Steve after he'd dropped by the Honeybee.

"I was simply trying to find out more
about the sale of Fagen Swamp, and he had
the information I needed," I said. "Well, his
dad probably has more, but I don't think
he'd tell me."

Declan was silent, and I realized I'd
misjudged my position; I couldn't see his
face, so now I didn't know how he was
reacting.

"But Steve would," he said. "Tell you, I
mean. Of course he would. He's still in love
with you."

"That's not true. In fact, I don't think that
he was ever in love with me. But it doesn't
matter. He asked if we could be friends, and
I said yes."

More silence, then, "Okay."

I sat up and turned to look at him.
"Okay?"

He shrugged, resignation on his face. "I
can't tell you who to see. And I have to
believe you. Trust you. Otherwise, where
are we?"

My arms snaked around his neck. "You're

kind of awesome, you know?"

His answer was lost as our lips met.

Mungo jumped up on the couch and wiggled between us. Declan laughed. "Sometimes I think you're jealous, little guy."

"No. He adores you. It's just that he'd rather *he* was the center of attention."

If a dog could give a withering look, I was on the receiving end of one.

Deck lifted Mungo onto his lap. "I know a guy who can fix your car. He'll do a good job for a decent price. We can take it by the insurance adjuster's first thing tomorrow morning."

"Can we wait? I have a few errands to run tomorrow."

"You don't want me to take you?"

I sighed. "As long as I have the time off, I thought I'd stop by Georgia Wild and clean the place up a bit. It's a real mess — fingerprint dust everywhere, and the police went through everything."

He pressed his lips together and looked at the floor. I realized he had been hoping we could spend the next day together. Dang it. Of course I wanted to spend a whole day with my sweetie. But I also felt drawn to help Wren any way that I could, and that whole figure-out-who-killed-Autumn effort wasn't going so well.

"Okay," he said. "I have to catch up on laundry and errands myself. We can reconnect later in the day."

This one's a keeper.

It was dark when I woke up the next morning. Without thinking, I swung my feet to the floor and reached for my robe as usual, completely unprepared for the pain — sharp pain by my elbow, dull throbbing pain in my hip, and a thump, thump, thump in my head that nearly brought me to my knees.

How could that have happened overnight?

Four ibuprofen, three cups of coffee, two hours, and one good slathering of arnica cream later, I felt better. For a brief moment, I even considered going for a run, but that seemed doubly foolish. My poor battered body deserved a break, and running in the early-morning dark could be dangerous if there really was someone out there who meant me harm.

I checked the protections already in the carriage house: willow broom leaning in the corner by the door, the rune Algiz carved near the locks on the windows, basil in a pot on the kitchen table, a silk bag stuffed with guardian herbs and sealed with beeswax placed on the built-in bookshelf in the living room. All were in place.

I gathered four white candles and tried a little scrying with a bowl of water from the stream in back.

Divination was Mimsey's bailiwick, but I kept trying despite the usually confusing results. This time all I perceived was a jumble of green. Green could indicate something to do with money or love, but since I had set the intention of the spell to identify whether I was in danger and from whom, neither made any sense.

I heard the sound of the shower starting and looked out the kitchen window to see the sun had crept over the horizon. My boyfriend could very well have walked in on me divining. It dawned on me as I put the bowl and candle away that I didn't really care. The divination had turned out to be a divi-no-tion anyway, and I wondered how he would have reacted.

Did Ben ever happen upon Lucy when she was casting?

I'd brought in the paper and was flipping through it when Declan came into the kitchen, yawning and reaching for the fresh batch of French press coffee I'd made when I heard him in the shower. Mungo was in the backyard, stalking the fence line for his second morning constitutional.

"Mornin', darling," Declan murmured into my hair before sitting down across the table and reaching for a section of the paper.

"Morning."

The paper dropped to the table as he examined my face. "What's wrong?"

Gesturing at the pages still gripped in his fingers, I said, "Autumn's murder barely made page four, but the hit-and-run yesterday is on the bottom of the front page. Someone took a picture of me lying on the sidewalk after I managed to get out of the way, and there's one of Wren, too, crying as she's getting in the ambulance."

"A reporter was there when it happened?"

"I can't imagine there was. Some looky-loo with a cell phone camera probably sent it — or more likely sold it — to the *News*." I couldn't keep the anger out of my voice. "Look — the Honeybee is right there in the background. It's terrible publicity."

Declan took a sip of coffee and said in an easy tone, "Katie, there is no such thing as bad publicity. I mean, other than the health department shutting you down or something like that, any mention in the paper will pique the interest of locals and tourists alike."

I harrumphed. "They found the SUV, too. It was a BMW. Apparently it was stolen right before the — well, I have to call it an attack now, don't you think? Anyway, the owner didn't even know it was gone."

He was skimming the article. "It doesn't say who the owner is, though."

"Right. They put our names front and center, not to mention a couple of really unflattering photographs, but they don't say who owns the BMW. I wonder if Detective Quinn would tell me."

"Probably. He seems to be pretty open to communicating with you regarding this case." Declan was staring at my picture, brow furrowed.

"Only because someone keeps shoving those stupid paper bats under doors and we don't know if they're a threat or . . . Well, what else could they be?" I reached for the French press to refill my cup, then thought better of it. More than three cups and my teeth would start to chatter. "Declan?"

"Hmm?" He finally looked up. The tenderness in his face arrowed through all my anger and frustration. "I guess I didn't realize until right now, seeing this picture, how close you came to being seriously hurt." He took a deep but shaky breath. "Or killed. Katie, I know you're tough, and God knows you're smart, but I couldn't take it if something really happened to you. I know it's not your fault that it was someone you knew who died and that you happened into the middle of the situation, but I don't like it." He rubbed his eyes with his fingers, and then his hands dropped into his lap. "Tell me again why you think this stuff happens to you?"

I traced a coffee circle on the tabletop with my index finger. "Remember what I told you about being a catalyst?" I asked. I hadn't told him about the whole lightwitch thing because Franklin Taite had left without informing me about any of the particulars other than I was a good witch — and apparently gave off flashes of light when under duress.

Declan nodded. "You said things tend to happen around you, that you cause them or attract them or something. Like when we found the body in Johnson Square. Are you saying that's what happened here?"

I shrugged. "Maybe. Kind of a coincidence for me to volunteer for Georgia Wild for less than three months and then someone gets killed."

"Makes it sound kind of dangerous to hang around you."

The words hit me hard.

"Oh, Katie," he exclaimed when he saw my face. "I was trying to make a joke. A bad joke, a terrible joke. Please don't think I feel that way."

I stood, shaken more by the thought that what he had just said might be true than I had been by someone shoving a maroon bat under my door. "How about some eggs? I have thick-cut pepper bacon and English muffins from the Honeybee."

"Katie." He stood and put his arms around me from behind as I stood at the stove, cast-iron skillet dangling from my hand. "Please don't turn away."

Leaning my head back, I smiled at him. "Get the eggs out of the fridge?"

He let go, apparently satisfied.

I, on the other hand, was anything but.

CHAPTER 19

Deck left after agreeing to call me later and making me promise to be hyperaware of my surroundings. Mungo polished off the extra bacon and eggs even though he'd eaten at the same time we had. Like a Hobbit, my familiar was a big fan of second breakfast.

Glancing at the clock, I saw it was late enough to call and so punched Mimsey's number into my phone. She picked up on the second ring.

"She's been up for hours," she said when I asked after her granddaughter. "The arm is very painful, but she doesn't like the idea of taking painkillers."

Maybe she'd give a few to me, then.

"Poor thing. I hope she feels better. Will you tell her Detective Quinn released the crime scene at Georgia Wild, and I'm planning to go over there to clean up this morning? Mama is filling in for me at the bakery."

"That's nice of you, darlin', but you tell

her yourself. She's right here."

Wren came on the phone. Her voice was quiet, and I thought I detected a tremble. I couldn't help wondering how much of that was from pain and how much from fear and worry.

When I told her I was going to the Georgia Wild offices she asked, "Oh, Katie, would you mind picking up the file on major donors? There should be copies of the donor contract in there as well as information on the current ones and the local businesses Autumn had been cultivating. Grandma is nervous about me leaving the house — and frankly, I don't want to — but if I don't have something constructive to do, I'm going to go nuts."

"You got it," I said. "I'll drop all that by when I'm done spiffing up the place for your return."

She was silent for a long moment. "I don't know if I'm ever going to be able to go back there."

I knew how she felt. "Well, now don't you worry about that yet. Just get to feeling better, okay? I'll see you later."

A few large drops splatted down on the windshield on the way to Georgia Wild, then stopped. Inside the nonprofit office I was happy to find that the smell of burnt coffee had completely dissipated. After lugging in the cleaning supplies I'd brought, I locked the door and opened the blinds all the way. The gray light outside barely made a dent in the gloom, so I flipped on all the lamps and the overhead light as well. Extracting a large white lavender-scented candle from my bag, I placed it on the small table next to the guest chair and lit it.

"Archangel Michael, I bid you lend your will to the flame, removing negative vibrations in this physical environment and on all surrounding dimensions. May the fire purify and cleanse. Let it be and thanks be."

It wasn't the most poetic incantation but one the spellbook club had used to effect before. At some point we'd have to get all the ladies together to smudge the whole building, but at least I could make a start.

Now that I'd begun tackling the metaphysical dirt, it was time to get busy cleaning up the physical mess.

Mungo settled into the chair by the candle to watch me work.

"It's too bad you don't have opposable thumbs," I muttered.

He didn't offer any comment.

It looked like the police had made yet another pass through the offices, because things were even more out of place than when Officer Feherty had let Wren and me in. First I cleaned up the broken glass still littering the carpet, toting the shards out to the trash in an extra-thick bag and then vacuuming. Then I tackled the fingerprint dust. It was as if someone had sprinkled printer toner all over the room. Even after I vacuumed, there were smudges of it on the light-colored carpet, which had already seen better days. Did the crime scene techs always make such a mess?

I swiped and wiped down everything on the desks and the coffee station, taking the coffeepot into the kitchenette to soak in the sink. Even that tiny room had been dusted, and I wondered whether the police had even checked for fingerprints on the toilet. Probably. I should be glad they were so thorough, but I'd save that for the next cleaning session.

Autumn's office, too. Wren wasn't ready to come to Georgia Wild at all, and I wasn't quite ready to spend a significant amount of time in the murder victim's office.

However, I was determined to do what I could. Back in the main office, I began working around the periphery of the room, using microfiber dusting cloths to smooth away the dark powder from the items tacked to the walls, the bookshelves, and door frames. Then I tackled the long, low desk return stacked with grant application materials and the printer table. Next to the printer was the file cabinet with the photos still scattered on top.

I'd forgotten about the satellite picture of Fagen Swamp. There was Evanston Rickers' cabin in the middle of the clearing, which I now knew was an island itself. Carefully, I wiped at the starburst pattern of fingerprint powder.

Most of it came off on the cloth, but the raylike design faintly remained, each strand slightly lighter than the rest of the photo, ghost fingers reaching out from a central point slightly higher and to the right of the cabin.

What the heck?

I carried the photo to the halogen desk lamp in order to see it better. The starburst appeared to be part of the picture, or at least the paper it was on. Could it have gotten wet? Or perhaps the printer was faulty?

Then I caught my breath. The center of the pattern, the nexus of the rays, was the giant cypress tree. A shiver ran like a mouse down my back. "Oh, my goddess," I breathed. "Mungo, do you think that means anything?"

He cocked his head to one side in puzzlement.

"Sorry. You have no idea what I'm talking about. I'll ask Mimsey when we go by there."

A sudden banging on the door made me jump. It could have been anyone, of course, but Mungo hadn't barked. Instead, he jumped down from the guest chair, silent as smoke. Hand over my racing heart, I dropped the photo and sidled to the peek hole.

Whoever was knocking stood too far to the side for me to see them.

On purpose?

Edging to the window, I carefully leaned around the frame and peered out. A Jeep Wrangler was parked on the other side of the street. It was dark green.

Hunter green.

Uh-oh.

I remembered the jumbled images of green I'd sensed when attempting my divination spell with the bowl of water earlier that morning. Craning my head a little farther, I could see Hunter Normandy standing on the wraparound porch. He shifted from foot to foot, obviously impatient. As I watched, he raised his arm and banged his fist on the door again.

"I know there's someone in there." The doorknob rattled.

Heart hammering against my ribs, I tiptoed over to the phone on the desk. I picked it up, only to realize I didn't have Quinn's number memorized. As much as I'd called him lately, it had always been on my cell phone. *Dang it.* I cradled the handset and was reaching for my phone when I heard the sound of metal in the lock.

I froze. *Oh, no. Autumn gave him a key.*

Hunter opened the door and stepped inside, eyes darting to me and then around the room. Evaluating. Assessing. He'd ditched the funky thrift-store clothes I'd seen him wear before for a Carhartt coat over jeans and hiking boots. His sandy hair was in disarray, and a few days' worth of stubble darkened his chin. Dark circles under his eyes accented irises so light blue they were almost gray. And unlike the other few times I'd seen Hunter, now I sensed an aura around him. It had the mental flavor of misery and fear. However, I couldn't know the cause. Autumn's death, sure — but had he been involved in it? Whatever he felt, it was different than Skip Thorsen's serious grief.

"Where's Wren?" His bellicose tone contradicted his dejected appearance.

"I don't know," I lied, barely managing to keep my voice from shaking.

His gaze settled on my face. "Is anyone else here?"

I didn't answer but glanced back toward the kitchenette to give the impression we weren't alone.

He didn't seem to buy it. "What's your name again? Kate? Is that right?" He paused. "I saw your picture in the paper, along with that other woman who works here."

Great.

"Now listen, Kate. All I need is for you to answer a question for me." He took a step in my direction.

Mungo shot out from under the desk, barking and snarling, stopping only inches from Hunter's leg.

Good boy.

"Call it off!" he yelled. "Call your dog off!"

"Maybe give him a little space," I murmured to my familiar.

Mungo backed off two terrier paces and lowered the volume of his growl a fraction.

"Please ask your question and then go." I took a couple of steps around a desk, putting it between us. "We're closed."

Never taking his eyes off my familiar, Hunter put his hands in his coat pockets. I tensed, and Mungo's lips curled back in warning. He jerked them back out so we could see them.

With apparent effort, he looked away from the canine threat and up at me. "Of *course* you're closed. You know Autumn was my girlfriend. My fiancée."

I felt my eyes go wide.

"She didn't say anything?"

I quickly shook my head to indicate the negative.

He sighed. "I guess she kept it to herself. I asked her two days before she . . . passed. She hadn't said yes yet, but she would have." Something hard entered his voice. "I know it."

Autumn hadn't given him an answer right away. I could certainly understand that, but her caution didn't seem like a very good motive for him to commit murder.

Providing, of course, that Hunter was telling the truth. Either way, he'd still gone to ground and managed to avoid the police for three days. There had to be a reason for that.

"Your question," I prompted, wanting him to leave me alone as soon as possible.

Hesitating, he glanced down at Mungo who had stopped growling but still held a combative stance closer to Hunter's leg than the man seemed to enjoy. I sent a jolt of gratitude to my familiar, but he was too intent to respond.

"Did you see her, um, after?"

My lips pressed together. "Yes."

"Was she wearing any rings? I mean —" He seemed to fumble. "She didn't generally wear much jewelry, so you might have noticed." His lips twisted, and a surge of pity eddied through me.

Sometimes I couldn't properly bring to mind the face of my fiancé of just a year before, his visage swamped by feelings of betrayal and anger, but when I thought of Autumn's body, I saw tawny hair tamed to a precise curl, white blouse, blue bruises, pink toe polish, and long fingers.

Long unadorned fingers, at least on the one hand that had been visible.

And yet — there was the diamond filigree ring I'd found among the mailers. "You gave her an engagement ring," I guessed.

"She was wearing it?" He looked unaccountably terrified at the thought. Weird.

"Not exactly. I found a ring tucked in with some promotional materials."

Relief slid onto his face. It was an odd reaction, really. Was the ring more important than the woman he'd hoped to marry?

"It looked really old," I continued, watching him carefully. "Antique filigree platinum with a diamond set in the middle and two on the outside. Is that it?"

"Yes, yes, that's it. I looked for it, but —" He ran trembling fingers through his already disheveled hair. "Okay. Okay, I can fix this. I can. Somehow."

What on earth?

My cell phone gave a good old-fashioned trill. It was sitting on the desk by where Hunter stood. He looked down and sudden fear shone from those eyes the color of water — deep fear mixed with desperation. "Oh, no!"

A low warning rumbled from Mungo's chest.

Hunter turned and ran outside, down the steps, and across the street.

Fumbling for the cell, I rushed after him. "Hunter! Wait!" It might be the only chance to question him. Glancing down, I saw what had spooked him. The caller ID said *Detective Peter Quinn.* The phone went silent before I could answer.

Hunter looked back over his shoulder but didn't slow. If anything, the desperation in his eyes had increased, and it scared me. I slammed the door and flipped the deadbolt, though a locked door hadn't stopped him before. Someone had tried to run Wren down, then given me the same warning she'd received, and I'd promptly gone and isolated myself in a place where I'd be easy to find. *Stupid.*

"Thanks for having my back, little wolf." I returned the phone call, picking up Mungo so we could both watch the green Jeep Wrangler speed down the street. He snuggled under my chin as if nothing had happened, nosing the phone as Quinn answered.

I told him about Hunter's visit, his preoccupation with the ring, and which way he'd been driving.

"Hang on," he said. "I need to alert patrol to watch for him in your area." He put me on hold.

While I waited, I gathered the cleaning supplies by the door to take out to the Bug. Then I grabbed the satellite photo of Fagen Swamp and tucked it in my bag. Surveying the main office, I was pleased with my work. Next time I'd hit the other rooms.

Including Autumn's office.

"Katie? You still there?"

"Yes — did you find him?" I asked, sinking into the guest chair by the window.

Mungo stood on his hind legs by the chair. I patted my knee and he jumped up.

"Not yet. Did he threaten you?"

"Not really. He had a key and walked right

287

in. I suspect he may have searched in here already." I'd blamed the extra mess on the police, but now I had to wonder. "He just wanted that ring."

"Oh, I bet he did," Quinn said.

"Meaning?"

"He stole it."

"Whoa. He stole a ring and then gave it to Autumn? That's downright rude."

Quinn made a noise of distracted agreement.

"At least the owner will get her ring back. Or did he take it from a jeweler?" I remembered the chain store box the ring had been in.

"The owner is dead."

"Hunter *killed* . . . oh, no. Wait. This is about his job at the mortuary, isn't it?"

"His supervisor found out about it. Apparently there was a problem another time, but in that case the, uh, client's missing possession turned up, and they simply thought it had been mislaid. This time they pinpointed Normandy as the culprit. I don't know how he found out — maybe one of his coworkers warned him — but that's probably one of the reasons he hasn't gone into work."

"One of the reasons?"

Quinn fell silent, and I could hear him

288

breathing. I waited.

"Katie, the lab called me this morning. They found something on those paper bats."

"What was it?" I tried not to sound too excited.

"Formalin and methanol. Formaldehyde."

"But . . . I don't understand. Formaldehyde isn't exactly a poison, is it?"

"It can be in large enough amounts, but there was only a trace on the paper. Katie, formaldehyde is a primary ingredient in embalming fluid."

I felt the blood drain from my face.

"If Hunter Normandy comes back, do *not* let him in. In fact, I'd prefer you leave Georgia Wild immediately since he already knows you're there."

But why on the good green earth would Hunter Normandy want to kill *me*?

Speaking of which.

"I saw in the paper that you guys found the SUV involved in the hit-and-run yesterday."

"We did," he said. "A BMW abandoned in an alley on the Southside. The front is totally trashed, and it has red paint on it that matches the Corolla it hit."

My heart gave a double thump in my chest. "And it was stolen?"

"At least that's what the owner said last

night. It took him that long to report it. Says he left it home all day and walked to work."

That sounded familiar. But no, that would be too much. "What's the owner's name?" I pushed.

"You're not going to believe this," Quinn said.

Try me.

"Logan Seward."

"Did that son of a . . . biscuit try to run Wren down? Or was he aiming for me?"

"He has a pretty good alibi for the afternoon — unless Heinrich and Steve Dawes are both lying."

They were fellow druids. How far would they go to protect one another? How far would *Steve* go? With an unpleasant feeling deep in my gut, I had to admit I really didn't know.

"So you believe Seward?" I asked. "Because that's kind of a crazy big coincidence, isn't it?"

"It is," Quinn agreed. "Any thoughts on that?"

"Not really."

"Me, either. At any rate, I'm going after Hunter with everything I can muster."

I hung up after promising to pass on the information to Wren. On the way out to my car, I spent more time looking over my shoulder than watching where I was going.

CHAPTER 20

Mimsey and her husband lived in a newer ranch-style home in Midtown. The lawn was an even, perfect green without a blade of grass out of place or a single weed. Even the edges along the sidewalk were precisely trimmed in winter. I pulled into the driveway leading to their two-car garage and got out. Mungo bounced to the ground, ran once around the yard, and came back to where I was retrieving Wren's file from the backseat.

All around the tasteful charcoal-gray house, winter shrubs unfurled in bloom. Bright yellow flowers dotted the witch hazel by the garage, while the wintersweet sported purple-brown and yellow petals. Winter jasmine flowed over the retaining wall that separated the Carmichaels' yard from their neighbors', and the winter honeysuckle flowers, though small, filled the slight breeze with their sweet fragrance. Pansies gamboled around purple ornamental kale in the pots on either side of the front door, and hundreds of spring bulb spikes reached upward from garden soil rich with compost and potential.

Mimsey's husband, James, answered the door. "Katie Lightfoot! You are a sight for sore eyes, sugar. Come on in."

"Good to see you, too." I followed him through the formal living room to the comfy family room off the open kitchen. Mimsey and Wren were seated on the floor in front of the hearth, surrounded by black-and-white photographs. Heckle snoozed on his perch by the window, training one fierce eye on me for a moment before letting it drift closed again. An oak-wood fire crackled in the fireplace, filling the air with warmth. The aroma of popcorn filled the room, and a bowl of fluffy kernels sat nearby. It would have been a scene of homey domestic bliss except for the cast on Wren's arm and the haunted look in her eyes.

Still, she smiled up at me. "Thanks for bringing over the donor file. At least I can make some phone calls now." She held up a picture of a young man in uniform. "Gran and I were going through some old family pictures. And I do mean *old.*"

"Watch yourself, young lady," James said.

"That picture is of me."

His granddaughter ducked her head. "Oops." But they were both grinning.

Mimsey smiled at them both, a bit of the twinkle back in her blue eyes, and beckoned for me to come over. "Join us here by the fire, Katie. Hello, Mungo."

James Carmichael settled on the sofa, and Mungo lay down next to Wren and put his chin on his paws, blinking up at her. I sat down cross-legged on the carpet and let the fire warm my back. "A few things have happened since I spoke with you this morning."

In answer to their quizzical looks, I told them how Hunter Normandy had come to Georgia Wild looking for the ring that Quinn said he'd stolen.

"From a dead body?" James said, obviously astonished. "That's low."

"The lowest," I agreed.

Mimsey blanched when I related the information about trace amounts of formaldehyde being on the origami bats, but Wren looked at me with tired eyes that seemed incapable of surprise any longer.

"So the police are on the lookout for him as we speak," I said.

"Golly!" Heckle squawked, apparently awake after all.

"Oh, hush." James glared at the bird. Heckle returned the favor. I barely managed not to smile.

"Do you think he killed her?" Wren asked.

Mimsey tsked.

I shook my head. "I don't know. I'm pretty sure that was his Wrangler leaving when I got to Georgia Wild, but you didn't see him that night, did you?"

"Nuh-uh," Wren said. "If he killed her, it had to have been before I got there. Why would he hang around?"

"Hard telling what goes on in the mind of a killer," James said.

"True." I grabbed a handful of popcorn as my brain worked. "I guess the ring could be the motive. Maybe he wanted it back and Autumn wouldn't give it to him. Or maybe she found out where he got it. I can't imagine she would have been pleased. She might have even threatened to report him to the police if she knew. And he could have stolen Logan Seward's BMW and tried to run you down. Us down."

"What?" Mimsey and James said together.

I explained about Seward reporting his SUV stolen shortly before the police found it wrecked and abandoned.

Wren nodded. "No one knows where Hunter's been, so he could have been the one who stole it. But why Logan Seward's car?"

"I've been wondering that. Autumn must have at least mentioned the maroon bats and her environmental battle over the sale of Fagen Swamp. Hunter could have left the origami bats to direct suspicion away from himself. Maybe he tracked down Logan Seward's vehicle for the same reason."

"Maybe." Mimsey looked thoughtful.

The others nodded slowly.

I pulled the satellite photo out of my bag and handed it to her. "Does this make any sense to you?"

She took it with a frown and settled her reading glasses on her nose.

Wren scooted next to her grandmother to take a look. "That's the swamp, of course."

"It is," I agreed. "But see those lines? They lead to a giant cypress tree out there. The biggest one in the area. Do you remember it?"

Wren nodded. "It's impressive."

"Do you know if it's part of the land that Fagen wants to sell? It looks to be on the far edge of the swamp."

"I don't know," she said. "I assumed it was, but I don't really know exactly where the boundary lines are for Fagen's property."

"That tree is —" I glanced at James. "It's powerful."

"Magic!" Heckle crowed.

James directed a dirty look at his wife's familiar. Somehow Heckle managed to look self-satisfied.

Mimsey handed the photo back and took off her glasses. She spoke slowly. "I'm not positive, but I think the satellite may have somehow captured a set of ley lines."

James stood. "I'll leave you all to your photographs. There's a game on that I'll watch in my den." Leaning over, he gave Mimsey a buss on the check and an affectionate look.

"What kind of game?" I asked as he walked down a hallway and shut the door behind him.

"It doesn't matter," Mimsey said lightly. "He gets bored with magic talk."

I squinted at her. "And that doesn't bother you?"

"Good heavens, why should it? We've shared a long life together, have a wonderful daughter and a wonderful granddaughter." She beamed at Wren. "But he isn't interested in magic, and I don't want to watch his Neanderthal football or have

297

anything to do with that silly game of golf. We have different interests, and after forty-nine years of marriage, we've worked out how to leave each other alone to enjoy them."

Well. That certainly put my worries about Declan not "getting it" into perspective. If I truly loved him, I shouldn't expect him to want to know all about my witchiness. It wasn't as though I wanted to convert him, and I already had plenty of people in my life whom I could share magic with.

Wren's phone rang, and she checked the number. "I have to get this." Standing, she went into the kitchen. Soon I heard murmuring.

"She forwarded the Georgia Wild phone calls to her cell," Mimsey explained.

"So tell me more about ley lines," I said, peering back down at the picture.

Mimsey leaned her back against the couch. "They are deep currents of energy that run through the earth, like a mystical energy highway. They have a force, a magnetic force, that's measurable by scientific instruments — or even by holding a simple iron rod in your hand. Stonehenge is famous for the lines of energy that emanate from the center, as are other stone circles. Some dowsers say ley lines affect how they find water." She stared into the flames lapping against the logs in the fireplace. "There's some which-came-first debate about whether they have been here forever, or whether they were created — by ancient trade routes, holy sites, or even the gods and goddesses. They supposedly emanate from the Bahamas, affect the area known as the Bermuda Triangle, and there are several places in the United States that are supposed to be built near these fields. Sedona, Arizona, is one."

"I guess I've heard that," I said. "Curious that Sedona is where Gart Fagen lives now, don't you think?"

"Perhaps he's drawn to them. I think of ley lines as the energetic nervous system of a living, breathing earth."

I stared at her. "And this set is coming from a tree that pulled me toward it as surely as if it had lassoed me around the neck."

She looked away from the flames to study me. "Really? I must see this tree. Because if those really are ley lines, there are a *lot* of them — and they're strong."

"You're never going to believe who that was," Wren said, reentering the living room.

I cocked my head to the side and waited.

"Evanston Rickers," she said.

"What did he want?" I asked.

"Bianca's phone number."

When I got back to the Honeybee, Declan and Ben were installing yet more shelves in the library. These were under the window. Since the books we offered drew in customers, I couldn't argue with using the last of the available wall space to house more volumes.

I paused under the LIBRARY sign, watching them. Declan looked up from the hole he was drilling in the wall and saw me. A huge grin spread across his face, and I couldn't help returning it.

"I like the new shelves," I said.

"Seemed like a waste not to put this area to use," Ben said.

"Hey, you." Declan put the drill down and came over to where I stood. He put his arm around my shoulders, giving me a quick squeeze. "How was your day?"

I gave him a peck on the cheek. "Interesting. I'll tell you all about it later, okay?"

"Deal."

"Now get back to work, mister."

"Yes, ma'am."

Laughter sounded from the kitchen, and I saw Lucy and Mama working side by side, filling muffin cups to go into the oven.

"Looks delish," I said as I went by to take Mungo into the office.

"Your mother even did a little *special* baking," Lucy said with a huge smile.

"Now, Luce," Mama said, but she smiled at me. "Sweetie, what are you doing here? I would think you'd savor a day off, especially after your day yesterday."

"Thanks for filling in for me," I said. "I really do appreciate it, and it gave me a chance to follow up on a few things this morning." I told them everything that had happened at Georgia Wild.

"You handled that very well," my mother said.

I showed them the photo of Fagen Swamp and told them what Mimsey had said about it. Lucy leaned over it for a long moment, then looked up at me and nodded. "I think she's right. They look like the images of ley lines that I've seen before in books. Mary Jane?"

Mama licked her lips. "They do look familiar. And you say you've been near this nexus?"

"Yeah. Bianca and Cookie, too. Do you think it might have something to do with maroon bats? Could they be surviving in the swamp because . . . No, that's silly. It just seems like it should *mean* something," I said.

"It does," breathed Lucy. "We just don't know what yet."

"We don't even know if that cypress is part of the sale. I imagine there's information about that in Autumn's office, but I'd rather stay away from there until Quinn finds Hunter Normandy. I'm going to make a phone call."

The sisters watched as I went into the office, but they didn't follow. Mungo snoozed on his chair as I got online and did a phone number search for Gart Fagen in Sedona. He had an actual landline, which I dialed. Unfortunately, I reached his voice mail. I left my name and number, but didn't go into details about why I was calling.

When I went back out front, Lucy was putting a slab of mocha shortbread on a plate for Jaida, and Bianca was in the library with Mama, helping to supervise the work crew. Declan said something, and Mama laughed. I could tell she really liked him.

Suddenly tired, I poured a cup of caffeine and slid onto the chair next to Jaida.

"Hey," she said. "Anything going on?"

I half laughed and filled her in on everything. "But you have to tell Bianca and Cookie. I'm worn out from giving updates."

Her look was wry. "I bet. You have quite the posse, don't you?" Her eyes cut to my mother giving advice on attaching the last shelf to the wall. "And now you have a new addition."

"Sheesh. You make it sound like I had a baby instead of a visit from my mother."

"How long is she going to stay?"

"I don't know. But you know what? It's been kind of great having her here," I said. "So far."

She gave a firm nod. "Glad to hear it. I know you two have had your problems."

I sipped my coffee, and she took a big bite of the dark, rich shortbread.

"So Logan Seward's SUV was stolen for an attempt on Wren's life. Maybe yours, too."

"Uh-huh."

"Suspicious."

"Uh-huh."

"And you're wondering where the boundaries are in the real estate transaction he's brokering."

"What are you getting at?" I asked.

She popped the last bit of shortbread in her mouth and chewed, then swallowed. "I mentioned that I've met Seward once. I wouldn't mind getting to know him a little better, being a fellow attorney and all."

"He's a druid, too," I said.

Her jaw slackened. "You're kidding. Why didn't you tell us?"

"Like you said, I have a lot of people to keep in the loop."

"Is he . . . ?"

"He's Nel's cousin. The one the Dragohs recruited from Kentucky."

"Holy crow. I was going to suggest that we go see him," she said. "But now I think I'll insist."

My watch said eight minutes after three o'clock. Where had the day gone?

"Shall we call him first?" I asked.

"Hmm. No. I don't think so. Do you know where his office is?" Jaida asked.

"Boy, do I."

CHAPTER 21

The sky still threatened rain, so we left
Mungo at the Honeybee and drove the Bug
to the building that housed the Dawes
Corporation and Logan Seward's offices.
The wind had kicked up by the time I found
a space to park around the corner, and we
hurried up the sidewalk to the front door. It
was open, and we stepped inside. A market-
ing firm took up the first floor and a soft-
ware mapping company the second. As we
climbed, the air seemed to become more
rarified, but maybe that was my imagina-
tion.

On the top floor, no one was behind the
reception desk. It looked extremely neat,
and I wondered whether they even had a
receptionist. Heinrich Dawes' office door
was closed. The other two were slightly ajar.
I heard the tapping of a keyboard as I
walked past Steve's to the one with LOGAN
SEWARD, ATTORNEY on it. Jaida followed,

took one look at the name, and rapped firmly three times before pushing it open.

Seward looked up and did a double take. He quickly turned his computer monitor so we couldn't see anything on the screen and stood. "May I help you?" he blurted.

Jaida closed the door behind us. We each took a seat in the chairs that sat in front of his desk.

"That would be nice," I said.

Seward blinked down at us and slowly resumed his seat.

His office was smaller and not as ostentatious as Steve's. His taste ran more to modern Danish furniture. Some Scandinavian furniture was quite beautiful, but he seemed to like pieces with weird angles and ugly color combinations. The chair I was sitting in was incredibly uncomfortable — the perfect guest chair if you didn't like guests. A shelf held what looked like old softball trophies, and the single painting on the wall behind his desk looked like an impressionist's interpretation of hell.

"I assume this has some kind of legal bearing since you brought your lawyer," he said.

"She's my friend," I said.

Elbows on the desk, he steepled his fingers. "Then what can I do for you?"

"It sounds like sale of the swamp is a

306

pretty sure thing," I said.

"It is." His voice was flat.

I took the aerial photo out of my bag and, standing, put it on his desk. "Can you tell me where the boundaries of the plot you're buying are?"

He barely looked at the picture. "We're buying the whole swamp, as well as the ring around it that Fagen owns."

"So this is included?" I pointed to the cypress tree.

Leaning forward, he finally looked at the photo on the desk. "Of course." Squinting, he said, "There's something wrong with your printer."

"Maybe." I looked at Jaida. She looked amused. I sat back down.

"Is there something else?" Seward asked impatiently.

"Your SUV was involved in a hit-and-run yesterday," I said.

His eyes narrowed. "How do you know that?"

"Because it nearly hit *me.* Naturally the detective in charge informed me when they found it."

He licked his lips. "It was stolen."

Jaida leaned forward. "Don't you think it's an awfully interesting coincidence that your vehicle was used to attack two people who have been working against your purchase of Fagen Swamp? After the founder of Georgia Wild was murdered?" She slowly raised one eyebrow. I could only imagine what she'd be like in court. Good thing she was on my side.

"Oh, please," he said, rushing to fill the silence. "You can't possibly think I had anything to do with your . . . accident. Or that woman's murder."

"It was *not* an accident. It was deliberately malicious."

"Listen," he protested. "I know you're friends with Steve Dawes. Why on earth would I try to hurt you?"

"Because you had to be sure we wouldn't stop the sale of the swamp," I repeated.

He shifted in his chair, obviously uncomfortable. "The Daweses both told the police that I was here all of yesterday afternoon."

I glanced at Jaida. "So you have no explanation for why your vehicle was used."

"Sometimes coincidences do happen," he responded.

"To some people more than others," I said.

"I'm not sure I —"

"Like druids and witches," I explained.

He blanched, eyes darting to Jaida. "I don't know what you're talking about."

"You're a member of the Dragoh Society," Jaida said.

His throat worked.

"See, our coven has a bit of a history with them. I think you should know that," she said.

I stood, and Jaida followed suit. "And I think you should know that even with Autumn Boles dead and Evanston Rickers evicted, it's still possible that Georgia Wild will find evidence of maroon bats in Fagen Swamp," I said. "If we do, we will do everything possible to save that habitat."

His face turned red, and he jumped to his feet. "Don't you threaten me, girl."

Next to me, Jaida stiffened.

A knock sounded behind us, and the door opened. "Logan?" Steve walked in without being invited. This was one time I was glad he had boundary issues. "What's going on?"

"This woman accused me of trying to kill Katie!" Seward pointed at Jaida. "And of murdering that Boles woman!"

"She didn't exactly accuse you," I said.

"And how does she know I'm a druid, Steve? Huh?"

"He didn't tell me, if that's what you think," I said. "It was your pinkie ring. I saw it when you kicked Dr. Rickers out."

"I didn't kick anyone out," he spluttered.

"All I did was serve a notice to vacate. The guy has two bloody months to find a new place."

"Settle down, Mr. Seward," Jaida said.

"Tell them I was here yesterday," Seward demanded.

Steve glanced at me. "He was. All afternoon after he got back from the swamp."

"In your car," I said.

Steve nodded. "In my car."

Logan Seward took a deep breath, which seemed to calm him somewhat. "Someone stole the BMW from in front of my house."

Jaida leaned her head to one side, considering him. "You park a BMW on the street?"

"The house I rent doesn't have a garage," he said through gritted teeth. "I'm still looking for the right place to buy."

She turned to Steve. "Did you and Mr. Seward here work together yesterday afternoon, then?"

He shook his head. "We were in our own offices."

"With the doors shut?"

"Part of the time."

"Did Mr. Seward leave to use the restroom?"

"How should I know?"

A humorless smile curved her lips. "Exactly. Good day, gentlemen."

We left them staring after us. Out on the street a light rain misted the air. We trotted to the car where I turned on the engine and started the heater. "Do you really think he's the killer?" I asked Jaida.

"I don't know, Katie. But if he is, then he has the power of the Dragohs behind him."

"Great."

Back at the Honeybee it was nearly closing time. We found Ben and Declan sitting in the reading area, drinking hot cocoa and admiring their handiwork. Lucy had re-arranged the books, and a few were already on the new shelving unit.

"Didn't want it to look empty, but it is good feng shui to have empty space to grow into," she said.

"Very nice work all around," Jaida said, and walked behind the counter to pour herself a cup of drip coffee.

I walked over and gave Declan a smooch on top of his head. "Hey, you."

A few customers sat at tables. Sometimes bad weather drove people inside and other times they just wanted to get home. "Where's Mama?" I asked.

"She went for a tour," Ben said.

"In the rain?"

"Those buses are covered. Two days in

Savannah, and she hasn't seen a single sight. I ran her down to the trolley tour office. Of course, we'll show her the real good stuff, but that's always a good overview for anyone who has never been here before."

Declan made a face.

I smiled at him. "You don't approve of the tours?"

"Necessary evils, I suppose. What we need to do is make your mother a real down-home meal tonight."

"Are you offering?"

He grinned. "Sure. How about shrimp and grits? Maybe some collard greens?"

"Yum," I said. "It's a deal." My stomach growled at the thought of creamy cheese grits cooked up with mushrooms, bacon, and fresh shrimp. Unaccountably, the collards, cooked down with a ham hock and a little vinegar, sounded just as good.

"Your mother and I made a coconut cake before she left," Lucy said. "Take some home for dessert."

"Hard to argue with that," Declan said.

The door opened, and Peter Quinn walked in, wearing a forest green slicker and carrying a furled umbrella. It looked like the rain had more or less stopped, at least for the time being. Ben and Declan both rose to shake his hand.

He nodded to Lucy and Jaida, then turned to me. "I was nearby, so thought I'd drop in rather than call."

"Cocoa?" Lucy asked.

"Sure. Thanks."

She bustled over to get him a mug.

"What's up?" I asked. "Did you find Hunter?"

"Unfortunately, no." He took the mug from my aunt and sipped the steaming chocolate with appreciation. "This hits the spot."

I glanced at Jaida before asking Quinn, "Does Hunter have any connection to Fagen Swamp? Or to Logan Seward?" After all, Seward could have hired Hunter to run Wren and/or me down.

But Quinn shook his head. "Haven't found evidence of either so far. However, we did find some other evidence. Since we spoke, I got a warrant to search Normandy's apartment. Sure enough, we found folded origami."

"Bats?" I breathed.

"Well, no. They were cranes, but still. And since you said he had a key to the Georgia Wild offices, I figured he probably had a key to Autumn Boles' apartment."

"Makes sense," I said.

"So I grabbed a couple of officers and

went back over there. We searched it the night after she died, but I hadn't been back since Sunday."

"Obviously he wasn't there, or you'd have him in custody," Declan said from the sofa.

"He wasn't," Quinn said. "The place had been tossed pretty thoroughly, however. And, Katie, I confirmed with the CSI folks that they had not gone back to Georgia Wild to reinvestigate. So I think you're right that Normandy had been there looking for something — presumably that ring, but perhaps something else as well."

The sure knowledge that he'd been in there was an effective curb to my appetite.

"We found a few prints that match his — they're in the system, so it was easy to check — but that doesn't prove anything. He no doubt spent some time in her apartment if he had a key."

I sank down on the arm of the sofa, and Declan put his arm around my waist. "Well, heck," I said.

"My point is that he's still out there, and he could be very dangerous. I want all of you to be extra careful. And, Katie? You especially. If he did steal Logan Seward's SUV and try to run you down, he could be capable of anything."

Including murder.

■ ■ ■ ■

I called Wren to fill her in on what Quinn had told us. She said both of her grandparents were home and that she had no intention of leaving the house. Soon after I hung up with her, Mama came back, bubbling over the Cathedral of St. John the Baptist and the house where Juliette Gordon Low, founder of the Girl Scouts, had been born. She was also thrilled to have seen Mercer House. "It was just like in the movie," she said.

Declan caught my eye and shook his head. Still, "the book," as Savannahians had come to call *Midnight in the Garden of Good and Evil* by John Berendt, had been instrumental in bringing countless tourists — and dollars — to the city.

When I told her Declan wanted to make her a real Low Country supper, she laughed with delight. "Grits? Good heavens, I've never had grits in my life."

"You'll love them," Declan said. He was leaning against the coffee counter, writing out a shopping list. "If you two will pick this stuff up on the way home, I'll do all the cooking. Try to get the collards as young and tender as possible. We don't have all

315

day like we'd need to cook up the big tough ones."

"We'll meet you at the carriage house, then?" I asked.

"Yep — and then I can give your mother a ride to Lucy's after dinner." He waggled his eyebrows in a terrible Groucho Marx impression, but I got the gist: He'd drop Mama off and then come back on his own.

"Sounds good," I said with a smile.

"First I need to swing by my house for a secret ingredient," he said.

"Can't I pick it up with the rest of these items?" I waved at the growing list.

"Then it wouldn't be a secret, would it?"

I pushed his shoulder playfully. "Fine. See you there. Come on, Mama. Let's pack up Mungo and that coconut cake and get going."

CHAPTER 22

The grocery store didn't take long, and soon we were pulling into my driveway. The clouds had scattered, and the setting sun painted the sky with a pastel brush as I got out and retrieved the mail before returning to help Mama with the grocery bags.

Mungo bounced to the driveway and trotted over to attend to business on the lawn. Finished, he stared, frozen, at the carriage house as if he were on point.

My heart sank. Now what? Maybe Declan had arrived before us. He had his own key, but his truck was nowhere to be seen.

Sure enough, my familiar suddenly charged the porch, barking harsh and low in his throat much as he had when the folded bat had been slipped under the door.

My mother's eyebrows knitted. "What's going on?"

Mungo reared onto his hind legs and pawed frantically at the door. I dropped my grocery bag and tote on the lawn and ran to him. He looked back at me over his shoulder, blinking rapidly.

Someone was inside, and it wasn't Declan. I turned the knob.

"Katie!" Mama cried.

I pushed the door open but didn't go inside. Mungo did, though, scampering to the bottom of the narrow stairs that led to the loft. Soft light shone down from above. Someone had turned on my reading lamp.

Then I saw with alarm that my secretary desk was open, my altar exposed. Not only that, but even from the open doorway I could tell the items on it had been rearranged.

How dare someone enter my home? How *dare* someone mess with my altar? Anger flooded through me, prickling every follicle on my scalp.

"Who's there?" I yelled, flipping the light switch on the wall by the door. The floor lamp by the fainting couch clicked on.

Behind me, Mama tugged on my arm. I pulled back but remained on the threshold.

A soft, gliding sound reached my ears. I recognized it as one of the storage drawers built into the wall of the loft. Whoever was up there had been going through my personal belongings. My anger turned to red-hot fury.

"Control yourself," Mama hissed.

"But —"

"Come *on.*" She pulled on my arm again. "Let's just call the police."

Hunter Normandy's head appeared above the loft railing. "No. Please don't do that."

My eyes blazed. "The hell I won't. You're wanted for murder, buddy, not to mention breaking and entering. You think we're going to just let you go?"

He'd blanched at the word *murder.* "I didn't kill her!"

Mungo lunged at the bottom step, lips pulled back to show his fierce, if small, fangs.

Hunter eyed him. "I only want the ring. Give me the ring and I'll go. You'll never see me again."

"Declan's here," Mama said. I heard her rapid steps as she ran down the sidewalk.

Glancing over my shoulder, I saw her hurry up to Declan as he got out of his truck. She gestured toward me, nodded, and hastened toward my tote bag, which I'd dropped near the sack of groceries. She was going for my cell phone.

In the brief time I'd looked away, Hunter had made it halfway down the steps.

"Don't you move," I threatened. "Not one

319

more inch. I don't have your ring. I gave it to the police, and they were happy to get it. Stealing from a dead body. Disgusting."

Panic infused his features, overcoming his fear of Mungo. He clattered down the last of the stairs. Mungo struck with his teeth, clamping down on the denim of Hunter's jeans. Hunter's foot moved, and Mungo caught air. He yelped but landed on his feet, quivering with indignation.

I started toward him, enraged, but Declan's hands closed around my arms, yanking me back and spinning me around. "Leave this to me."

"Put me down!" I cried, though he hadn't, technically, picked me up.

Hunter, now at the bottom of the stairs, was cornered too near my bedroom to access the back door. His eyes cut left and right, looking for a way out.

Declan moved toward him, slowly, hands raised. "Now, come on. You know the police are on their way."

"Let me go," Hunter panted. "I thought she had the ring. I never hurt anyone. Let me go."

"Sorry, but that's not going to happen. Just settle down. They'll be here soon." Declan spoke with the smooth tone he'd used to soothe me after the hit-and-run the day before.

Unfortunately, the effect was lost on Hunter. Reaching into his coat pocket, he pulled out a Swiss army knife and quickly unfolded the largest blade.

The guy was actually pointing a knife at my boyfriend. I shuddered. I hated knives as much — or more — than I hated snakes.

Declan stepped forward, and this time when he spoke his voice held real warning. "Drop it."

"I didn't do anything," Hunter said.

"I don't know if you killed anyone or not. That's for a court to decide. Same for that ring Katie told me about. But right now, even if you haven't taken a thing from this house, you're upping a charge for breaking and entering to assault with a deadly weapon. And you know what? That's not a good move."

A frisson of desire thrilled through me as I watched Declan, all calm and cool, reasoning with this jerk who had invaded my home, this jerk who was holding a knife pointed right at his solar plexus.

However, Hunter wasn't interested in reason anymore. Waves of frantic desperation rolled off him.

"He's not listening," I warned. Mungo ran outside.

Good boy.

Hunter thrust the blade at Declan. My man was fast, dodging to the left, but that gave Hunter a slight opening. He rushed past Declan, heading straight for me, still holding the knife.

I spun out of the doorway, into the room so he could escape and no one would get hurt, but Declan grabbed Hunter's coat from behind, turned him around, and slammed his back into the wall. The whole carriage house vibrated. Something crashed to the floor in the kitchen. Hunter fell to one knee. He stayed down for a few panting breaths, then came up again with vengeance in his eyes. He drew his hand back, and I knew with all my heart he meant to stab Declan.

"Stop."

The tableau in front of me froze as if I'd hit the pause button on a DVD.

Taken aback, I stared at the two men, unmoving, for a long moment.

Mama appeared in the doorway. "What on earth . . . Katie! What did you do?"

"I — I used my Voice. I didn't mean to, not like that —"

She took me by the shoulders and shook me. *"What did you say?"*

"I said, 'Stop.' "

322

My mother ran to Declan, and my eyes widened as she put her ear to his chest. "He isn't breathing."

"What?" Terror gabbled in the back of my mind. Oh, good goddess, what had I *done*?

She glanced at the other man. "Neither is he. Their hearts have stopped, too." She grabbed the knife out of Hunter's hand.

"Commence!" Mama yelled with her own Voice.

Nothing happened.

"Katie — you have to reverse it! *Commence.*"

Scared out of my wits, I screamed the word, throwing everything I had into it.

In a flash the men moved again, catching themselves and gasping, shock on both their faces. They stared at my mother, then at me. Tires skidded to stop in the street out front, but neither one seemed to hear. Blue and red lights flashed through the gloaming outside. The police had arrived faster than I could have imagined.

"What the . . . ?" Hunter breathed.

Declan looked like the proverbial deer caught in the headlights.

"What the hell was that?" Hunter managed to get out. The whites of his eyes were bright. I saw them flick up to my altar, still open in the loft. "What are *you*?"

323

I ran to Declan and put my arms around him. "Oh, honey. I'm so sorry. So, so sorry."

His arms remained at his sides. I looked up at him, and he met my eyes with a mix of wonder and horror.

"Are you okay?" I whispered around the tightness in my throat. "Tell me you're okay."

A single, slow nod was his response, and his hand went to my shoulder. Relief gusted through me, and I buried my face in his chest.

Two officers appeared in the still-open doorway, Margie hovering behind them.

Mama marched over to them. She pointed at Hunter Normandy, who seemed to have lost all desire to escape. "We came home to find this man had broken in and was going through my daughter's things. He is also wanted for murder and theft. Please arrest him now."

Defeat slumped his shoulders, but he still didn't look away from me. The officers looked somewhat amused at my mother's imperious demand, at least until she added, "He had a knife." She held out the Swiss army knife, still open, to the nearer officer, the woman. It looked small against her palm, a paltry excuse for a weapon. Declan was a trained firefighter. He would have been able to handle Hunter Normandy with no help from me, twenty-twenty hindsight and all.

"He gave it to you?" the policewoman's partner asked, approaching Hunter with what looked like a giant plastic zip-tie.

My mother and I looked at Declan. He still hadn't said a word, and his face had gone an odd shade of gray.

"No," Mama said. "He dropped it."

"Declan? Are you sure you're okay?" I asked again, afraid that I'd really hurt him. He seemed to have caught his breath, though.

Hunter shook his head as the police officers pushed him toward the porch. "There's something wrong with her," he said. One of them began reading him his Miranda rights. He tossed one last baffled look over his shoulder as he stumbled out to their patrol car.

Margie stood aside to let him pass, her expression marked with curiosity. Then she came up and peered in at us. "Is everyone okay? I heard a ruckus over here and called 911."

That explained how quickly the police had arrived. I went over and gave her a hug. "Thank you, neighbor. You saved the day."

"Why, Katie, you're shaking like a leaf.

What in creation happened?" She was right. I was shaking right down to the tips of my chartreuse high-tops. But I didn't want Declan to know how scared I was — not of Hunter Normandy, but of him getting hurt. And of me being the one who caused it.

Makes it sound kind of dangerous to hang around you. His words from the night before flooded back, and I hugged Margie a little tighter before releasing her.

"That man thought I had something of his, and he was trying to get it back," I said. "I didn't, of course, but that didn't stop him from looking."

Margie frowned in confusion, looking at my mother for an explanation.

"He broke in before we came home," Mama said.

My neighbor's hand flew to her mouth. "Oh, heavens. I didn't see a thing."

"You can't be expected to see everything," I said gently. Like whoever had slipped that bat under my door — when we *were* home. Had it been Hunter Normandy?

Quinn showed up then, and Declan came out of his daze long enough to haltingly relate what he'd found when he arrived shortly after Mama and I had gotten there. Mama confirmed his story and added how I'd come inside to find Hunter going through my possessions.

"He was looking for the ring," I called down to Quinn from the loft. As soon as I could, I'd high-tailed it up there to close the secretary desk and hide my altar. "He left Georgia Wild before I could tell him I'd already given it to you. It doesn't look like he took anything else, though."

"Have you checked your room?" my mother asked.

"I guess I'd better." I clambered down the stairs and went into the bedroom, disturbed more than I wanted to admit by the notion that Hunter Normandy had spent any time in there. Declan followed me.

Flipping on the light, I took a quick survey. "Nothing looks out of place."

"Katie." Declan stood by the window. The lamplight cast his eyes into shadow. "What did you do to me?"

Did he remember? I didn't know because others' Voices had never worked on me. Did he have a blank for the time he was out, or had he been aware the whole time? Either way, I had to tell him the truth. Guilt arrowed through me, so strong my knees felt weak.

"I'm sorry," I whispered. "I didn't mean to do it."

"Everything all right in there?" my mother called.

I put my hand on Declan's arm. "We'll talk."

Quinn appeared in the doorway.

"I don't think Hunter got this far in his search for the ring," I said.

"Are you sure that's all he was here for?" Quinn asked.

"That's what he said. You think he was here to harm me?"

He stroked his chin with thumb and forefinger. "I think he killed Autumn Boles and threatened you and Ms. Knowles with those bats, but I don't know if he actually planned to hurt you today. The bats seem more like misdirection. If we're lucky, he'll confess and we'll finally learn the truth."

"Will you tell me what you find out?" I asked as the three of us returned to the living room.

"If it pertains to you, of course." Quinn smiled.

I considered asking him to stay for supper again, but I refrained. It would only be putting off the inevitable conversation with Declan. At least Mama was here to defuse the situation.

A week ago I'd never have believed she'd be the one to help me.

She'd saved Declan's life, too.

The thought made me start shaking all over again, so I was glad when Quinn took his leave.

CHAPTER 23

It turned out Declan had been only vaguely aware that I'd yelled something and his world had stopped — including his breathing and his heart. His *heart.* I'd stopped the heart of the man I loved.

But he'd seen Mama moving, heard voices, so he knew something had happened. When he came back, he'd felt disoriented and confused, and, though it was hard for him to admit, afraid. This was not the effect I wanted to have on Declan. Ever.

Or on anyone else for that matter.

We'd settled into the living room, Declan and I on opposite ends of the couch with Mungo in between us. Mama sat on one of the wingbacks. She had explained to him what a Voice was, and how some people have it and some don't. She was very direct and down-to-earth on the surface, but I could tell that even talking about it made her uncomfortable. Nonetheless, she plunged on — as much for my sake as Declan's, I suspected.

"Mine isn't very strong," she said. "That's why I couldn't reverse what Katie Commanded. Do you know anyone else with a Voice?" she asked me in a bright tone.

"Cookie, but it doesn't last very long," I admitted. "Heinrich tried to use his on me. So did Steve."

Declan's eyes narrowed. "What did he try to make you do?"

I looked ceilingward and shook my head. "Nothing improper, if that's what you're thinking. Besides, it doesn't work on me. I'm immune, at least so far."

He was looking at me as if I were an odd bug under a microscope. "I don't understand. You told me magic was about manifesting intention."

"It is," I said.

"But that sounds like some kind of New Age take on positive thinking. This thing you're telling me about is real. I mean, you can actually *do* things. Tell me what else." He looked wildly around the room as if I were going to manifest a unicorn.

"Having a Voice is kind of like being born with red hair," Mama said.

He rubbed a hand over his face. "You mean she got it from you."

"And her father."

Declan let out a long sigh.

"I told you my powers were hereditary," I said, trying to tamp down my frustration — and remorse. "Mostly the Craft is about intention, and mostly I place that intention into herbs and spices when I'm cooking. I mean, I can't twitch my nose and go to Paris or anything. I can't say abracadabra and come up with a murder suspect, either. Believe me, if I could, I would. Heck, half the time I can't even find my keys."

He didn't smile.

I went on. "See, I can't *make* things happen, only . . . open the door for them. I'm just a little more . . ." I trailed off, wishing more than anything that the sick feeling in my stomach would go away. With it came the sense — no, the knowledge — that using my Voice on Declan had irretrievably broken something between us. I looked helplessly at my mother.

"What you did to me was a whole lot more than opening a door," he grumbled.

"Katie is a catalyst," she said quietly. "And . . . well, she's powerful. Be clear, however, that what happened to you today is as much my fault as hers."

My chin jerked up in surprise.

"Maybe more my fault."

"Mama."

"No. I knew you had ability, real, tangible power, but I ignored that because I didn't want to face raising you as a witch. I was frightened of what people would think, of losing my small-town community. I abdicated my responsibility as your mother, and you went into the world untrained."

Declan couldn't keep the distress off his face. When he turned and looked me in the eye, I saw something else, too: distrust.

There is no going back from this. He knows magic is real and not some game. At least for me.

My mother said, "I'm going to remedy my mistake, though. My Voice may not be as strong as yours, but at least I can teach you how to control it."

I tried to smile and rose. "If we don't get going on supper, we won't be eating until ten o'clock."

Declan blinked. "Yeah. Okay."

"I'll help, okay? Mama, I think the coconut cake is still in the car."

Supper was a quiet, subdued affair. I asked about Daddy and his hardware store and Mama's volunteer work at the hospital. She answered without detail, and I felt myself struggling to keep the conversation going.

Declan hardly talked at all. When the dishes were done, he said, "Ms. Lightfoot? Do you mind if we leave a little early? I'm bushed."

She bit her lower lip and looked at me. "I guess that would be fine. Unless you want me to stay, Katie?"

I shook my head. "I'm pretty tired, too," I lied. "At least I don't have to worry about Hunter Normandy anymore."

Mama went into the living room to get her purse, and I grabbed Declan's arm. "You're coming back as soon as you drop her?"

His blue eyes searched my face. "I don't think so. Not tonight. I need to think about things. I'll call you."

"Tonight?" I pushed.

He gave a slight shake of his head. "Probably not. I need a little time. There was a time when you asked me for that, and I gave it to you."

I dropped my hand from his arm. "Of course. I understand." Which was true. In fact, I was afraid I understood too much.

After they left, I sat on the sofa and listened to the silence. The space didn't feel as tainted as it had when my home had been invaded before, but the air felt empty with my mother and Declan gone.

Maybe it wasn't the air. Maybe it was my heart.

Mungo jumped up and searched my face with his warm brown eyes.

"Well, I may have solved that whole problem of what to get my boyfriend for Valentine's Day," I said, "because I think there's a pretty good chance I won't have a boyfriend by then."

He laid his head softly on my lap as I began to cry.

Later as I desperately tried to sleep, my cell phone gave a soft chirp. The clock said 1:14 a.m. The text read, *Another stroke for justice. Congratulations. Glad you're safe.*

It was from Steve.

Between running the events of the last few days over in my mind, curiosity about the cypress tree and the ley lines in Fagen Swamp, and thoughts that kept returning to Declan over and over, sleep largely eluded me. Finally, I got up and went into work at four the next morning. Mungo immediately began snoozing in his office chair, and I settled in to my usual morning routine. An hour spent sifting and mixing, tasting and baking, netted a half-filled display case and a calmer me. At a bit after five, Lucy arrived at the Honeybee with Mama. In the last two days, the bakery had become even more of a family affair, and I was glad for the help.

"Looks like you've been here for a while, honey. How are you doing?" Mama asked with concern.

Lucy came up and gave me a hug. "Your mother told me what happened with Declan. I'm sure he'll come around."

Inhaling her spicy scent of patchouli, I returned her embrace but tried to keep my tone light. "He has a right to know what he's getting into. We should look on the bright side — Autumn's killer is in custody, and now things can get back to normal."

Lucy laughed. "Normal, huh?"

"How are the plans for the bake sale going?" I asked.

My mother's face lit up. "We've made a lot of progress — the mailers went out, and the Downtown Business Association has started some buzz going around town. We decided to have it in two days. Your uncle arranged for us to set up someplace called Rousakis Plaza."

Nonna would like that. I wondered if she'd talk to me again if I went into the echo chamber. I hadn't smelled even a hint of gardenia during the confrontation with Hunter.

"I'll stay for the sale," Mama said. "Then I should probably get back to your father. He called last night, and apparently he misses me." Her eyes flashed with pleasure.

"Of course he does," I said.

"Oh, and I forgot to tell you yesterday, but I contacted the newspaper. They said they might want to do a feature on Georgia Wild. They were resistant at first, but then I mentioned the murder, and that made their ears perk right up."

I gaped. "Gosh, Mama. That's kind of mercenary, isn't it?"

She shrugged and tied a flowered apron over her black slacks and pearl gray sweater. "I know it was a terrible tragedy, but a story in the *Savannah Morning News* will really help get people to come to the bake sale."

Lucy looked over at me. "Mary Jane, did they tell you who's going to write the story?"

"Dane . . . Dawes? Yes. Somebody Dawes."

I sighed. "Steve Dawes."

"You know him?" she asked. As much as I'd seen of him lately, Steve still hadn't met my mother.

Dolloping a mound of almond chocolate chip cookie dough onto a baking sheet, I said, "I guess you could say that."

337

"Well, he's supposed to call me today to set up a time to talk to Wren. I'll tell him you said hello."

Lucy's lips twitched as she turned to the row of aprons on the wall and selected a white waist apron to cover her tie-dyed skirt. "I'm sure he'll be glad to hear that."

The phone lit up as the news of Hunter Normandy's arrest spread. Mama told Wren when she called about Steve wanting to interview her, and then Wren called me. I gave her all the details I knew about Normandy, though I fudged a bit on my role in his apprehension. No reason to go into that, though I was sure the coven would hear all about it in time. The relief in Wren's voice was palpable, and she sounded downright excited when I updated her on the bake sale preparations.

"The bank called late yesterday and said the short-term loan has been approved," she said. "But I haven't heard anything about those two conservancy grants yet. I'm hoping the bake sale will make some money, of course, but that it will also get the word out about what Georgia Wild does. Maybe we'll get more donations as a result."

"So my mother told you all about the newspaper feature," I said.

338

"Yes! Isn't it wonderful?"

I agreed it was wonderful. Then Mimsey got on the line, and I told the Hunter Normandy story all over again.

Quinn called an hour later. "Normandy lawyered up," he said. "But we're continuing to build the case, don't you worry."

"I don't suppose his lawyer is Logan Seward?"

He laughed. "No, it's someone who has nothing to do with this case at all."

Jaida and Bianca came in at lunchtime, and I was happy to learn Mimsey had already called the other members of the spellbook club so I didn't have to repeat it again. Every time I told the tale I thought of Declan, which made me want to call him to find out if everything was all right between us or if there wasn't an "us" anymore. But I'd agreed to let him call me, so I resisted.

Bianca took off her coat and hung it over the back of a chair. Something moved in the pocket, indicating Puck's ferrety presence. As long as he didn't jump out and run around the bakery, I was fine with her bringing him in. I certainly wasn't in any position to object.

Even though it wasn't on the menu, I brought my friends bacon, lettuce, and tomato sandwiches on grilled sourdough and tall, sweating glasses of sweet tea.

"Yum," Jaida said, and dug in.

Bianca took a sip of tea and beamed at me. "Guess what?"

"What?" I asked.

"I have a date tonight. Well, this afternoon because Colette will still be in daycare, but still — a date!"

"With one of the guys on Savannah Singles?" Jaida asked.

I looked at her in surprise.

She waved her hand in the air. "I know all about it."

But Bianca was shaking her head. "No, not with any of those bozos. With Evanston Rickers! He called me last night and asked me out for a drink at Rocks on the Roof."

"Nice!" I grinned. "I was there when he called Wren for your number. Guess you made as much of an impression on him as he did on you."

She giggled.

My jaw dropped. Tall, elegant, fashion plate Bianca Devereaux was not one to *giggle.*

Jaida laughed and took a swig of sweet tea. "I'm happy for you, B. Have you decided whether or not to tell him you're Wiccan?"

Bianca lifted one shoulder and let it fall, still smiling. "I'll just play it by ear."

"And have you told Cookie yet?" I asked.

"Nope. She'll probably disapprove, but it's my life."

I looked over my shoulder. The reading area was packed with customers, and Mama was busy at the register with a group of tourists. Ben was manning the coffee counter while Lucy talked with a woman who looked familiar. With a start, I realized it was the rude woman who had demanded a fancy coffee drink two days before. As I watched, Lucy handed her a wrapped loaf of olive sourdough and a bag of pastries. No doubt this time the woman would get the help she needed.

It was gratifying to see the uptick in business. The Honeybee was busy, but no one sat near enough to our table in the corner to overhear our conversation.

I turned back. "When are you going to meet Evanston?"

"Three o'clock." Bianca's eyes narrowed. "Why?"

"Because if we know he's going to be here in Savannah, it would be the perfect opportunity to go out to Fagen Swamp and cast a location spell."

"For the maroon bats?" Jaida asked.

"Exactly." I didn't mention how much I wanted to check out the cypress tree.

Uneasiness replaced the smile on Bianca's face. "I don't know. It seems wrong to trick him on our very first date."

"We're not tricking him," I said. "We'd be, um, saving him from the difficult situation of dealing with a bunch of witches casting in his backyard. It's not like we'll be going in his cabin or even onto his little island there. We'll work near that tree where he said he saw the maroon bats."

Jaida looked intrigued. "I like it. If we can actually find some of those bats, we might still be able to nix the sale of that land. And Bianca, if that happens, your new love interest will be able to remain for the rest of his sabbatical."

Bianca's eyes sparkled. "Well, when you put it like that . . ."

CHAPTER 24

I made some calls, and everyone agreed to meet at the bakery at two o'clock. Wren would be around earlier since Steve had called and asked to interview her at the Honeybee at one. I told Mama about our plan and invited her to come with us, but she declined.

"I'm not ready to cast yet, and certainly not with a coven. I've always worked solitary — or with your father — and while I know you have a great group in these ladies, it's not for me."

"Okay," I said, happy enough to hear she was at least thinking about taking up the Craft again.

"I'll stay here with Ben so Lucy can go," she said.

"Perfect," I said. "And thank you."

Steve walked into the bakery right after Wren. I was in the kitchen, slicing gingerbread. He caught my eye and lifted a hand in greeting. I nodded to him but didn't go out front. Wren looked relaxed for the first time since Autumn's death. Her cheeks had pinked, and she had on a different pair of glasses that flattered her face. The cast on her arm even had a few signatures on it.

They got their coffee and dry cappuccino and retired to a table to chat. Steve took out his notebook, and Wren began to talk with excited animation. If he wanted a passionate interviewee, he had one.

Cookie came in as they talked, the royal blue of her beret mirroring the blue highlights in the dark curls surrounding her heart-shaped face. She wore practical jeans and boots with a turtleneck and blazer. A frilly scarf softened the look.

She returned my wave, and Lucy took her a cup of tea. When I'd finished restocking the sandwich cookies for the second time that day, I went in to where Cookie was sitting by the new bookshelf in the library. Pulling over a poufy chair, I perched on the edge.

"Do we need to talk?" I asked.

Surprise flashed behind her eyes before she could stop it. "About what?"

"About why you've been avoiding me."

"I haven't —" She stopped. "I guess I

haven't been around much, have I?"

"Did I do something to hurt your feelings or make you angry?" I asked.

"Nnno." She drew the word out.

"Is it because Franklin Taite said I'm a lightwitch?"

She didn't say anything.

"It is! Listen, do you know what a light-witch is?"

Slowly, she shook her head. "Only what he said — that you can't do dark magic."

"Well, for Pete's sake, Cookie. I don't want to do dark magic anyway."

What did I do to Hunter and Declan, then?

I pushed the thought away and went on. "As for what else being a lightwitch might entail, I really couldn't tell you. Taite left before elaborating on the subject. So I'm just as much in the dark, pardon the pun, as you are."

"You don't seem any different," she admitted.

"That's because I'm *not*. Besides, if there is a Goody Two-shoes in our group, it's Bianca, and you two get along great."

"She didn't tell me she was meeting Evanston Rickers until it was too late to stop her," Cookie grumbled. "He got a good look at her Jag the other day, and professors don't make that much money."

I laughed.

After a few seconds, she did, too. "I suppose I did overreact to the whole lightwitch thing."

"What about the other stuff that's going on in your life? Did you hear back about the job?"

She nodded happily. "I didn't get it."

"That's a relief," I said. "Even I could tell it was the wrong thing for you."

"Well, I found the right thing."

I scooted back on the chair and crossed my legs. "Do tell."

"I'm going to Europe with Xana and Brandon. It turns out he doesn't want to be away from me so long, and when Xana heard I was willing to come, she said she'd keep me on as her assistant."

"So they weren't running off together after all."

She looked at me as if I had suggested she swallow a goldfish. "Of course not. Where did you get that idea?"

Where *had* I gotten that idea?

"Anyway," she went on, "it's time for me to move on, but in this case it's a change of location rather than a job."

Or a man.

"You sound happy," I said.

Her lips turned up and a soft laugh escaped. "Oh, I am."

"Good. Then I am, too — though we're going to miss you while you're gone."

"It will only be for three months," she said.

"Are you ready to find some bats this afternoon?" I asked.

"Absolutely."

Mimsey showed up next, then Jaida with a bag I knew contained four aquamarine candles scented with jasmine and a wineglass. We'd decided to keep things simple for the location spell. As for the cypress, I didn't know what I hoped to learn, but I was determined to get nearer to it. Given the way it had pulled at me before, I was glad my friends would be with me.

Steve and Wren finished up their interview, and Wren joined everyone in the library. I went into the office to get my denim jacket and pack up Mungo. I looked down at my outfit. I hadn't known I'd be tramping in the swamp when I'd left the house that morning and had dressed in light khaki slacks with a long-sleeved heather T-shirt and Simple sneakers. They'd be all right to walk in, and we wouldn't be in the swamp all that long.

Stopping in the kitchen, I pointed out to Mama what I'd left undone to get ready for the next day's baking. She gave me a hug. "Good luck, honey. If you're not back by the time we close, come over to Lucy and Ben's. I'm making dinner."

I grimaced, remembering last night's supper. She saw my expression and understood. "Lucy's right. Declan will come around. You can't let what happened yesterday distract you when you're casting. It'll contaminate your spell."

Magical advice from my mother. Wow.

Steve was waiting when I went out front. "What's going on?"

"What do you mean?"

He gave me an oh-brother look and nodded at the ladies milling in the library area. "Your coven is gathered, minus one member and plus another, but still."

I took a deep breath. "You can't tell your dad. Or Logan."

He searched my face, then shrugged. "Okay."

"We're going out to Fagen Swamp."

His forehead cleared. "The tree?"

I glanced at the others. "That's one reason I want to go. We're also planning to cast a location spell for maroon bats to see once and for all if there are any."

"I see." Steve pivoted on his heel and walked toward the reading area. I hurried to catch up.

"Ladies," he said, "would you mind terribly if I joined you?"

Wren's eyes went wide. "Um, I don't think —"

"He's a druid," Mimsey said. "Remember when I told you about the one who was killed a few months back? One of them."

I heard Mama's quick intake of breath and realized she'd followed me out of the kitchen. I hadn't told her anything about Steve when our lines of communication had fallen apart during the last year. Now I turned to see her eyeing him speculatively.

Wren blinked. "Oh. But he's a Dawes."

"I'm not directly involved in the land deal, and I promised Katie I wouldn't tell my father about the location spell." He put his hand on my shoulder. "You can trust that I won't break my word to her."

Mimsey looked around at the others. "What do you say, ladies? It's a little out of the ordinary, but we've worked with him before."

Jaida nodded. "Fine by me."

Cookie said, "Excellent!" and directed a dazzling smile in his direction.

"I'm not a member, so I'll happily go along with whatever you think will work best to find the bats," Wren said, looking at Steve with new eyes.

"Of course" was Lucy's warm response. "We know he and Katie have worked well together in the past. It can only help for him to come along."

I threw up my hands. "Well, okay, then." Apparently I'd already been outvoted. Secretly, though, I was glad he would be there. We did have a magical bond, even if we weren't romantic, and I wanted his take on that tree as much as anyone's.

Mama's face was inscrutable as we left. Ben's was downright unhappy.

The afternoon sunlight seemed brighter than usual, washed clean by the showers of the day before. We all piled into Lucy's Thunderbird since it was the only one of our vehicles that could accommodate seven people, a Cairn terrier, and a ferret. Even then it was a tight fit, and Cookie ended up sitting on Steve's lap.

I ignored them, telling myself that she was sticking with her current boyfriend after all, and even if she wasn't, I had no right to have an opinion about Steve's love life.

Or the fact that he had his hand on her knee.

Reaching into my pocket, I extracted my cell phone. Declan still hadn't called.

Following my directions, Lucy turned onto the road that led into Fagen Swamp. "Pull over here," I instructed when we reached the curve before the bridge to Dr. Rickers' cabin.

She pulled to the side but stayed on the pavement rather than risk getting stuck in the marshy ditch. We piled out of the car, pausing to take in the heavy smell of fertile compost and standing water, the sounds of the birds calling, the odd warmth of the microclimate within the swamp. The air thrummed with life energy.

"Mungo, I need you to stay in the car, okay?"

He made a sound of disapproval.

"Honey, I can't hold you while I'm casting, and I don't want you to be eaten by an alligator."

That seemed to change his mind, and he settled into the backseat with a tiny grunt.

I could see the top of the giant cypress now that I knew where to look for it. The pull I'd felt before was there, but not irresistibly so. "Do you feel that?" I asked everyone.

Cookie nodded. "It doesn't seem as strong."

"What are you talking about?" Mimsey asked.

"The ley lines." I pointed. "That's the tree at the nexus, if that satellite photo is right."

Steve squinted. "Ley lines?"

"Mmm-hmm." I reached in beside Mungo, took the picture out, and handed it to him.

He whistled. "I wish we'd known about this before. I'm sure my father will be very interested."

"Interested enough to buy the land and *not* develop it?" Wren asked.

"Honestly? I don't know."

I took out my cell phone again — this time to check in with Bianca. It was three o'clock on the dot, but I wanted to make sure Rickers wasn't running late. If he caught us now, I'd simply introduce Steve as one of the parties interested in the land, and he'd have to deal with it.

Except I couldn't call Bianca.

"No service," I said.

"That's hardly surprising," Steve said, turning the picture in his hands. "Magnetic energy like this would mess up any cell signal. In fact, from the looks of this, we might have a problem with the magnetic strips on our credit cards when we get back."

"Oh, Steve," Lucy said.

He looked up at her. "I'm serious."

The smile dropped from her face. "Is it dangerous?"

"Of course not!" Mimsey said, the happy twinkle fully restored to her eyes. "It will augment our working, I'm sure."

Jaida grabbed the bag with the candles in it. "Let's get going, then. I doubt Bianca will have more than one or two drinks if she's picking Colette up from daycare after meeting her date."

"Hang on," I said. "I want to make sure he's gone."

I took off at a lope, happy to have the air rushing in and out of my lungs. As I ran around the curve, the wooden bridge came into view. Slowing, I crossed to the other side. Sure enough, the old Chevy pickup was gone, and no smoke drifted from the cabin's chimney. I turned away, then paused.

Evanston Rickers had been awfully upset when he'd discovered Logan Seward had gone inside his cabin without asking. It was hard to blame him; in the same situation I'd have been furious. Still, it made me wonder if there was something the professor was trying to keep secret.

It's not like we'll be going in his cabin or even onto his little island there. That was what I'd told the others. I wouldn't go

353

inside, but curiosity impelled my feet until I stood by the corner of the building. It was small, perhaps only one room. I walked around to the rear and found more than a cord of firewood stacked against the wall. Then I saw the outhouse tucked back in the woods.

It was primitive living for a man with a doctorate degree. He must be awfully devoted to his work. I smiled to myself as I thought how Bianca would react to such facilities.

There were five windows, and all were curtained. The one on the end, however, had enough of a gap in the fabric to be able to see a chair, the corner of a table and the computer monitor on it, a small stack of logs on the floor, and a shelf of specimen jars full of coiled figures in liquid.

Snakes. Ugh.

Well, what did you expect? Stop being so nosy.

Quickly, I ran back to where the others waited. Panting in the humid air, I said, "We're good."

Cookie led the way to the dead tree where Dr. Rickers said he'd seen the bats. I scanned the ground for snakes as everyone filed into the clearing. A clump of grass to my right rustled, and I froze, staring into the shadows. Suddenly a bird took flight in a flash of feathers.

"Oh!" I laughed and put my hand on my chest, waiting for my heart to stop pounding.

"Nervous?" Steve asked.

"There are lots of snakes here," I said. "They're Dr. Rickers' specialty."

"I haven't seen any," he said.

"Good."

Jaida took the candles out of her bag, and she and Cookie set them at each of the compass points. She'd brought protective votive holders to keep the wind away. I looked up to see high clouds scudding across the blue of the sky, but the air down in the swamp was preternaturally still. Wren, too, looked upward, but at the trunks of the bald cypress trees, eyes searching for wee furry bodies among the drapes of Spanish moss. Using her good arm, she raised the fancy camera she'd brought along, using the telephoto lens to search more thoroughly. After a minute she lowered the camera and shook her head.

Mimsey dipped the goblet into a pool in the nearby marsh. "Natural water is good, but natural water from the place where you are working is best."

Lucy and Cookie lit the candles. We

gathered in a circle around the half-full glass Mimsey held at arm's length.

"All right, ladies." Her eyes cut to Steve. "And gentleman. Breathe." She closed her eyes. "Concentrate."

I closed mine, too. Lucy took my right hand. Steve took my left. His flesh felt so hot it was almost uncomfortable, and I had to make an effort not to flinch. Gathering my focus, I slowed my inhalations and allowed my center to become calm. The thrumming energy around us brightened. It seemed to increase in volume, though it was nothing I could physically hear.

"Wren," Mimsey said, "because you have the clearest notion of what we're looking for, perhaps you should focus our scrying."

"All right."

I opened my eyes as Wren took a step forward, camera still around her neck. She stared into the water in the glass. Used to working solitary, she moved her lips silently. Nonetheless, I knew she was invoking the element of water to reveal the location of any maroon bats in the swamp. I reached out mentally to merge my intention with hers.

"Katie!"

I whirled to see Bianca picking her way down the path. She was breathing heavily, the light cloak she wore hung open, and the watered silk skirt she'd chosen to wear on her date with Evanston Rickers had a rip in it. Lucy's hand flew to her lips, and Mimsey broke contact with Jaida and Cookie on either side of her.

CHAPTER 25

Hundreds of dragonflies exploded from a treetop behind Bianca. Lucy gasped. A feeling of dread settled across my shoulders.

"What's wrong?" I asked Bianca. Urgency rushed my words. "Why are you here?"

She stopped outside the circle we'd defined. "I had to warn you, and no one would answer their phone. I think Evanston came back here."

"Why? What happened?"

Bianca looked disgusted. "I don't think he was ever interested in me. He started right off talking about you."

Me?

"Question after question about where you came from and what you do at the bakery, and then he asked if I knew whether you had any special abilities."

Lucy put her hand on my arm. "Was he talking about magic?"

"I don't know, because he changed the

subject to Autumn's murder investigation. I started to tell him about Hunter Normandy, but all of a sudden he excused himself and said he had something he'd forgotten he had to do. The creep ran out of the bar like his hair was on fire *and* stuck me with the check." She paced back and forth, fuming.

Cookie said, "I told you —"

"We can figure out her love life later," I interrupted. "Right now I want you to think back to what you were talking about when Dr. Rickers suddenly got itchy feet."

She stopped pacing, and her eyes moved to the left as she searched her memory. "I think it had something to do with Hunter being an embalmer. About how the police found formaldehyde on the origami."

A dragonfly drifted past.

"Anyway, I came right out here to let you know. Broke the speed limit the whole way, but I don't know whether I beat him or not."

"Ladies," I said, "I do believe there may be more to Evanston Rickers than meets the eye. We'd better pass on the location spell for now and get the heck out of here. I don't know how he'd react if he caught us casting." And I really didn't like that he'd asked Bianca about my "special abilities."

"But we might have time to finish," Wren protested. "I thought I was picking up on something." She pointed up at a nearby tree. "There."

"I don't see anything," I said.

"We'll come back, another time, Wren." Mimsey thanked the water element and poured the contents of the goblet back into the swamp. "This Rickers fellow sounds fishy."

"He probably knows we're here already," Steve protested as Mimsey and Lucy hurried to reverse the circle. "But listen — Rickers only rents the cabin, not the whole swamp. We have every right to be out here. Gart Fagen gave Dawes Corp. permission to come on his land, and I'm giving it to you."

My mind was racing. "Mimsey's right. We can come back later," I said as things began to come together in my mind. "Hunter Normandy is in custody for Autumn's murder because of formaldehyde and the origami cranes the police found in his apartment."

"And because he's a thief," Jaida said, gathering up her candles.

"That, too. But he doesn't have any real connection to the bats, and Autumn was holding a folded bat, not a crane. He'd just asked her to marry him, and then turns around and kills her?"

"What if she found out about the ring?" Jaida asked.

"You're right — that's a possible motive. But he doesn't have any connection to Logan Seward — and no reason to steal his car. That's been bothering me ever since he was arrested. You know who does have a connection to Seward, though? As well as to the bats?"

Wren looked skeptical. Bianca had gone white as she listened.

"Remember when Seward came out here with the eviction for Dr. Rickers? He was driving Steve's car."

Steve tipped his head to one side. "And?"

"And I asked him about it. Seward said he'd walked to work and left his vehicle at home, so he'd had to borrow your car to drive out to Fagen Swamp. Rickers had had previous contact with Seward, enough that he probably knew what he drove. I think he stole the BMW and tried to run Wren and me down. All he had to do was find out where Seward lived and take the BMW later that same afternoon."

"Why?" Mimsey asked.

"I don't know why, but it must have to do with the bats. I can tell you this though — in his cabin Dr. Evanston Rickers has jars and jars of preserved snakes."

"So?" Cookie said.

At the same moment Bianca said, "How do you know that?"

"Looked in the window before we came down here," I said. "So what do you imagine he uses as a preservative?"

Wren's head jerked up, alarm written on her face. "Formaldehyde."

A frisson of fear passed through the group. Even Steve seemed convinced that we needed to leave. Together, we moved swiftly toward the path that led back to the road and our waiting car.

"Why would he kill Autumn?" Jaida asked as we fast-walked. "She was helping him."

I opened my mouth, then closed it again, stumped. "I don't know. She was talking about giving up Georgia Wild's fight for this swamp habitat."

"From what I've heard, Dr. Rickers doesn't sound like a rabid activist. Would extinct bats be adequate motive for him to commit murder?" Jaida asked.

"What if it wasn't about the bats?" Steve asked. "What if Dr. Rickers' main interest in preserving the swamp involves something else?"

I grabbed his arm. "The tree."

He nodded. "The tree. Maybe he can feel its pull, too."

"Katie Lightfoot," a deep male voice called from the direction of the cypress. It sounded far away.

"Speak of the devil," I whispered, and gestured for Mimsey to hurry.

She fanned her face. "I'm not as young as I used to be, dear."

"Sorry." I slowed to her pace. Bianca in the lead, we made our way down the path toward the road, away from Rickers.

"Where are you?" the voice came again. "I know you're out here someplace."

In a low voice I asked Steve, "Do you think he's a druid or some kind of sorcerer?"

"No idea. Though this place would be great for someone like that to live."

I brushed aside a curtain of Spanish moss and shuddered. The ripe smell of the swamp suddenly seemed more rank than fertile.

The path widened as we approached the road, but Bianca suddenly stopped. Cookie almost ran into her, and the rest of us slowed. Skirting Lucy and Mimsey, I made my way to her side, senses on high alert. My stomach dropped when I saw the horrified look on Bianca's face. She stared, unmoving, at the ground. I followed her gaze with my own.

Ten feet away a snake lounged smack-dab in the middle of the pathway. It was four feet long, two inches in diameter, and a dark charcoal color. As we watched, it reared its heads to look at us.

Heads. The thing had *two heads.*

Panic froze my body and scrambled my brain. Along with the others, I stared stupidly at the two reptilian heads swaying to and fro. Then Lucy's sharp intake of breath broke the moment.

Do something.

I tried desperately to focus my attention, which was still scrabbling to hide away so I wouldn't have to accept the freakish thing that blocked our way. With an effort, I raised my hand and willed the monstrosity to *move,* the same way I'd made Logan Seward back off in the stairwell.

Except nothing seemed to happen. I pushed harder. Steve's hand gripped my elbow, and I felt a surge of power. The creature began to turn away, then stopped. It began to move.

Toward us.

Bianca took a step back. A white flash darted out of her coat pocket and down to the ground.

"Puck!" she screamed.

Her new familiar attacked with liquid speed, flowing over and around the snake, biting, dodging, confusing his opponent

364

who always seemed to strike where Puck had just been.

Terrified, Bianca looked on helplessly, her hands fluttering by her sides.

"Go." Steve pushed me. "Get past it."

Before I could move, Evanston Rickers stepped onto the path on the other side of the melee. "There you are!" He poked at the warring animals with his walking stick. Puck disengaged and ran back to Bianca, who scooped him up and held him while she still visibly trembled.

Rickers lifted the mutant reptile with the end of his stick and tossed it into the marsh. "And it seems you brought friends."

I let out a whoosh of air and pasted an innocent smile on my face, hoping he couldn't tell I suspected him of murder. "Wow. Thanks! That thing was scary."

He wore rubber boots and jeans along with the same plaid shirt he'd worn the last time I'd seen him. *That's how you go on a date?* On the other hand, it didn't sound like he ever intended for his conversation with Bianca to be a real date.

"We thought we'd try one more time to find evidence of maroon bats," I said brightly.

"Oh, really." His tone was wry. He pointed to Steve. "And you brought the enemy along to help?"

Mimsey bristled. "He's not our enemy."

"And who, pray tell, are you?" he asked.

"We're . . ." She squared her shoulders. "We're friends of Georgia Wild." She put her arm around Wren's waist. "This is my granddaughter."

His eyes narrowed, and he shook his head. "I know why you're really here. You shouldn't have come."

"It's really none of your business," Steve said.

"Everything in this swamp is my business," Rickers hissed. "*Everything.* And now that you're here, you're my business."

"Was Autumn Boles your business?" I asked. Lucy pinched me.

"She betrayed me," he grated.

"Because she was going to give up looking for the bats? You killed her out of revenge for *that*?"

"Of course not," Rickers scoffed. "I couldn't care less about the stupid bats. I strangled her and left a clue so the police would blame the investment group that was going to buy this land. I couldn't let them kill . . ." He trailed off.

The cypress.

"You were . . . really? You were trying to frame the investment group? It didn't take

366

long for attention to focus on her boy-friend," I pointed out. "Despite the folded bat you put in Autumn's hand after you killed her."

His nostrils flared. "Stupid cops. Stupid press. The paper didn't even investigate the connection between Georgia Wild and the Dawes Corporation's investors."

Steve stepped forward. "You thought you could crucify our investment group on the cross of public opinion?" He snorted.

"Don't laugh at me!" Rickers held his walking stick up sideways. Something about it snagged my attention — something other than that he was using it to block the pathway.

"Oh, please," Steve said. "There are eight of us. Unless you plan —"

"Steve," I interrupted. "The staff."

"The . . ." He trailed off.

"What?" Bianca asked.

The others looked equally baffled. But I could feel the staff tugging, subtle, weaker than the tree it came from but with the same flavor. "He's holding a piece of the nexus."

Rickers' laugh was a truly unpleasant sound. It ran down my spine, weakened my knees. The women around me looked ill, and even Steve had paled under his tan.

"Well, I'm not surprised you know about the nexus, Katie. Katie Lightfoot." He sounded a little crazy, and I wondered how living so close to the tree for so long might have affected him. "Because you're special like me, aren't you? Do you all know how special she is?"

"Katie?" My aunt sounded terrified.

I stepped to Steve's side. "Special like you? Because of the tree? I can feel it, sure. But so can everyone here to some degree." I thrust authority that I didn't feel into my voice. "The ley lines are highly magnetic. Anyone would feel it. It's an energetic force."

Rickers regarded me with assessing eyes before suddenly smirking. "Nice try. But I saw you. I felt *you,* pushing that huge metal vehicle with your mind . . . or something. I saw the flash of light you threw to send me off course."

I looked around at the others. Only Wren seemed fazed by his words. Everyone else, including Steve, had seen me glow in the dark. No wonder they weren't overly surprised.

He nodded. "I see your friends know what I'm talking about."

The sun was low in the sky, and the temperature was dropping. My friends were in danger. Quinn needed to handle this nut-case. If Rickers really killed Autumn, there would be some kind of evidence. At the very least I could testify to seeing the specimen jars through the cabin window.

"I'm sorry, Dr. Rickers. We need to be going now."

"After I told you I tried to kill you? Fat chance."

The staff in his hands began to move, writhing like a gnarled brown snake. The atmosphere twanged, the air pressure changing with a sharp, explosive sound. Without warning, Evanston Rickers let drop the veil that had kept his true nature hidden, the veil none of us had known was there. The cloying, rotting stench I associated with the origami figure Autumn had been clutching in death blasted over us, a tangible wave of distorted and debased intent.

Power thrummed through him, growing in intensity — pushing, pushing, *pushing* at us. Steve staggered. My head throbbed. My vision blurred. I clamped my eyes shut and threw a protective mental circle around the group. Channeling the force of the tree, Rickers breached it in seconds. Mimsey cried out.

I redoubled my efforts, reaching for the power of the tree myself. Down through the earth, seeking access through the roots.

There.

The sudden influx of energy drove me to my knees. I held on to it, riding the vigor of the nexus, pure and unadulterated by Rickers' sickness. Light flared through my closed eyelids. I knew I was the source, or at least the outlet, but it didn't matter. Wrapping my intention in my passionate, savage desire to protect my friends, I lurched to my feet, lashing out at Rickers.

He countered, surprisingly strong. I gasped, and tried again.

A hand touched mine. Steve's? I couldn't look, but instinctively I opened to the help.

Darkness swirled into my light, twisting through it, touching the tree's power, flinching, then shooting toward our attacker.

I opened my eyes. Cookie grasped my fingers with one hand and sketched figures in the air with the other. A low, guttural sound issued from her throat as she stared at Rickers, her eyes wide and black in the silver illumination of . . . me.

"Cut him off!" she shouted.

The others clasped hands and reached out to us with additional support.

"Cut him off!" she growled. She wasn't talking to us.

She was Commanding the tree.

370

I joined my voice with hers. *"Let him go."* Over and over. *"Let him go, let him go, let him go."*

"No," Rickers moaned. Then he screamed, and the staff fell from his hands. He fell and lay on the path, unmoving.

The sense that my head was on the verge of exploding stopped instantly. The silvery quality in the clearing faded, leaving us in the gloaming. Taking deep, shaky breaths, I assessed my companions.

"Mimsey?" I rushed to her at the same time Lucy and Wren did.

Slowly, she sat up. Her complexion was gray, but she grasped her granddaughter's arm and allowed herself to be pulled to her feet. "I'm all right. Is everyone else okay?"

"Shaken and stirred," Jaida said, "but intact. What the heck happened, Katie?"

I looked at Cookie. "A battle of light and dark," I said with a small smile. I didn't explain that they had both been on the same side. "Thanks. I couldn't have done it without you."

She blinked, then slowly nodded. "You're welcome."

You must trust that you have whom you need in your life.

The difference between good and evil had become even more complicated. Or maybe

371

it hadn't. Maybe it really was all about intention.

Steve approached Evanston Rickers and knelt beside him.

"Is he dead?" Cookie asked.

"No, he's still breathing. His eyes are open, too." He took hold of Rickers' shoulders, and we all tensed as he pulled him into a sitting position. Lucy frowned, puzzled, then looked at me.

The man who had killed Autumn Boles and tried to kill my friends — and me, twice — stared at nothing. There was no longer any connection to the tree, but something else had been severed as well. His will? His . . . soul?

Whatever it was, I had done that to him. With Cookie's help, I had done that.

Squaring my shoulders, I walked to where Steve sat beside him and looked down into those blank eyes. Maybe it wouldn't last. Maybe it would. Either way, I'd do it all over again to save my friends.

"Who wants to come with me to find some cell service?" I asked.

CHAPTER 26

Two long tables groaned under the rows and platters of scones and cookies, biscotti and brownies, tea and coffee cakes, and a big batch of peach pecan mini-pies as Mrs. Standish had requested. The morning had been cool but sunny, and attendance at the bake sale sponsored by the Honeybee Bakery was brisk. Cookie and Mama were handling the regular bakery business while Ben, Lucy, and I worked the booth on Rousakis Plaza. We'd stretched a canopy overhead in case of rain, but now the early-afternoon sun warmed the air and the shade was welcome.

Mama and Ben had done a great job getting the word out about the Georgia Wild fund-raiser in a short amount of time. People who worked in the historic district dropped by, and the normal tourist traffic in Rousakis Plaza made a beeline toward the plethora of goodies we had on offer.

Several customers also mentioned the feature Steve had written about Georgia Wild that had appeared in that morning's *News.*

Nearby, Wren had set up a table with a large sign with Georgia Wild's motto — SPACE AND A PLACE FOR ALL — and had spent a lot of time answering questions and handing out literature. A few people had written checks on the spot.

The loan officer at Bianca's bank had given Wren the short-term loan, and one of the grants had come through the day before. She was still waiting for the second one, a little worried because she had to repay the loan in sixty days. She also wanted to hire some full-time help and arrange for more volunteers than yours truly.

The last few days had been busy. Lucy, Mama, and I had spent long hours at the Honeybee getting all the extra baking done for the sale. We'd still found time to meet with the ladies of the spellbook club at the Georgia Wild office. We'd finished the cleaning job I'd started, and then my mother had given the whole place an organizational makeover. The former living room of the renovated house was now Wren's office, and Autumn's office had been converted to a storage and file room. Finally, we'd smudged the whole place with white sage and French lavender to get rid of any of Evanston Rickers' lingering influences. I was happy to report there was no remaining trace of the unpleasant, intangible essence I'd perceived from Autumn's origami bat.

As for Dr. Rickers, he was still being evaluated in the hospital. So far he'd only sat and stared at the wall, saying nothing. According to Quinn, one doctor had speculated that his apparent catatonia may have resulted from a mental break caused by guilt over killing another person. Quinn himself thought Rickers was faking it to get out of going to trial. The police had found ample physical evidence that he was guilty of Autumn's murder. Besides the formaldehyde he used to preserve his snakes, they'd discovered a packet of maroon origami paper stuffed under his mattress, and his fingerprints matched some found in Autumn's office as well as in Logan Seward's smashed-up BMW.

Of course, there was also the fact that he'd confessed to eight people who were willing to testify to that effect.

I didn't think it would come to that, however. Something had happened in the swamp that cut Evanston Rickers off from more than the tree. I'd been a part of what happened, even if I hadn't been entirely responsible. Thoughts of going to visit Rickers had gone through my mind, but I couldn't bring myself to do it. At least not yet.

Hunter Normandy had been released after his deceased client's family agreed not to press charges. They only wanted their mother's ring back. He did lose his job at the mortuary, however. Peter Quinn told me Hunter planned on moving to the West Coast and starting over. He might not have been a killer, but after the unfortunate episode with him in my carriage house, I was glad to hear he would be leaving town.

"Thank you," I said to a petite, dark-haired woman who had purchased a baker's dozen of chocolate-filled sandwich cookies. "You have a nice afternoon."

"Oh, I will." She winked. "Starting with eating at least two of these in the car on my way home."

As she walked away, a tall man with a shock of sandy blond hair approached the Georgia Wild table. Skip Thorsen appeared much better than when I'd talked to him in the Old Familiar — clear-eyed and ruddy-cheeked. He stopped in front of Wren, said something, and held out his hand for her to shake. Instead, she stood and gave him a hug. He blinked away tears as she sat back down, then pulled a checkbook out of his back pocket and began writing.

After he left, I sidled over. "Autumn's ex made a donation?"

She blinked up at me with a stunned expression. "He just wrote me a check for a hundred thousand dollars."

"Holy cow!"

"He said it was the amount Autumn's life insurance policy will pay out. He knew she'd want Georgia Wild to have it."

"Wow." I shook my head. He hadn't been kidding about still being in love with his ex.

Declan still hadn't called. The day before, Ben had pulled me aside and asked what was going on. How could I tell my uncle what I'd done to his protégé — and one of his favorite people? But he'd pressed me, and I'd settled on saying that something had happened to make Declan realize that my being a witch involved a lot more than burning incense and dancing around a fire. It was something that he'd found very alarming and had needed time to think over.

Margie stopped by with Baby Bart in a backpack carrier. He grinned at me over her shoulder.

"Where are the JJs?" I asked.

"At my sister's. She watches them once a

week so I can run my errands. Oh, my *God,* Katie. Those are the cutest little pies I've ever seen!"

My neighbor turned to my aunt. "You make cakes for special occasions, don't you?"

"Of course," Lucy said. "What did you have in mind?"

"My mother-in-law's birthday is coming up, and I wouldn't dare try to make her a cake myself." Margie was a self-proclaimed disaster in the kitchen, while Redding's mother was a culinary genius.

"Oh, now," I said. "I happen to know you make a mean Coca-Cola cake."

She made a face. "That's fine for the kids, but not exactly proper fare for Evelyn Coopersmith."

I waved at Lucy. "This is your gal, then."

"What kind of a woman is your mother-in-law?" Lucy asked.

"Kind of formal. Not snooty-formal. More like . . . precise."

They discussed a few designs, deciding on one that featured Mrs. Coopersmith's favorite pastel colors.

"How about if I add some iridescent candy pearls?" Lucy suggested.

Margie laughed. "She'll love it. Heck, *I* love it."

Steve came up to the booth. "Hello, Ben," he said to my uncle.

"Steve." Ben's monosyllabic response was stiff at best.

"I'll take a dozen of anything," he said. "The guys at the *News* will go through whatever I bring back like a panzer division."

Ben nodded and began loading up a bakery box. I noticed he chose the most expensive items we offered, and I suppressed a smile.

"I took my father out to the swamp," Steve said to me.

"Finally," I said. "I can't believe he's going to purchase the property without even looking at it."

"Oh, he'd seen it," Steve said. "However, as you might guess, he's not one to tromp through swampland, so he'd checked it out from the air. Helicopter."

"Naturally." I rolled my eyes.

"This morning I took him to see the cypress in person."

"And?"

"He's already steered the other investors to another property they'd been considering for the golf course, and he's buying the entire swamp from Gart Fagen."

My jaw dropped. "You're kidding. Talk

about moving fast. What's he going to do with it?"

"Nothing. He wants to preserve it. Learn more about the tree and the ley lines."

I rushed out of the booth and gave him a big hug. "You are awesome." Stepping back, I found myself grinning so hard it made my cheeks ache. "Go tell Wren. She'll be over the moon."

On the other side of the booth, Mimsey's granddaughter was going over a Georgia Wild brochure with a long-haired teenager, oblivious that even more good news was headed her way.

"I want to show you something first. Ben, do you mind if I borrow Katie for a minute?"

"It's up to Katie," he said.

"I'll be right back," I said.

Steve led me to a nearby bench and we sat down. He opened his messenger bag and took something out. It was the old *Life Magazine* I'd seen him flipping through at the Honeybee, the one with Kim Novak on the cover.

"Look at this." He opened the magazine and handed it to me. "It's about the area around Fagen Swamp."

"It's about more than that," I said, skimming the story. "This confirms that someone else knew about the ley lines as far back as 1958. A PhD, no less."

He nodded. "Dr. Seymour Gold. The story makes him sound like kind of a wacko, but enough people took him seriously that a magazine of that stature wrote about his theory."

Our eyes locked for what felt like a long time. Finally I said what we were both thinking. "Could that be how the cypress tree became so powerful?"

"Maybe." A smile tugged at the corner of his mouth.

"Do you think it's dangerous?" I asked.

"It was for Evanston Rickers," he said. "And at least some of the animals in the swamp were affected."

"Mutated," I said. "Like those snakes in Dr. Rickers' specimen jars were." Quinn had told me they all had mutations, some freakish and some practical. "Your father isn't going to rent that cabin, is he?"

Steve shook his head. "No way. Rickers may or may not have been nuts to start with, but it seems likely it was the extended exposure to the tree that sent him over the edge. No one is going to be living in that swamp."

"Good." I glanced over at the bake sale booth. "I'd better get back. Mind if I take the magazine and show Uncle Ben?"

He handed it to me.

"Do you think Dr. Rickers really saw maroon bats?" I asked as we walked.

Steve shrugged. "I doubt it. They were just an excuse to keep the swamp the way it was. And to keep his privacy. I wouldn't be surprised if he planned to stay there instead of returning to Oregon."

"Wren mentioned going back out there to set up cameras in places the bats would likely roost. Just in case. Do you think Heinrich would let her do that?"

"I think so."

Steve went to tell Wren the good news. Ben was looking over my shoulder as I approached the booth, and I turned to see what had caught his attention. Declan strolled down the redbrick sidewalk. Steve saw him, too, and veered into his path. He stopped and held out his hand. He said something I couldn't hear. Declan paused, then shook Steve's hand before continuing toward us.

Well. Will wonders never cease?

When my boyfriend — could I still call him that? — turned and caught my eye, I realized I had stopped breathing. Ben heard my sudden inhalation and gave me a knowing nudge.

"Declan," he said, "what can we get you?"

"Nothing at the moment, thanks. Katie? Can we talk?"

This time Ben practically pushed me out of the booth.

We walked to the edge of the echo chamber and sat down on a retaining wall. We were near enough to the Savannah River to hear the water lapping at the shore. Butterflies flapped like bats around the sandwich I'd had for lunch. I ducked my head and looked surreptitiously at Declan's face. Was he here to break up with me?

"Ben called me last night," he said.

I sighed. "I'm sorry. Yesterday he asked what was going on with us, and I told him . . . a little. I didn't expect him to bug you. You should take all the time you need to decide what to do about me."

He smiled. "What to do about you, huh?" He looked at the toes of his work boots. "You tried to tell me. I didn't take you seriously enough, I guess. But you did try."

"I'm sorry I hurt you."

"I know you are." He was quiet for several seconds. "And I know you'll never do anything like that again. Ben pointed out that he's been with Lucy for almost thirty years, and some weird things have happened. But he loves her, and that's stronger than anything else."

The butterflies in my stomach returned to a more manageable size. "But . . . how should I put this? Lucy's 'weird things' and mine might be a little different."

"Because you're a catalyst. And something else, from what Ben told me. I still don't entirely understand what that means."

"Honestly, neither do I."

"And I don't know how I'll react to future, um, situations, but I'd like to give it a try and see what happens."

I leaned my head against his shoulder. "Deal."

He put his arm around my shoulders and pulled me close.

"You're a brave man," I said.

He smiled. "Shut up and kiss me." A trace of sweet gardenia swirled around us as Declan bent and touched his lips to mine.

RECIPES

MOCHA SHORTBREAD COOKIES

1 1/4 cups flour
1/4 cup cornstarch
1/4 cup unsweetened cocoa powder
2 teaspoons instant coffee or espresso powder
1 cup softened butter
1 cup confectioners' sugar

Preheat oven to 325 degrees. Sift together flour, cornstarch, cocoa, and instant coffee; set aside. Beat butter with an electric mixer until it is creamy and lighter in color — about 5 minutes. Add confectioners' sugar gradually, beating into butter until thoroughly incorporated. Add flour mixture and mix just until smoothly blended.

Spread parchment paper on a large cookie sheet. Divide the dough into three portions and, covering each portion with plastic wrap, press each one into a circle that is 5–6 inches in diameter. Be sure to press the rounds into place on the parchment where they will bake. If your cookie sheet is two small for all three rounds, use two smaller sheets with two rounds on one and a single round on the other. Remove plastic wrap.

With a very sharp knife, score each round into eight wedges. Bake for 25 minutes or until the shortbread feels firm to the touch (it will puff up a bit first). Remove from oven and rescore each round while it is still quite hot. Slide the shortbread, still on the parchment paper, onto a wire rack to cool. After they are completely cool, break or cut the rounds into wedges along the scored lines.

These are fabulous served with vanilla ice cream!

CHOCOLATE CHIP GINGERBREAD

2 1/2 cups flour
2 teaspoons baking soda
2 teaspoons powdered ginger
1/2 cup butter
1 cup sugar
2 large eggs
3/4 cup molasses
3/4 cup boiling water

2 tablespoons grated ginger (or use pre-grated ginger found in the produce department)

1/3 cup crystallized ginger cut into 1/4-inch dice

1/3 cup dark chocolate chips

Preheat oven to 350 degrees. Butter and flour a 9-inch square cake pan.

Sift together flour, baking soda, and ginger; set aside. Beat butter with an electric mixer until it is creamy and lighter in color — about five minutes. Add sugar and beat until fluffy. Add the eggs one at a time and beat well.

Combine the molasses, grated ginger, and boiling water. Blend gradually into the butter mixture. Add in the flour mixture and combine thoroughly. Stir in the crystallized ginger and chocolate chips.

Pour into pan and bake for 35–45 minutes or until a cake tester inserted in the middle comes out clean. Cool slightly; then turn gingerbread out onto a wire rack to cool completely.

Delicious with a simple sprinkling of confectioners' sugar or a dollop of whipped cream on top. Or both!

ABOUT THE AUTHOR

Bailey Cates believes magic is all around us if we only look for it. She's held a variety of positions, ranging from driver's license examiner to soap-maker, which fulfills her mother's warning that she'd never have a "regular" job if she insisted on studying philosophy, English, and history in college. She traveled the world as a localization program manager but now sticks closer to home, where she writes two mystery series, tends to a dozen garden beds, bakes up a storm, and plays the occasional round of golf. Bailey resides in Colorado with her guy and an orange cat that looks an awful lot like the one in her Magical Bakery Mysteries.